DEFEN
OF THE GIAI

Over at one cart, which was filled with green beach ball–sized melons, a large toddler was lifting one of the things to put in a customer's basket. He accidentally dropped it, the melon cracking into a hundred gross, gooey pieces. His mother began kicking him in the ankles, while his father climbed atop the cart and cuffed him on the back of the head.

Looking around, I noticed the same kind of thing going on all over the marketplace. And if adults weren't dumping on their own kids, they were encouraging others.

Bellowing like a wounded lion, I laid the bike down and hurried to the melon cart. The little guy noticed me coming but was too surprised to react. I grabbed him around the throat and lifted him straight up, like you see Schwarzenegger do. It might've been my adrenaline—or maybe the creep weighed twenty-six pounds—but I did it real easily. His eyes bulged as I shook him like a terrier . . .

"What's wrong with you people anyway? These are your *children*! How can you—"

"Interloper!" a woman exclaimed.

"Meddler!" a little guy added. "Mind your own business!"

"We'll show him what we do to meddlers!" another shouted, and there was a chorus of approval . . .

PRAISE FOR
BICYCLING THROUGH SPACE AND TIME:

"A funny SF novel with a combination of craziness and good craftsmanship . . . Cheerfully gonzo!"

—*Amazing*

Ace Books by Mike Sirota

BICYCLING THROUGH SPACE AND TIME
THE ULTIMATE BIKE PATH

THE ULTIMATE BIKE PATH

MIKE SIROTA

ACE BOOKS, NEW YORK

This book is an Ace original edition, and has never been previously published.

THE ULTIMATE BIKE PATH

An Ace Book / published by arrangement with the author

PRINTING HISTORY
Ace edition / October 1992

ISBN: 0-441-84391-3

Ace Books are published by The Berkley Publishing Group, 200 Madison Avenue, New York, New York 10016.
The name "ACE" and the "A" logo are trademarks belonging to Charter Communications, Inc.

PRINTED IN THE UNITED STATES OF AMERICA

10   9   8   7   6   5   4   3   2   1

For a bunch of Excellent people:

Karen Climenson
Syd & Dave Covey
Mary Kennedy
Danny McCarthy
Cathi Paul

And for John Fiscella—One of the neatest and most courageous people on this or any other planet

CHAPTER 1

Where Are You, Old Guy?

Yeah, well, it's me again. Told you I'd be back.

Today being Thursday, I'm into my fifth day of reality time. Actually, I'd kind of lost track, because it's gone so fast. It's been pretty neat, too. Why? you ask. Or maybe you didn't ask; you already know.

Right, Holly Dragonette.

Remember the bells and whistles and Tchaikovsky? Okay, I've got it figured out. See, by last Sunday night I was *definitely* hearing some major league bells. I'm talking the Bells of St. Mary's, Notre Dame Cathedral with Quasimodo going ape, the Good Humor man, a Bell for Adano. If I'd rattled my head, a bunch of churchgoers would've probably showed up at the door of my condo.

Small wonder. After helping Holly look for a place to live (she eventually rented an apartment *four blocks* from me!), we'd biked forty miles up and down the coast. The lady barely broke a sweat! She thought it was great, especially the well-marked bike lanes, something they lack along the farm roads of Iowa. Getting to know each other so well that day, the bells just happened. And the best part was, I know she heard them too.

Now I could've heard whistles, and in the natural course of things old Peter Ilyich would have followed. Something soft and romantic from *Serenade for Strings* or *Romeo and Juliet*; or something stirring from the *1812 Overture* or *Marche Slave*. But no, I drew the line at bells.

This is the part I said I'd figured out. In the first place, hearing bells was wonderful enough. When you begin a relationship with more than that—like what they used to call, among other things, *head over heels in love*—there are two ways you can go. The first is to sustain those lofty expectations, which isn't easy. And the second way is *down*, falling *out* of love after you discover that the person of your dreams is inordinately devoted to mama, snores and mumbles all night, hates most of the food you like, has a Silly Putty fetish, whatever.

But give the relationship time to develop, and whistles and Tchaikovsky will follow. Then, when you finally hear the horns and strings of that haunting love theme from *Romeo and Juliet,* wow!

So what did I do with the rest of reality time? Like I had told you, I went to the beach . . . with Holly. I caught a Padres game . . . with Holly. She's a White Sox fan (*see* the kind of things you find out?), but that can be worked on. I even called my mother, Mrs. Rose Miller Leventhal, in Florida. Didn't tell her about Holly yet. (*No, Ma, I don't think* Dragonette *is a Jewish name.*)

And as also advertised, I continued to write down what had happened to me along the Ultimate Bike Path and beyond. One thing about reality time was that the longer the stretch, the more you begin to question whether your experiences were real or not. The writing helped to deal with that.

The reason I was even thinking about the Path today was that, earlier, I'd driven Holly to the airport. It was going to take her a month to finish the chapters of her life in Iowa, then she would drive out with her things in a U-Haul truck. Guess what, I'm going back there to help her.

Okay, I suppose that sounds like *true love* or something, but there's more to it. I've always wanted to bike cross-country, and while Cedar Rapids isn't exactly on the East Coast, it's far enough. So on Sunday I start riding.

Actually, I *did* think about the Ultimate Bike Path during the last couple of days, when we shared some of our *friendlier* moments. That was because I kept remembering the Old Guy and his cronies, and the fact that they could watch me whenever they wanted. Yeah, I know they'd promised to be discreet about my personal life; still, Holly had to wonder if I was looking for spiders on the ceiling or something.

So now, late Thursday afternoon, I was thinking a lot about the Ultimate Bike Path, which meant I was more than ready to ride it. That was when I made the first of two major league dipshit mistakes.

Dipshit mistake #1: I decided not to enter the Path from what the Old Guy called the Starting Point, down the Stuart Mesa hill in Camp Pendleton. After all, I figured, the Torrey Pines grade was only a couple of minutes from my place, and by now

I was a pro traveling the *mhuva lun gallee,* so why not use it? I'd gotten on the Path from lots of different hills coming back, and *they* hadn't caused any problems.

Dipshit mistake #2: I would leave for the Ultimate Bike Path without being sure the Old Guy and his pals were watching me. This, I swear, wasn't for lack of trying. While getting changed I glanced out my bedroom window at the sky.

"Hey, Old Guy, can you hear me?" I asked, feeling sort of stupid. "I'm ready to hit the *mhuva lun gallee.* Just hope you're looking over my shoulder."

No response; no divine voice, no white room, *nada.* Didn't faze me, though. I rode the Nishiki to the coast, paralleled the ocean going south, and within a few minutes was climbing the Torrey Pines grade.

Let me tell you about this *mother* of a hill! Though about as steep as the one on Camp Pendleton, the Torrey Pines grade goes on for a mile and a half, *three times* as long. Average riders avoid it like a diseased rat. Going up, you induce yourself into semiconsciousness and think about anything *but* pedaling. And *flying* down you try to remember if your life and health insurance premiums are paid up. Once, when a usual headwind was absent, I got near forty mph before deciding not to look at the speedometer anymore.

In case you're thinking that *Torrey Pines* sounds familiar, you might recall this golf tournament that comes on in the middle of winter, when you're freezing your buns off in Bemidji, Buffalo, or Bangor. You know, where it's sunny and seventy-three degrees, and you see hang gliders and surfers and gray whales on their way down to party in Mexico? Yep, it's the one held at the Torrey Pines Municipal Golf Course. Makes those of you from the aforementioned ports of call wish you were here; makes those of us who spend *all* our days in (overpopulated) paradise wish it were never shown.

Speaking of that tournament, back in simpler times it was called the San Diego Open, then the Andy Williams San Diego Open, or AWSDO, to those in the know. The old crooner, taking a cue (or was it a four-iron?) from Bing Crosby and Bob Hope, would play in the celebrity pro-am, sing a song or two, and in general grin a lot. After that, when corporate sponsorship became a necessity, it was the Wicks Andy Williams San Diego Open, then the Isuzu Andy Williams San Diego Open.

Eventually the singer's name became disassociated from the

tournament (possibly because a whole new generation was asking the question, "Andy *who*?"). Corporate sponsorship changed, so that in one of its most recent incarnations it was the Shearson Lehman Hutton Open. But it's probably not over. If more celebrities and organizations wish to be associated thusly, we could wind up with the Oprah Winfrey Mitsubishi Jose Canseco Church of Jesus Christ of Latter-Day Saints Leonard Nimoy Hebrew National Boris Yeltsin Coors Light Sierra Club Stephen King Pepto-Bismol Open. You never know.

Anyway, here I was at the top of the hill, *near* the golf course, and only moderately breathless. Once again I waved my arms and addressed the heavens (a couple of northbound riders thought that was interesting). Nothing. Still, not to worry; the Old Guy and his pals would tune in before long.

Scenario: Study Group Old Guys *not* paying attention to Jack Miller.

Study Group Old Guy #1: "When was the last time anyone checked on Jack?"

My Old Guy: "I did, not long ago. He was with the female again."

Study Group Old Guy #2 (grinning impishly): "Were they . . . ?"

My Old Guy: "No, this time they were riding their bicycles. Jack appears to be quite fond of her."

Study Group Old Guy #1: "I'm afraid he won't be of any use to us for a while."

Study Group Old Guy #2: "I think you're right. Do we have another diversion?"

My Old Guy: "Oh, indeed! At this moment a Demgrimma-jin offal worm is emerging from its cocoon to begin its twenty-four hour life cycle, always a fascinating one. We can observe every minute of it!"

Study Group Old Guy #1: "That is wonderful. We'll check on Jack when we're done." (Scratches head.) "Er, he wouldn't undertake the journey on his own, would he?"

My Old Guy: "No, he won't. Jack may be a lot of things, but he's not—" (Inserts finger in ear.) "—a dipshit."

I started down the Torrey Pines grade.

The last riders had gone by a minute ago, and no one else was coming. Someone in a car could see me wink out for that split second, I suppose. But in general drivers hardly paid attention to bicyclists, and down this crazy winding hill they concentrated on the lane in front of them.

Even with a headwind I was quickly hurtling along at thirty-two mph. Could've shifted then but decided to wait until at least halfway down . . . which is when I suddenly had these thoughts relevant to aborting the whole thing. Didn't listen, though.

At thirty-four point five mph I shifted into the Vurdabrok Gear . . .

. . . and for the first time was absolutely one hundred percent sure I had made a *large* dipshit mistake.

This play-by-play is of what went down in the next one point three seconds . . . if that long. What *went down*, actually, was *me*. The first thing I became aware of upon emerging onto the Ultimate Bike Path was my speed, which felt faster than all prior entries. And second, I was moving headlong toward one of the tunnel's walls—*one of the rust-red, solid-looking walls!*

I squeezed the brakes hard, pulling one foot free of the toe clip as I tried to veer off.

Too close; too late.

The Nishiki went down; so did I, after somehow pulling out of the other clip.

The mist-covered floor of the Ultimate Bike Path felt grainy and weird under me.

Still hurtling forward the bike bounced once, then struck the wall, where it was *absorbed* with a sound like that of bacon sizzling.

I bounced, too, then rolled toward the same wall, unable to stop.

Oh, shit, where are you, Old Guy?

CHAPTER 2

". . . A Land of Both Shadow *and* Substance . . ."

It sounded worse than it felt, and let me assure you, it didn't feel good.

My flesh wasn't being fried off; I could see that. But the feeling was like fishhooks scratching me, on the verge of puncturing the skin before being pulled away, replaced immediately by more. I kept waiting for the hooks to set, all the while seeing that guy in *Hellraiser*.

You think this wasn't worth a good scream?

But it was a weird scream, like after you've sucked helium and sound like Jacques Cousteau or Donald Duck. Not an impressive scream, which didn't matter, as long as the Old Guy or somebody heard it.

Nobody did.

So I kept "rolling" through the wall, not really sure if there was a "floor" below me. Thinking about it, I could've just as easily been falling. I don't know if air was rushing past, or if there were *any* sounds, the scream accompanying me throughout my journey.

Ahead (or below? above?), I saw the Nishiki. Didn't seem any the worse for wear, but how could I be sure? Gaining on it slowly I was soon able to grab the rear tire. As I pulled it toward me, the fishhooks seemed to scratch deeper into my arm. Tough; I had to have the bike.

Somehow (don't ask me, I don't have a clue) I was able to climb atop the Nishiki . . . or maybe I pulled it under me. Whatever the case, man and machine were together again.

And racing toward something that could have been the gateway to Perdition itself.

It was either big and right in my face, or bigger yet and farther off, but either way, it was *there*. Blue and yellow and orange flames the size of western Canada, snapping, crackling, and popping amid equally enormous crystalline stalactites (the ones that hang down, right?). And weaving through all this, like the Angel of Death on Passover, was a grayish-black mist, long and serpentine. In a crazy moment I imagined it forming a one-word message in cursive script: *toughshitjack.*

To shift down, or not to shift? Who cared? Everything was screwy; I didn't know if I was going into or out of somewhere. And those fishhooks, I swear, were about to snag me.

I shifted out of the Vurdabrok Gear . . .

. . . and this time was falling, *definitely* falling, fortunately not very far.

But enough to stun me for a few moments, during which I remember thinking—despite a possible concussion—how nice it was to lie atop something substantial and not be moving.

The ground (floor, whatever) was black, solid, with the coldness of ice. Thinking about that, I sat up; but slowly, afraid my flesh was stuck to it. Not so, thankfully.

As my head cleared, I assessed the damage to both the bike and me. Nothing wrong with the Nishiki; a few scratches, chain slipped off the chainwheel, that was it. *Takes a lickin'* and all that. And I had survived, too, other than a bump on the side of my head and a bruised knee. No fishhook injuries; that was probably in my brain. All in all, none the worse for wear.

So why couldn't I stop shaking?

Jesus, Miller, did you really have to go out of your way to prove you were the world's largest posterior orifice?

Satisfied I was still all together, I looked around at wherever-I-was; which, to tell you the truth, didn't seem to be *anywhere.* Now that sounds weird, right? But I couldn't make out a hell of a lot, not because it was dark, but because it was *black,* like the floor. Sounds like I was in a room, or some other enclosure, but I *know* that wasn't so, because I could sense the openness all around me. It was unnerving, to say the least, especially looking up and seeing not a single star or other dot of light.

Nice going, O great Jack-o. Here, let me shove those two dipshit mistakes in your face again. First, you leave without informing certain interested parties of your plans; second, you choose a hill to Hell. At least you're still alive, and when you get back on the Ultimate Bike Path . . .

When you get back on the Ultimate Bike Path, *what?*

Did I say *two* dipshit mistakes? I did say *two,* right?

Make that three.

Make that the *universe's* largest posterior orifice.

Even if I'd had a moment—which I didn't—to glance behind me at the gate I came through from the Torrey Pines grade, I would have forgotten to do it. *I didn't have a clue which way was back!*

All right, let's discuss options here. Assuming I return to the *mhuva lun gallee,* I could look for the old familiar gate to the Stuart Mesa hill in Camp Pendleton. But since it was no longer *my* time and place in the universe, finding it might take forever, or longer. And I'd probably return there in the past, anyway.

Next option: find a gate that shows up again and again. Yeah, you think *that's* easy? The blue Earth doors, with their pyramids and such, are very similar. How many would I have to memorize before I made the first match? Uh-uh; you could go crazy doing that.

I could ride the Path until I got the attention of the Old Guys by waving and shouting and stuff. Maybe they'd show me the way back, gratis. Then, I could be all humble and apologetic about messing up. I mean, haven't I *exceeded* their expectations so far? How pissed off can they be about one foul-up? Okay, so I won't draw the anticipated crowds to observe my further exploits. Screw it.

The last option I had from the *mhuva lun gallee* was to rub the Bukko. Wouldn't that be great! Until now I've survived some nasty stuff *without* touching the thing. So instead of it saving me from something two hundred feet long and reptilian that's about to bite me in half, or from a free-fall into a swimming pool full of toxic waste . . . I use it because I'm *lost!*

Now, all of the aforementioned options hinged on the *large* assumption that I could get back to the Ultimate Bike Path. No guarantee there, right? I mean, look at this freaky place! No *normal* gate—isosceles triangle, Elmer Fudd, Gorbachev birthmark, whatever—brought me here.

I came through a blasted wall!

Nothing about getting here was right. For all I know this place doesn't *exist.* It might not even be in the jurisdiction of the Old Guys. I could rub the Bukko until I got a skin rash and nothing would happen.

Maybe I *had* punctured the portal of Perdition after all. Oh, great!

Yeah, you're right, it's my pessimistic mode again; not the

first time, huh? So why didn't I start doing something about it? First off, I was still woozy and hadn't totally stopped shaking, which made it a bit hard to stand up. And second, the exploration of this weird place was an enterprise I unabashedly admit I was trying to put off for as long as possible. It really gave me the creeps.

But finally, still wincing from assorted aches, I got on my feet. Now normally your eyes adjust to the dark, right? Uh-uh, not here, because like I said before, this wasn't darkness, this was *blackness*. As an experiment I took four steps away from the Nishiki. Gone, like it didn't exist! I hurried back to the bike, stood it up, and held the handlebars more tightly than usual. *No way* would I do that again.

Standing around was useless, so I started walking. The direction I chose was *straight ahead*. Below my feet the black smooth floor went unchanged; I could actually feel the cold through my Avocet bike shoes.

I walked for what, by my guess, was an hour, but could've been either six minutes or three days. *Almost* everything stayed the same during that time. The floor was black and cold, unbroken by rifts or holes, and it was level, not sloping up or down in the slightest. All that seemed to change was the engulfing blackness, which *lightened* to an ugly ash-gray. That was my perception, at least. I still couldn't make out a thing, even nearby.

By this time my head was clearer, and I figured as long as the surface was smooth, why not ride? I got on the Nishiki but pedaled slowly. Not being able to see past the front tire, I wasn't of a mind to have a sheer drop suddenly be there. Actually, free-falling off one could be just what I needed, but I at least wanted the option of thinking about it first.

Unlike the *mhuva lun gallee,* I could hear my tires gliding on the smooth surface. But otherwise the silence was really unnerving. Unable to stand it anymore I shouted, "Yo, is anyone around?"

I *thought* I'd shouted something.

Jesus, was *that* weird! The words didn't come out of my mouth but detoured up into my head, where they bounced around for what seemed like half of forever before fading away. I stopped the bike and covered my ears, which was dumb, since the echoes were *inside*.

"Holy shit," I muttered, real softly this time, but the same thing happened. Okay, so I knew to keep my mouth totally shut.

I rode on through the ash-gray gloom, and now *nothing* changed; this place was totally flat! Before long I was tired and had to stop. Fortunately the Gatorade in my bottle had survived the trip. There was also a granola bar, one which had been in my seat bag for some time and tasted like oat-and-honey particle board, but I ate it anyway.

Somehow I managed to fall asleep sitting up; didn't want to stretch out on the icy ground. At some point I had this dream about trudging through ice and snow across a frigid wasteland, Siberia or something. The only thing I wore was a fluorescent pink muscle shirt that said LIFE'S A BEACH in green letters. My buns were blue, but the rest of me seemed okay.

Up ahead James Arness was frozen in a block of ice. As I got closer he sat up suddenly, the upper half of his body cracking through the ice. He pointed a carrot at me and said, ''You're sled dog meat, Jack.''

I hauled my (blue) ass out of there quick.

Farther along, atop a frozen lake, hockey players were shooting pucks into a net with deadly accuracy. There was one jersey from every National Hockey League team. Being a fan, I sat my bare buns down on a rock to watch. But all of a sudden *I* was standing in front of the goal. I had a stick, but no pads, no helmet, not even a Jason Voorhees mask.

Twenty-odd guys, who *were* wearing Jason Voorhees masks, started firing pucks at my personage.

I woke up.

Things vaguely shaped like hockey pucks but unquestionably bird turds were falling from the sky, splatting on the ground all around.

Splatting on me and the Nishiki.

I stood and looked up; one splatted on my head. Fortunately these things slid off like oysters going down your gullet.

A few seconds later the offensive rain ended. I heard no flapping of wings, no chirps or squawks.

Still groggy, I climbed on the Nishiki and pedaled away. Too fast, but then, the ground was smooth, right?

Holes were suddenly there, and I bounced through a couple of small ones but managed to avoid going over on my head. I got off the bike, which was a good thing, because subsequent holes were more the depth and dimension of unfilled graves.

So, grounded again. For the next hour (day?) I weaved through what looked like the aftermath of an aerial bombing. Twice I nearly stumbled in a depression, and once I lost hold of the bike, which was really a talented thing on my part.

Christ, where was I going?

I mean, this place, it was . . .

A shadow fell over me.

Now how the hell, in this gloomy place, with no source of light, *could a shadow fall over me*?

But I swear, that's what happened. I actually *felt* it pass, and knew it was both darker and colder in that moment. Then, it was repeated . . . a number of times.

I started shaking again and almost reached for the Bukko. *This* was a bit much, huh?

Give me *some* credit, I didn't rub the ugly coin. Graves or not I hurried away, and before long the black floor of this place was again smooth.

But the shadows kept falling over me without pause, and my *angst* was doing the Watusi in my throat!

Maybe the shadows were being cast by whatever it was that had dropped the hockey puck turds. If so, I should probably have considered myself lucky nothing was coming down. In any case I got back on the bike and rode off, this time *real* slow. I concentrated on the ground in front of me, but could still see and feel the unending shadows.

Then, finally, something significant! Still in a high gear, I started pedaling effortlessly. Without a doubt the ground was sloping down.

This ended, and I had to climb briefly, but that was okay; at least *something* was happening. And when the next declivity was both longer and steeper, I was sure of it. Still, the cold and the unnerving shadows—not to mention the uncertainty about what good this was going to avail me—tempered my enthusiasm.

Three valleys later I decided it was time to take a chance. Each had been longer, which was good. The bad part was the grueling climb out of the last one; didn't need that anymore.

So when I felt the ground sloping down again, I stopped. No way was I rushing into it without getting psyched first. Going down the last one I'd hit twenty mph, and that was with riding the brakes. By my guess, I could've easily exceeded twenty-five. The problem was, since you couldn't see a damn thing ahead of you, it was a scary trip. I *had* to overcome that if I was going to get past thirty.

Another shadow fell over me. (Could this be the Valley of the Shadow of . . . ? Naah, never mind.) Now *there* was motivation. I started down.

Oh, great, this was great! Plummeting into oblivion, what a way to go. Twenty-two point five mph. My hands were twitching around the brakes, but I fought the urge to squeeze. Twenty-five mph. Even at this speed I was aware of passing shadows. *Please, don't distract me with hockey pucks!* Twenty-eight mph. I was hunched over the bars, staring straight ahead, although from what there was to be seen I might as well have had my eyes closed.

Thirty mph. I tried to shift into the Vurdabrok Gear.

Nothing happened.

Thirty-one point five; still nothing. Oh, jeez, don't do this to me!

Was I doomed to stay in this shadow world? If so it might be a brief sojourn, considering the valley floor was not too far below and I was rushing toward it at speeds in excess of . . .

Thirty-three mph. Which in one way or another would cause serious damage to my anatomy.

Try not to scream, Miller. If it stays in your head, you could reverberate to death.

Thirty-four point five. The lever began to yield!

I pushed harder and slipped into the twenty-second gear . . .

. . . and this time, when I burst onto the Ultimate Bike Path, I took a quick glance behind me. Guess what, I'd come out of the wall!

I was near the middle of the Path, slightly angled, but that was correctable. A long run of Bart Simpson heads passed on both sides, and they looked fine to me. As screwy as that shadow world was, I had survived it and gotten back. Everything was okay again.

Almost everything.

I'll never find the gate to the Torrey Pines hill.

Whoops, the old pessimistic mode again. I hadn't figured on getting this far, right? So how about seeing what happens before I freak?

The portals to the numerous Afterwards ended, and the

random pattern began. Seeing the first blue door, I memorized it. Same for the second and third, which were different. But the fourth caused some problems, and the fifth got even more confusing. And by the time the sixth, seventh, and eighth rolled past I had muttered two short words that rhymed with "bucket." This was impossible.

You won't *believe* what happened.

There was a message over the next blue door, one of those wanna-be neon things. It said, HOW ARE YOU DOING, JACK? and was signed O.G.

Could it be? Slowing, I memorized the pyramid pattern, then began looking in earnest for a match. Quite some time passed, and many more blue doors.

But finally, there it was.

No message over this one, but everything matched, and unlike the others it was beckoning me. Turning sharply I passed through the blue haze dead-center . . .

. . . and shifted out of the Vurdabrok Gear as I hurtled down the Torrey Pines grade. No doubt I'd only been gone for an instant, because a red Mazda I'd noticed coming up the hill was still coming up the hill.

I'd overcome my dipshit mistakes and gotten back without screaming for help, rubbing the Bukko, or losing any of my extraterrestrial fan club!

CHAPTER 3

Baby Huey Revisited

"So, Jack, you had a good ride?"

"Yeah, sure did."

The Old Guy (mine, singular) was waiting at the bottom of the hill, across from the entrance to the Torrey Pines State Reserve. He still rode the old black Schwinn, but this time was dressed more appropriately. Too much so, in fact, his outfit being *identical* to mine, right down to the Campagnolo cycling socks. We resembled a cutesy father-and-son team. Much as I liked him, I hoped we could get this meeting over with quick.

"I didn't expect you'd be going back before we were again in touch," he said.

"Well, I tried to call but you weren't home," I told him, and he looked at me strangely.

"Yes, uh . . . Why did you use *this* hill, instead of the regular one?"

"Because it was *there*," I said dramatically, and smiled. He did, too, even though he didn't know about what.

"You mean nearby to your home, of course. Yes. But, Jack, did you not encounter any . . . uh, problems?"

"Nope, none. I got on the *mhuva lun gallee* and rode around for a while until I heard from you."

How much did he *really* know? I wondered. Was this scenario all so I could save face? Or had I truly made out like a bandit and retained my hero status? Assuming these guys were as incapable of lying as Mr. Spock, I'd say the latter.

He glanced up the Torrey Pines hill and shrugged. "Well, that's good," he said dubiously. "And you were able to resist the lure of the gates?"

"Oh, yes, I didn't go anywhere. Stayed right down the middle of the Path." *Please, Blue Fairy, don't make my nose grow!*

The Old Guy nodded, so I guess he believed me. "Well, I'm glad you enjoyed yourself," he said. "But, Jack, do me a favor."

"What's that?"

"Wait for me before you enter the *mhuva lun gallee,* and please, unless we discuss it beforehand, use the Starting Point."

I thought to myself *Oh hell yes!* but said, like a whiny kid, "Do I have to?"

"We of the study group would appreciate it."

"Oh, okay."

He smiled. "Well, that's that. By the way, where is the female? We thought you were still with her."

"Holly left yest— A few hours ago, for Iowa. She's probably still on the plane."

"So! You'll be going right back to the *mhuva lun gallee* then?"

I was beat but wasn't about to tell him that. "No, think I'll wait till morning. Don't feel like driving north in rush hour."

He stuck a finger in his ear and learned all about *rush hour.* "Oh, understandable," he said, nodding. "Tomorrow morning then, at seven?"

"Sounds good."

"You won't see any of us at the Starting Point, but we *will* be with you. And as I predicted, two others will be joining us for observation."

Study Group Old Guys #3 and #4. *That* was the anticipated throng? Guess I had to do some more impressive stuff.

The Old Guy waited while I rode away. Watching him in my little mirror, I realized he was handling himself a lot better than ever before on his bike. A good thing, too, considering the load of traffic now zooming past on the coast road. I wondered if anyone would see him wink out or fade away or whatever.

Soaking in the spa alleviated much of the soreness from my ill-fated excursion to wherever-the-hell-I-was. I wrote the whole thing down, then tried forgetting about it, which wasn't going to happen.

I don't think I told you this: Izzy McCarthy, my agent, called earlier in the week. Yes, he'd gotten my latest completed gem, *Mutant Bats of Krimmia,* to the publisher, and they'd make a decision on it in their usual time, which meant somewhere between when Saddam Hussein donates half his holdings to B'nai B'rith and 2 Live Crew is invited to do a benefit concert for the National Organization of Women. But that wasn't the *big news,* of course. The *big news* was that due to the *enormous* popularity of *Tree Men of Quazzak,* they wanted me to do a sequel. Was that exciting, or what! Yeah, I know, I'd just about sworn off writing fantasies after Murlug, but what the hell, a contract was a contract. Their suggested title, based on two chapters from Book One about these gigantic wood-devouring beasties, was *Termite Terrors of Quazzak.* I suppose it might work, especially if I had a spaceship crash-land on the forest world with the Orkin man aboard.

So while I was contemplating the potential of such a literary masterpiece, I got a call from Holly. She was safe and sound back in Cedar Rapids; plane wasn't decorating a hillside in Colorado or something. Said she missed me, was looking forward to being together again, which is pretty much what I told her. Wonderful stuff.

My dreams that night were a weird amalgam. Part was of Holly, and that was nice. But others were of sinister creeping shadows, flying hockey pucks, and a humongous flaming door with a sign that said, ENTERING HELL—WATCH YOUR STEP AND HAVE A NICE DAY. I woke up every time that door started to open, which got to be a real pain.

Anyway, it wasn't a dream but my body alarm that got me up at 5:56 the next morning. I actually felt great and considered cycling up to Camp Pendleton. But memories of recent experiences won out, and I drove instead.

Not a single Old Guy was roaming around Stuart Mesa. But there was plenty of traffic, bike and otherwise, and it took me three runs down the hill before I could wink out. A woman cyclist changing a flat near the lone sycamore ("No, I don't need help, you think I'm some impotent goddamn female or something?") kept wondering what I was doing up there. I told her that going down big hills made me horny.

After what happened yesterday, entering the Ultimate Bike Path from this hill was . . .

. . . a piece of cake, but even so I glanced behind to make certain I knew which door I'd come through. Almost immediately I was running a gauntlet of Florida gates, with an occasional Elmer Fudd. Not in any big hurry, I rode them out. It took a long time to find the random pattern.

Feeling a bit giddy (or maybe *assholish* would be a better word) I grinned at the ceiling of the tunnel and waved one hand. "Good morning, Old Guy," I said. "Hello, old Old

Guys, and an especially warm welcome to you new Old Guys. Hope you enjoy your observations.''

Well, they were definitely tuned in, because farther along was one of those glittery silver signs in front of the tunnel wall, like when the Old Guy showed me the way to Hormona the Vulvan. Brief, this time; HI, JACK was all it said.

I have a long-held fantasy about that message. Writers tend to create all sorts of weird scenarios around various stimuli. See, I'm now a famous bestselling author, and I land at an airport in *your* city as part of my national tour. As I'm coming off the jet, a chauffeur assigned to meet me with a limo holds up a sign saying *those* words. He is promptly blown away by Security. Strange, huh?

A note to myself: I really want to know how to travel in the Afterwards without being dead. I've been especially looking forward to a return visit to the Rock-and-Roll Afterward, where I could spend more time with Harry Chapin and get to meet the others there. Is it the Old Guy who "prepares" me for this? Is it someone else? Or does it just "happen," and if so, what do I look for? How do I know?

A fellow traveler appeared on the Path ahead. In all respects it was an elephant, save two: Its fleshy trunk was obscenely long, and it had a face that more closely resembled a common housefly. It "rode" along on fire engine-red "boots," each of which had two wire wheels the size of Frisbees.

My apologies to Dumbo, but I finally saw an elephant-fly.

Pulling up parallel to the creature, but two yards away, I threw it a salute and said, "Hey, how's it going?"

The thing looked at me and grinned (I think). Its pink proboscis reaching for me, it said, "I can't wait to pull out your heart and intestines and feed on them, yum!"

Was this some sort of practical joker, or did they allow cosmic psychos on the *mhuva lun gallee*? I guess so, since Atoris the Evil once traveled it. So, assuming the UT6 was functioning properly and not misinterpreting what the elephant-fly was saying . . . *I got the hell out of there, fast!*

Didn't slow down for a long time, either. When I finally did the random pattern was past, and the tunnel walls were dominated by those old isosceles triangles with the exploding fireworks. In-between were a few of the lemon-colored Gorbachev birthmarks, all with a uniformly strong pull. Never having tried the latter before, I'd pretty much decided that one of them would be my next port of call.

Then, a triangle "grabbed hold," and you know the way things work on the Path. Gorby would have to wait. I raced headlong into the fireworks display . . .

. . . and shifted down as I came to a nice easy stop (for a change) on a meadow of four-inch-high, thick-bladed grass.

Compared to other gates I'd been through this place didn't rate particularly high on the scale of *weird,* at least not initially. Everything—hills behind me, sky above, forested valley below—was pretty much the right color, with only slight variations thereof. The sun—directly overhead—appeared quite large, and it was warm here, but tolerable, not humid at all.

Two dwellings stood on the far side of the meadow, one hundred fifty yards away. While not exactly New England Colonials, these houses were a few notches above the huts of Kamamakama. Walking the bike I angled toward them, soon intersecting a narrow, tightly packed dirt path. There were tire marks of some kind in the undisturbed dust. At least these people had figured out the wheel.

Before continuing along the path to the houses, I noticed people coming from the other direction. From this distance it looked like an adult and two children, the former walking behind. I decided to wait for them. They saw me, for sure, but didn't slow down. Apparently my presence wasn't fazing them.

Or maybe they had Uzis and could blow my head off before the first word of greeting escaped my mouth.

The "smaller persons" in front were *not* children, I realized, as they came nearer. Nor, thank heavens, did they appear to be armed. The woman, dressed in a dun-colored sack dress, stood about four feet eight; the man, who wore trousers and a shirt of the same awful material, was an inch taller. A stogie shoved in his mouth was the size and shape of a football, I swear. They didn't appear to be midgets or dwarfs, but normally proportioned adults who had simply . . . grown smaller, like the Incredible Shrinking Man, or the kids in that Disney movie. Which was crazy, of course. The woman was pulling a small wooden cart with a tall basket in it; the man's hands were free, except for when he took the stogie out of his mouth and blew these foul brown vapors into the air. From their scowls I surmised that neither was glad to see me.

The "larger person" behind was something else altogether. First thing I thought of was an old comic book character called Baby Huey. Yeah, this was a kid, but *what a kid!* He stood over six and a half feet and was bottom-heavy; butt and belly really waddled with each step he took. His only garment, made of the same sackcloth, was . . . a pair of short pants, I guess, but they were pinned on him in the manner of a diaper. He had this cherubic face with a sort of toothless half smile, half grimace as he stared at me. Not much hair on top of a pink, knobby skull. And unlike the adults (his parents, probably) his arms were laden with bags and baskets, the load appearing quite heavy.

Considering his size, if these *were* his parents, this kid was one hell of a freak of nature!

"Good morning," I said when they were near.

"Yeah, what's so good about it?" the little guy replied. I swear, he sounded like Edward G. Robinson in those old gangster movies.

"Uh, nothing, just trying to make conversation."

"Well, that's a crock," the woman said wearily. "No time for it. Too busy." She was glancing at the Nishiki, but whatever the extent of her curiosity, she didn't ask a thing.

"Skneezulgrix," the giant kid said.

"Shuddup, Harlan," the little man said, and you know what he did? He leaned over and bit the kid on the thigh.

"Waaaa!" the giant kid cried.

The woman looked up at Harlan, stamped her foot and waved a fist. The kid stopped crying. The little man glared at me.

"You was gonna say something?" he asked in a sort of growl.

"Other than to compare your face to a mound of sea gull splat, nothing. I don't suppose there's a town around here?"

He began to sputter, but the woman said peevishly, "Oh, give him directions, Lemuel, so he'll leave us alone."

"The town is called Warithess," Lemuel said. "Follow the trail in that direction we just came from. You get to a wider road, turn left. Takes you down to the valley, five miles. Can't miss it. Now get lost!"

"Yeah, you have a nice day, too," I said dryly, but they

were already on their way. Harlan, still toting his load, looked at me and smiled. Cute kid, considering his size.

"Blabbafab," he said.

Lemuel wagged a beckoning finger at Harlan. The giant baby bent way down. Lemuel grabbed one earlobe, twisted it, and led the kid away.

"Waaaa!" Harlan cried again.

Assholes!

Walking along the trail I thought, *Do I really want to hang around this place?* But then, I was beginning to understand more about the gates along the Ultimate Bike Path. When you were *invited* in, there was usually a reason, even though it might not be evident at first. Okay, so I'll stick it out.

Sometime later the trail ended at a wider road, as advertised. Had I been riding, I would've gotten there a hell of a lot sooner. I don't know, maybe it was thinking about that poor giant kid . . .

Anyway, this time I *did* get on the bike and began the easy descent to Warithess.

CHAPTER 4

Anyone Here Teach Lamaze?

Actually, the second and third miles down were fairly steep, but the road was in good shape and didn't pose any problems. Until now I hadn't seen a single house since the meadow, but the last two miles into Warithess made up for that. Dwellings similar to the first ones, with barns or storage buildings in the rear, were on both sides of the road, initially spaced over a hundred yards apart, the distance narrowing the closer I got to town. Crops grew everywhere, but in rather haphazard "rows." This place wasn't going to pose an economic threat to the heartland of America.

I caught an occasional glimpse of someone working in a field or walking around a building. No one seemed the least bit interested in me or my transportation, even though I doubted whether they'd seen anything like the Nishiki before. But that ended when I passed this one particular farm.

A girl stood on the other side of a low picket fence at the edge of the road. She was tall, five-ten or so, and gangly. Probably a teenager, I guessed, except her face had this sort of tomboyish little-kid look; reminded me of a Cabbage Patch doll, an image enhanced by her curly orange hair. She was waving and smiling, so I decided to stop.

"Hi there, young lady," I said, smiling back.

Her voice was a squeaky high C, and you won't believe what she said without a single breath: "Hello who are you my name's Daphne what is that nice thing you're sitting on are you going to Warithess how do you make that thing go did I say my name is Daphne that's such a wonderful thing oh I wish I could ride on it who did you say you were I'm eight years old are you from around here it's a very shiny thing it's almost time for lunch would you—"

"*Daphne!*" a voice shouted with a thunder that made me think of the Jolly Green Giant.

Guess what, it was a guy about the same size as Lemuel, maybe even an inch or two shorter. He was standing in front of a cottage thirty yards back, gesturing impatiently. Daphne's smile faded; turning, she hurried her gawky body between rows of rutabagas (or something). When she passed the little guy he raised a hand, as if to hit her, and she cringed. I was about ready to hop the fence and kick some ass, but he let her by, and she disappeared inside the cottage. The creep went on to the barn, though not before waving an arm at me in what looked like an umpire signaling a home run, but probably wasn't. Undoubtedly he didn't recognize *my* hand gesture, either.

What was with these people anyway!

I kept on riding toward Warithess, and before long there were lots of people on the road. Enough, in fact, that I decided to walk the bike rather than weave between them. The adults, all of them small, were either surly or indifferent. Their large children (yep, this seemed to be the way it was) were curious about me, as Daphne had been, but they didn't dare say a word.

Then, I saw something *really* strange. There was this couple, each about five feet two. The woman was pregnant. No, let me rephrase that: she was *PREGNANT!* By Earth standards she was easily in her seventy-third month, give or take. Her distended belly sat atop a wheelbarrow, which she pushed along in front of her. A tent-sized maternity sackcloth dress was straining at the seams.

Do I have to tell you the lady was in a bitchy mood?

She harangued her husband; she harangued her unborn child; she harangued anyone within earshot.

Me included.

"What are *you* staring at, you anus of a maggot?" she said, none too sweetly.

Yo, outta there! I found out how quickly I *could* weave.

Now, lest you think this was an isolated incident, it wasn't. As the cottages (shabbier, now) drew closer together, each practically leaning on the next, more *PREGNANT!* ladies began turning up. The top of the wheelbarrow in front of this particular one closely resembled the Chrysler Building.

There was a lot of commotion at the door of one hovel. I stopped to have a look, and while there were at least a dozen people, none were any taller than five feet three. Even so, the door was only slightly ajar, and I couldn't tell what was happening.

Suddenly, from inside, there was a scream, one that would have put Fay Wray's first meeting with Mr. Kong, or Vera

Miles's with Mrs. Bates, to shame. Two women entered, joining others already there. I still couldn't see what was doing.

A second and third scream came with hardly a pause, followed by silence.

Then, a different sort of scream, deeper, more resonant: *"Waaaaaaa!"*

"It's a boy," someone said in a tone of voice one would use to announce "I have cancer."

The door opened wider, and there he was: a nearly seven-foot baby boy, cheesy stuff, clipped umbilical cord, the whole nine yards. I would have loved to see the mother deliver *that.*

On the other hand . . .

So obviously, giving birth to jumbo children here was not uncommon. Still, I hadn't seen any large grown-ups (that's *grups* to you Trekkies) yet, or for that matter even normal-sized ones, and there were plenty of people around. Really weird.

Okay, this was definitely the heart of beautiful downtown Warithess. Hovels *were* on top of each other, two and three stories. Many were storefronts, although you really couldn't tell what they were selling inside. People vended stuff off carts in the "marketplace," where half a dozen or so twisty roads came together. There were a few wheelbarrow ladies, and lots of oversize kids. The noise level, needless to say, was up *high,* but the sounds weren't happy ones. This might be a stupid cliché, but the tension really *was* thick enough to cut with a knife.

Over at one cart, which was filled with these green beach ball-sized melons, a large toddler about the size of Harlan was lifting one of the things to put in a customer's basket. He accidentally dropped it, the melon cracking into a hundred gross, gooey pieces. His mother began kicking him in the ankles, while his father climbed atop the cart and cuffed him on the back of the head.

Nearby, in front of a store, another couple was doing a similar number on a skinny girl who resembled Daphne, except her Cabbage Patch hair was black. The poor kid was sobbing; it was pathetic.

Was this bullshit, or what! Looking around, I noticed the same kind of thing going on all over the marketplace. And if adults weren't dumping on their own kids, they were encouraging others. *Jesus!*

All right, enough! I wasn't bound by the Prime Directive,

and even if I was, there was no way this should be allowed to happen. Fuck it!

Bellowing like a wounded lion, I laid the bike down and hurried to the melon cart. The little guy noticed me coming but was too surprised to react. I grabbed him around the throat and lifted him straight up, like you see Schwarzenegger do. It might've been my adrenaline—or maybe the creep weighed twenty-six pounds—but I did it real easily. His eyes bulged as I shook him like a terrier and tossed him to the ground.

"Why don't you pick on someone your own . . . age?" I said, kind of stupidly.

I broke up a few others like it; even shoved some of the women aside when they came at me. Now I was really getting into it. Some of the kids were watching me curiously. Deep inside each one, I was sure, were unspoken *Aww-right*s! and *Yeah*s! and stuff like that just waiting to burst forth.

Then, as I slowed down for a moment, I realized that two dozen of these people had formed a circle around me, and man, did they look pissed! Okay, they were little, but you think I could take them *all*? I started wondering what in hell I'd gotten myself into, although when I looked at the faces of those poor kids, I knew.

Deciding to keep on pressing the issue, I yelled, "What's wrong with you people anyway? These are your *children*! How can you—?"

"Interloper!" a woman exclaimed.

"Meddler!" a little guy added. "Mind your own business!"

"We'll show him what we do to meddlers!" another shouted, and there was a chorus of approval.

Hoo boy!

Their cries became louder; the circle tightened. So there I was, in my spandex and Padres cap, about to be assaulted by a whole shitload of mini-people. Okay, what the hell; I'd made my point, and I *wasn't* going down without taking a bunch of them along.

Think fast, how did Chuck Norris do it in *Good Guys Wear Black?*

CHAPTER 5

The Dark Time

Two figures burst through the crowd, and I quickly deduced they weren't after me. One man was short, like the others, and stocky, in a walrusy kind of way. He reminded me of an English bobby. But the other was different. He was about my age *and* my height. His blond hair was wild and frizzy, like Dr. Emmett Brown in the *Back to the Future* movies. Yeah, and he was wearing a white lab coat.

"There, Constable, that's him!" he told the walrus, pointing at me. "These fools were about to rip him apart!"

"He's right about that," I quickly added.

The people all started shouting at once. The walrus waved his arms to quiet them.

"All right, all right, it's over," he said, *not* in a cockney accent. "Go back to whatever you were doing."

They grumbled but began to disperse. *Whew!*

The walrus cast a dubious eye at the man in the lab coat. "This is your *guest*, you say?"

"That's right, Constable Heywood. He's from . . . out of town and isn't familiar with our ways. I'll take him now."

The walrus looked me up and down. "Probably as daft as you, Ambrose. Well, don't let him out of your sight again."

"Wait a minute," I said, really pissed, "didn't you see what these people—?"

"Oh, no, sir, I won't," Ambrose interrupted, throwing me a shut-the-hell-up look. "You can count on it."

"Probably another daft *thinker*," Heywood muttered, walking away.

"Idiot," Ambrose said when the walrus was gone.

The people *had* gone back to what they were doing, except for one thing: At the moment none of them were dumping on the kids, physically or otherwise. That was good. I still got my share of dirty looks, but it beat the alternative.

Turning to my wild-looking rescuer, I started to say, "Guess I owe you—"

But he interrupted: "Save it till I've taken you home. Best to get away from the marketplace."

He led me to my bike. I thought the little creeps would have done a number on it, but surprisingly it was untouched.

We passed between dozens of people, headed for this one twisty road. On our way, I noticed a boy keeping pace with us. Now, I was growing reluctant to guess ages in this weird place, but facially I believed the freckled kid was about ten or eleven. He was the same height as Ambrose and me.

Just before we started up the road, the boy hurried around to stand in front of us. Smiling tentatively he said, "What you did back there was a wonderful thing. I don't think I'll let my parents hurt me like that anymore."

This pleased Ambrose no end. As the boy started off he grabbed his arm and said, "Tell other children the same thing you told us! You'll start doing that, won't you?"

The boy nodded; first reluctantly, then with more conviction. Ambrose practically did a dance, he was so happy.

Now we were headed up the road, passing only a handful of people along the way. I saw my first senior citizens, gnarly folks under four feet. Whether they knew what had happened or not, they sure as hell scowled at me.

When Ambrose finally came down to earth he said, "I'm sure by now you're thoroughly confused. You were going to thank me back there, when it is *me* who should be thanking *you*. I may be a genius in many areas, but *courage* it not one of them."

"Wait a minute, I don't have a clue what you mean. Since you figured out that I'm a stranger in these parts, why don't you start at the *very* beginning and give me an education?"

"Yes, that would make sense, wouldn't it? Very well. Once, this world was an ordinary place. Adults were like you and me, and children were little people who, in time, grew into those adults, which is as it should be.

"Then, the Dark Time of our history came. This was about one hundred and fifty years ago. *Something* covered our sun, and for countless days the people lived in terror, until finally the darkness went away.

"But the Dark Time caused something to happen. Children, although they continued to age, ceased to grow, while adults started getting smaller."

No shit, *The Incredible Shrinking Man*! See, I was right. And

I also had a good idea what Ambrose was going to tell me next.

"After that, when a woman became pregnant, the fetus expanded to unbelievable proportions within her. A child does not grow up after it is born, but rather grows *down*.

"You've likely seen women carrying their babies here. Can you imagine how uncomfortable that must be! And after it's born? Both parents taking care of a seven-foot infant!"

Yeah, I thought, must be a million laughs changing the kid's diaper!

"I suppose it's understandable why these people are so ill-tempered," Ambrose went on. "It's not only the difficulties of child-rearing, but spending your own entire life *shrinking*. Not much to look forward to."

"Yeah, it does sound bleak, but I still don't think it's an excuse for hurting a little kid, no matter how big that little kid is."

"Neither do I . . . here, this is home!"

We'd walked about a quarter mile out of town on a bumpy road. Dwellings here were few and far between. Ambrose's "house" was a ramshackle thing standing twenty-five yards back from the road. Both it and a small barn were surrounded by all kinds of junk, which made the place look like a landfill. The interior did, too, though at least it didn't smell, and there were no creepy-crawlies that I could see.

"I'll have to clean this place one day," he said unconvincingly. "But my hospitality is genuine, so make yourself at home."

"Thanks. Since I think I'm safe in assuming you're not a kid, how come you're normal-sized?"

"To answer that, the first thing I must make you understand is that most of the people here are doers. I, on the other hand, am a *thinker*. My parents were semithinkers, which was why my childhood was not as difficult as most. Even before my teens I was performing all sorts of scientific experiments."

He waved a hand around at the walls, where shelves were crammed with beakers, jars, tins, things that resembled petri dishes, and little tubes similar to what your 35mm film comes in. Messy, but impressive.

"With one of my formulas I was able to halt the shrinking process," he went on. "This just happened to be my size at the time."

"You . . . *stopped growing smaller*?" I exclaimed.

"Yes, just as anyone else here can. I also have a formula that can shrink a child to the proper size for its age, and another that works inside the womb. Afterward, the child will grow normally. I'm even working on a variation of the original one to enlarge a small adult. Whatever the case, within a generation everything would be normal again, as it was before the Dark Time."

Assuming this guy wasn't pulling my chain . . . he *was* a genius! "But why isn't any of this happening yet?"

Ambrose shrugged. "As I said before, these people are doers, not thinkers, and what they *do* is what they've always done, what their parents have done before them. They are scared to even talk about anything like this. So I'm considered *daft,* as Constable Heywood says, and am treated like a pariah, a carrier of some contagious disease. That's why your actions in town, and the response of the boy, are so significant."

"Yeah, are you ready to explain that now?"

"One of the many disadvantages of being a pure thinker is a total lack of courage, or at least the ability to understand it. I could never have stood up for those children like you did. Despite their hostility, it's gotten a lot of the people *thinking* . . . something they're surely not used to. And that boy's reaction, oh, how wonderful! Even as we stand here he is spreading the word among others of how the stranger defied the grown-ups, and how *they* could also do the same thing, seeing as how much bigger and stronger they are. We'll go back later, and you'll see what your actions have begun."

"I hear what you're saying, Ambrose, but don't underestimate your own courage. You *did* walk into the middle of the whole mess to bail me out, remember?"

He thought about that for a moment, then grinned. "I did, didn't I? Well, this calls for a celebration! I hope you're hungry and thirsty."

Yes to both. He shoved junk off a table I didn't even know was there and served up all kinds of stuff. I'm not sure what I was eating or drinking, but most of it was pretty good. The closest thing I could make a comparison to was this amber liquid in a pitcher, which tasted like alcoholic Tang.

Having a fondness for weird people, I enjoyed talking to Ambrose. His weirdness only enhanced his likability. Naturally he was curious about me, though he stopped short of asking where I came from. Everything else, however, was fair game:

my spandex wardrobe, the bike shoes, the Gargoyles I'd worn earlier against this world's bright sun. And you can imagine how much the Nishiki turned him on! With my permission he drew diagrams of it from every angle. Probably be seeing mountain bikes all over Warithess within a year.

After a couple of relaxing hours, Ambrose decided it was time to check out the town. When we went outside I noticed the sun was in the same place it had been all along. Ambrose said it was midday; by our time sunset was probably a week off. O-kay.

Beautiful downtown Warithess was in a mild state of turmoil. Conflicts between big children and little adults were going on in a number of places. The creeps still had the upper hand, but the kids were making strides. One huge five-year-old, probably imitating me, was holding his abbreviated father high overhead. The boy we'd run into earlier stood defiantly in front of his parents, arms crossed. Seeing us, he threw a double thumbs-up. Needless to say, Ambrose was ecstatic.

"This needs a bit more time to fester," he said, "*then* we'll hit them with something dramatic. Hmm, let me think . . ."

"Ambrose, if you gave your formula to one of the giant kids, how long would it take for the shrinking process to begin?"

"Oh, the change is almost immediate. No sense to prolong it."

"Then I have an idea. We'll need to go into the hills. I have transportation, but . . ."

"Don't worry, Jack, I do too. Come on!"

But before starting out we were confronted by Constable Heywood. The little walrus was really pissed.

"You see what you've started?" he said huffily. "Why I've a good mind to—yaaargh!"

Ambrose lifted him up Schwarzenegger-style. "You haven't seen anything yet!" he exclaimed. "Now out of our way!" and he threw the walrus atop a cart filled with what looked like cotton.

"See?" I told him. "You can be a thinker *and* a doer at the same time."

On our way back to his house Ambrose said, "After the Dark Time most species of animals seemed to disappear. A while back I made a journey to some distant valley, where I found a rather exotic pair of what I call swajjas. I've been breeding them ever since. There are six now, and two are pregnant.''

While I wheeled the Nishiki across the landfill . . . er, yard, Ambrose got some stuff out of the house, then went into the barn. He emerged with something that looked like it had hopped off the page of a book by Dr. Seuss. For the most part it was an enormous pink pig with purple mottling, except for the fuzzy head, which reminded me of Sam I Am from *Green Eggs and Ham*. Friendly-looking thing, too. There was a blanket across its contoured back, but no saddle, bridle, or anything. Ambrose straddled it, grabbing a double handful of its thick mane.

''Would you like to ride one?'' he asked. ''It'll be a lot easier going uphill.''

''No thanks,'' I said, even though the swajja was grinning at me. ''I'll stick with the bike.''

We cut across some fields and eventually joined the road I had first come in on, though much farther out of town. Now I suppose you already know what I had in mind. All this time I hadn't been able to stop thinking about poor little (??) Harlan, getting bitten, tweaked, dumped on, whatever. I'd explained this to Ambrose, and he agreed wholeheartedly with my choice.

Okay, so I *should've* ridden a swajja up into the hills. But what the hell, I survived, and pretty soon we were making time on the path across the meadow. Approaching the first cottage we saw Lemuel, stogie still in mouth, standing on top of a bale of hay and whapping Harlan across the back of the head.

Yeah, I'd made the right choice.

''Hey, Maisie,'' the little creep hollered, ''it's that guy again!''

Harlan stopped crying long enough to smile at me and gawk at the pink pig-thing. His mother appeared at the door. Lemuel glared at us.

''I thought I told you to get—!'' he began, but I cut off his wind and lifted him high. The stogie smelled like a rat-and-bean fart, so I pulled it out of his mouth and heaved it about twenty-five yards with a perfect spiral that would have impressed Joe Montana.

''*Bliffil*,'' Harlan said happily, petting the swajja.

''*Mmruggh*,'' said his father, less happily.

''Now let's talk about how you treat this poor kid,'' I said, ''because as of today, it's gonna stop.''

I suppose Maisie should've been pissed about everything, but instead she had a real anguished look. Echoing some of Ambrose's earlier words, she said, "You're a stranger, and a man, also, so what could you know about how it was to bear a child of this size. Or for the two of us to raise him . . ."

"Mmruggh," Lemuel said again, and I noticed he was turning blue, so I put him down.

"Only after having our own did we understand why *our* parents treated us as they did," Maisie went on.

"Yes, she's right," Lemuel said, gasping.

"No she isn't!" Ambrose told them sternly. "It hasn't been *right* for an eternity. Do you know what it was like before the Dark Time?"

"We've heard the legends, like everyone else," Maisie said. "But what good to bring it up? Even if it *had* been true, it could never be again."

"But what if it could?" Ambrose asked. "Please, answer me."

Maise looked at Lemuel, shrugged, and said, "I suppose it would be wonderful . . ."

"Then I'm going to ask you to trust me." Ambrose dug into his bag and pulled out something that looked like a pink Necco wafer. He gave it to Harlan.

"Fruufata," the big baby said, and put it in his mouth.

"What was that?" Lemuel exclaimed.

Ambrose unpinned the diaper and stood back. Harlan sat down. Five seconds later he began to shrink. Now I'm telling you this because I was standing there and watching, but I still don't believe it! He just kept getting smaller and smaller, grinning the whole time. Maisie covered her mouth; Lemuel's eyes bugged out.

In less than a minute a cute, pudgy *little* baby was sitting there. He sort of looked like Marvin from the comic strip. Maisie's eyes softened; so did Lemuel's, for that matter. The happy mom scooped up her son and hugged him.

"Can this truly be?" she exclaimed.

Ambrose nodded. "He'll grow normally now, maturing in his time."

Lemuel was grinning. "How can we repay you?"

"You can come to Warithess and share this with others," I said, "so Ambrose can do the same thing for them."

They agreed to this wholeheartedly. I put Lemuel on my bike

seat and rode the pedals. Maisie sat behind Ambrose, Harlan in front, making sure the swajja went in the right direction.

Needless to say, by the time we reached the densely populated outskirts of Warithess, people on both sides were noticing the little guy. Ambrose was happy to hold him up for all to see. Finally, one small woman with Mt. Everest on a wheelbarrow in front of her pleaded for help. Ambrose, like a priest offering communion, slid a green Necco onto her tongue. Her belly shrank, and she was no longer *PREGNANT!* but pregnant, like any normal woman in her ninth month. She was elated.

Others might have kept us there indefinitely, but we had them clear a path into beautiful downtown Warithess. There, the revolt of the little big kids had reached its peak. No longer were they taking *any* shit from their parents. The adults, quite chastened, were ready for some kind of assistance. When they saw Harlan and heard the words of his parents they said sure, make our kids normal-sized.

But guess what, the kids were dubious about this, especially after having a taste of power. Things went back and forth for a while. In the long run, however, the adults were truly sincere about having learned their lesson, and the kids really wanted to be kids. The first few "shrinkings" brought about some wonderfully emotional scenes, like families were discovering each other for the first time. It was neat. I knew everything was going to be fine.

"Well, Jack," Ambrose said during a lull, "I truly wish you could stay longer."

"My part is done, and I have to be moving on. But I'm sure you'll find plenty of willing assistants."

"Oh, indeed! Constable Heywood has already volunteered, and Maisie and Lemuel—and Harlan, too—are proving indispensable."

"I hope you have enough of all the formulas."

"If not, I'll make more! I'm a *doer* now too, remember?"

We shook hands, and I started away from the marketplace, this time to a hero's send-off. As I did, a little eight-year-old Cabbage Patch kid with orange hair stepped in front of the bike and said, "Hi I'm Daphne and I know who you are now aren't I cute in this size I still think that's a neat thing you're riding on can I—"

I scooped her up and gave her a big hug. With her parents'

permission I put her on the bike seat and pedaled out to their farm, where I dropped her off. The kid was beside herself.

With Daphne happily babbling and waving on the road behind, I started up into the hills.

CHAPTER 6

Dream a Little Dream a Little Dream a . . .

A thought for concern while riding along the Ultimate Bike Path: We already know this is some great *universal* artery, right? So it stands to reason that the different physical characteristics of life-forms with access to it is infinitesimal. They could be twenty feet tall, fifteen feet across, and fill up a lot of the tunnel.

Or they could be *really* small.

Bug-small, or germ-small. Small enough to be concealed under the mist covering the floor of the *mhuva lun gallee*.

Small enough to be turned into road splat when my tires ran over them.

Isn't that a bummer? Jack Miller, mass murderer; killer of seven intellectual centipedes from the planet Terminex III. Oh, great.

On the other hand, if these centipede beings, amoeba-folk, whatever, *were* intelligent, they would stay far away from the center of the Path; probably inch (or millimeter) their go-things along the bases of the walls. I hope so.

Maybe there was another *mhuva lun gallee* just for wee life-forms, about the diameter of a toilet paper tube, where . . .

Okay, Jack makes himself crazy again. Accept the last idea as gospel and leave it at that.

So of course, just as I'm reconciling this, I come across a small rider.

Not under-the-mist small, since I could obviously see it. Still, I overtook it quickly and would have caused serious pain had I not slowed down and veered off to the side.

Paralleling it now, I had a better look at this traveler. It was a skinny rat with horn-rimmed glasses and dreadlocks. Reminded me of half the erstwhile Milli Vanilli. Maybe it would lip-sync when it spoke; I'd have to see. It was about twelve inches from end to end, most of it a pink fleshy torso, the rest a gross rodent's tail, what you hate to see disappearing around the corner of your baseboard. Its go-thing looked like a green bedpan with eight Tinkertoy wheels, which it pedaled (I think) from the inside.

"Nice weather we're having," the rat said in a voice that, I swear, sounded like Peter Jennings. It reached out a tiny paw, which I leaned down and shook.

Looking around at the tunnel walls and ceiling I said, "Uh, right, nice weather." At least he was more personable than the elephant-fly.

The rat's beady eyes looked me up and down. "I don't think I've seen anything like you before."

"Likewise, I'm sure. Are you traveling the Path for fun and adventure?"

"Oh, hardly. I've been to dozens of worlds already and will travel to as many as I have to until I find someone who can cure my wullat."

Say what? "Cure your wullat? What's that?"

"It's a disease; very rare one indeed, but I have it."

"Is it . . . contagious?" I asked nervously.

"Yes, but only through direct skin contact, so you don't have to . . . whoops!"

He looked at his paw.

I looked at my hand.

The diseased rat had touched me!

"Sorry about that," he said sincerely as I frantically wiped my hand on my pants. "But maybe it only affects our species, so you need not worry."

Yeah, but did I want to take that chance? Jesus, *wullat!* I didn't like the sound of it. Suddenly I had this overwhelming compulsion to wash my hands.

"Well, I *am* worried, no thanks to you," I said sharply. Then I noticed his pained look, which was hard to determine on a dreadlocked rodent's face. "Listen, here's what you do. Start thinking Hazel the Healer, Hazel the Healer, over and over; really put out the vibes. When an Elmer Fudd gate beckons, take it. Hazel will solve your problem. Just tell her Jack sent you."

"Elmer *what*?" the rat asked.

There was a run of them on the left wall. I stopped wiping my hand long enough to point one out.

"Yes, I'll look for this Hazel," he said, "and thank you. Again, I'm sorry if—"

But I was already gone like a bat out of hell. I'd been pedaling slowly, so the slightest increase put a mile (or maybe a thousand) between me and the diseased rat in seconds. My course was a shaky one, steering as I was with only one hand.

There was a voice inside my head, repeating the same thing, *wash your hands, wash your hands,* and it sounded like Darth Vader, who of course was James Earl Jones, although David Prowse was inside the costume, but when he was revealed to be Anachin Skywalker it was actually . . .

Oh, yeah, you're right, I was freaking! Water, I had to have water! A bar of Lava would've been fine, too. Or even Ivory, which is nice, because it floats, and wasn't it Stephen King who said that we all float down . . .

Jesus, the wullat was affecting my brain!

The nearest portal was a black circle with the laser bread slicers. I burst through . . .

. . . and shifted out of the Vurdabrok Gear (at least I remembered to do that) to find myself in the middle of a blistering desert. Swirling winds raised dozens of little dust devils all around me. Nope, no water in these parts.

Arrakis . . . Dune . . . desert planet . . .

Worse, no hill from which to get back on the Ultimate Bike Path. The nearest mountains were at least a mahooga . . . at least fifty or more miles away.

Wash your hands, James Earl Jones *noodged.*

Turning, I noticed a rift that effectively divided the desert in two. It was narrow, maybe two yards across where I stood, but deep, descending into oblivion. At least I hoped so, because I didn't think twice about free-falling into it . . .

. . . which put me back on the *mhuva lun gallee* at a slightly skewered angle, easily correctable. The next gate was a Gorbachev birthmark. I penetrated its lemon-colored mist . . .

. . . and found myself atop a denuded, sheer-walled promontory that rose like a smokestack out of a dark green, ominous-looking sea. Water—*water*—lapped the base of the outcropping . . . over two hundred yards below. Big deal.

*Water. Wash your hands, Luke. Let go the hatred that burns
within you, and you will know the power of the Dark Side.*

My bike bottle! I had Gatorade; *wet* Gatorade.

Yeah, two big squirts. I poured out what was left, rubbed and
rubbed, until friction dried them up.

No good. I was convinced I still had wullat.

Wash your hands, my son.

Father, what the hell is wullat?

*It's what you use to soak your sweaters and other fine
washables, my son.*

I don't think so, Father.

Straddling the bike I leaped off the promontory . . .

. . . whizzed past two Bart Simpsons and dove into an
isosceles triangle . . .

. . . onto a grassy meadow, where an idyllic pond beckoned. *Yes! Gretzky shoots, he SCORES!*

I pedaled like a madman, even though the pond wasn't all
that far away. Naturally I was going way too fast when I
reached the edge and squeezed the brakes. Momentum (and
stupidity) carried me over the handlebars and into the cold
pond, which shimmered with the color of the stuff that you run
through your bathroom bowl. Now for all I knew this "water"
could have been battery acid, and my flesh could have gone the
way of those Nazis in the first Indiana Jones movie. But
nothing happened, and after a few seconds I figured it was
okay.

Standing waist-deep now in the pond. I began washing not
only my hands but all the rest of me, too. I mean, if wullat was
contagious, it must be spreading all over. Anyone watching me
thrash around would have been inclined to call for the nut
wagon, or someone from Animal Control to fire a tranquilizer
dart into my ass. I didn't care; I just wanted to get rid of
whatever-it-was. In retrospect I can't say why I freaked out so
much. Maybe that was one of the symptoms of the disease,
although I don't recall the rat in the bedpan go-thing acting
weird.

Whatever the case, I thrashed and splashed and wiped and
rubbed for a while. I must've been getting somewhere, because
eventually Darth Vader's voice faded away like that disembod-

ied chorus at the very end of Gustav Holst's *The Planets*. It was then that, drained, I dragged myself out of the pond.

Oh, nice going, Miller, jumping in with your bike shoes on! I took the squishy things off . . . which was the last thing I remember doing, because the frenetic minutes following my encounter with the diseased rat on the Ultimate Bike Path had exhausted me. Laying my head down on the soft earth, I either fell unconscious or asleep . . .

Don't ask me how long I was out. A small, pinkish sun was directly overhead when I opened my eyes, but since I hadn't noticed where it was when I'd gotten here, its location didn't mean a thing. Whatever the time frame, I felt refreshed and calm. My body was dry; so were my Avocet shoes, and I put them on. Maybe I'd slept for a couple of days. I was also convinced that the wullat was gone. Time to get on with business.

Rule-to-Live-By #326 When Riding the Ultimate Bike Path: Never shake hands with a rodent unless you're certain he's had all his shots.

Should I get back on the Path, or check this place out? I couldn't tell much about it from the little I could see. The yellow-green meadow was ringed by drab hills. There was another pond fifty yards across, and a few stunted trees scattered about, wanna-be maples and junipers with leaves showing autumn colors. No birds sang in these trees, and now that I thought about it, I didn't hear a sound coming from anywhere. It was quiet here . . .

Too quiet.

Is it a universal law that *deathly stillness* always precedes some cataclysmic event? A second later the tranquil, shallow tidi-bowl pond in which I'd bathed began to churn like Dr. Jekyll's magic elixir. Standing, I grabbed my Nishiki and started backing away.

Bubbles began popping over the frothing pond.

A hand emerged from the small body of water, rising atop an arm that was thicker than your average three-hundred-year-old redwood. The hand itself was about the size of Wrigley Field. Fifty yards above my head, it stopped. It swiveled around for a moment, then "looked" down at me. The index finger wagged, saying *you've been a bad boy jack.*

Then, the hand came reaching for me.

No Olympic sprinter on steroids would have been a match for me. Seven seconds later, when I leaped on the seat of my Nishiki, the bike computer was registering sixteen point five mph. I immediately got that up to twenty-three. But the arm continued to emerge from the pond, and the hand, fingers aflutter, came down from the sky.

Dropping a few gears, I pedaled furiously across the level, grassy surface. Twenty-nine point five; couldn't keep that up too long. For some reason I thought I was making progress.

Which of course was when the hand flicked the rear tire, toppling the bike and sending me sprawling (yet again). Stunned, I hardly noticed the hand fall, getting ready to pulverize my personage into the loam . . .

I snapped awake and was still near the tidi-bowl pond, and my bike shoes were still a little damp, but I put them on anyway. Hell of a dream that was, because it felt so real. Without hesitation I got away from there fast, even though everything was tranquil, and this time birds *were* singing.

My destination was the nearest hill, long and steep enough, I was sure, to get me back on the *mhuva lun gallee*. No, I wasn't interested in exploring this place. I'd cured myself of wullat (I guess) and had no desire to hang around.

The hill definitely *was* long and steep enough, because I was breathing hard when I got to the top. I'd walked all the way to check out the ground, which seemed to be debris-free under a short layer of grass. The trip back to the Path should be easy, right?

So just as I'm hitting thirty mph these six little blond girls in white taffeta dresses and saddle shoes skipping rope and tossing a ball appear . . . *less than ten yards ahead*. Veering too sharply I (all together now) fell off the bike and rolled down the hill. The brats pointed at me and laughed their heads off. I couldn't stop myself, not even when I saw this giant bear trap with *really* nasty teeth pop up. The guy who used to play Grizzly Adams stood next to it, nodding at me benevolently.

My butt end tripped the damn thing . . .

I woke up next to the tranquil pond. My bike shoes were pretty wet, but I put them on anyway.

It's just possible that I have this figured out. In that great comedy-horror flick *An American Werewolf in London*, the main character is in a hospital room recovering from all sorts of trauma at the hands (claws?) of a lycanthrope. He has this dream about a bunch of Nazi-style, armed-to-the-fangs monsters who come into his house, blow away his parents, his kid brother and sister, Miss Piggy and Kermit on the tube, before cutting his throat, which is when he wakes up. His sympathetic nurse goes to get him something; another one of the monsters appears and stabs the shit out of her. Our hero wakes up *again* from a dream within a dream. Really freaked him out.

Yeah, and this really freaked *me* out.

So was I awake now, or what? I used the old tried-and-true method of pinching myself on the arm. Hurt like hell. Yeah, but so did falling off the bike in both "dreams." Whatever. I *know* I was awake; standing in soggy shoes was enough to convince me of that. This time, by Crom, I would get out of here.

Forget the hill where I almost ran down those nasty little girls; there were plenty more. Casting a few wary glances at the tidi-bowl pond, I rode half a mile to the base of an especially steep one. I tossed aside a few bits of rubble on the way up, but no big deal. It would be a smooth run.

But needless to say, I was wary on the way down. At thirty mph I started pushing on the thumb lever. It gave way at thirty-one point five, and there was still nothing in my path. A moment later I was in twenty-second gear . . .

. . . and bursting *not* onto the *mhuva lun gallee* but something that could've been a dungeon of the Spanish Inquisition or an especially deep tunnel in the New York City sewer system. Dank, evil-smelling, with a two-inch layer of sludgy stuff on the floor that splattered up my legs. Along crumbling ledges on both sides of me, huge rodents (without dreadlocks) scurried in an unending line. Nasty place, wherever this was.

But it didn't make sense! I was in the Vurdabrok Gear for sure, and if universal law held sway then I *had* to be on the Ultimate Bike Path . . .

I *was* on the Ultimate Bike Path, just like that. No dungeons, no rush-hour rodents, even though I hadn't popped *through* a gate. But my speed was excessive, and I was moving *across* the Path, not along it, toward a blur of gates. No way could I stop in time. My only hope was to hit one of the gates, *not* the wall.

I *did* hit a gate, a Gorby (I think), at a crazy angle . . .

◆   ◆   ◆

. . . and shifted down absently as I looked around.

There was nothing to see.

Nothing but sky and clouds.

I was in free-fall, and this *wasn't* a module at Galaxyland.

Between the clouds I could see the spiraling peaks of a mountain range pushing up to meet me, and I could almost hear them saying *oh jack we would deem it an honor to have your guts splattered all over us.*

Yeah, well, no problem, right? In free-fall I could shift and get the hell out of . . .

I couldn't shift. Not because the lever was stuck, but because it had turned into a worm. Thick ugly thing it was, and it gyrated crazily; it was either doing the conga or tossing me the bird.

The tallest peak was closer than I had thought.

Oh, shit . . .

I snapped awake by the tidi-bowl pond. My bike shoes, still next to me, were full of water, from which minnows leaped, but I put them on anyway after pouring all of it out.

I was ready to rub the Bukko and put an end to this, because it was getting weird. Another dream, huh? But there, look at my arm: still a trace of the red mark where I had pinched it before.

Yeah, pinched it in my sleep.

If at first you don't succeed . . . screw it. No, that was a lousy attitude. Still . . .

How many times was this going to happen?

Next hill. Good easy unimpeded descent. Shift . . .

. . . and appear *along* the Ultimate Bike Path, right in the middle . . .

. . . but upside-down, on the ceiling.

A Florida gate wearing a Stetson looked more like Texas from my point of view.

Bart Simpson and Elmer Fudd looked weird.

A quartet of riders resembling Alaskan king crabs on skateboards clattered their pincers at me from below. At least I didn't have to deal with them.

I started floating down toward the pissed-off crustaceans. As the claws groped for my ass I remember thinking, *Someone pass the melted butter and lemon juice . . .*

◆ ◆ ◆

I woke up (or came to) under the Santa Margarita River bridge. The Old Guy (mine, I'm pretty sure) was kneeling by me. My bike shoes were on a rock, drying in the sun.

"Am I . . . dreaming this too?" I asked.

He smiled. "No, this is for real, Jack. We decided it was time to pull you out of there."

"So I don't have wullat anymore?"

"You never *had* wullat, Jack."

"I never did?"

"And even if you had contracted it, the only symptom— which lasts a couple of days—is a tingling in the tips of your whiskers."

"The tips of my . . . Darned rodent never told me that! So what happened to me?"

"It was the water in that pond. Dangerous stuff."

"Yeah, the water; that figures. But all that happened to me . . . I mean, was it live or was it Memorex?"

"Was it . . . ?" The finger went to the ear. I stopped him. "Was I hallucinating or what?"

"Oh, I see! Tough question, Jack. Why don't we just include it in the half you wouldn't understand?"

That wasn't good enough, but I suppose it would have to do. "Yeah, well . . . But I'm okay now, for sure?"

The Old Guy nodded. "My only advice is to let your shoes dry out more. After that you can get right back on the *mhuva lun gallee,* if you wish."

I followed him up to Stuart Mesa Road, where both our bikes were propped against the bridge railing. He smiled, waved, then climbed atop his Schwinn and wobbled off. Five hotshots in identical jerseys flew past him, and he nearly wound up in the turkey mullen.

Watching my favorite extraterrestrial struggle with the complexities of an Earth-born ten-speed, I decided that for sure I wasn't dreaming anymore.

I went back under the bridge, stretched out on a rock near my bike shoes . . .

. . . and fell asleep.

CHAPTER 7

Gypsies, Curses, and Such

I snapped awake under the Santa Margarita River bridge. My bike shoes, still on the rock, were dry. Only trouble was, a bunch of swallows from the mud condos had done a strafing run on them—and me. Gross! You'd think that, on a Marine base, someone could've called "Incoming!"

After wiping off the mess in the mucky river I put on the shoes and climbed up to the road. To tell the truth, even though I was absolutely unquestionably positive the dream was over . . . I *still* wasn't sure. That makes sense, right? Who knows, maybe life itself is one big dream that we keep snapping awake from, over and over. In which case, not to worry.

One thing for certain, my watch was ticking off the minutes and seconds. (Do LED watches really *tick*?) It was still Friday morning, but past ten-thirty, over three hours (of real time) since I'd begun this latest round of excursions into the unknown. That was about how long I'd been asleep. Not something I usually did; must've really needed it.

The Nishiki was right where I'd left it. Can't believe I forgot to lock it up; I mean, it's only *expensive as hell and has an alien-implanted extra gear*. No big deal.

There were a few bicyclists on Stuart Mesa Road. Muriel and Walt, haranguing each other, were starting up the hill in advance of three other seniors. Great; might as well go back under the bridge and catch a few more Zs.

Actually, I wasn't sure if I was ready to be back on the Ultimate Bike Path. In my head I knew that was stupid, but . . . So I stood on the bridge, watched the water fowl and did some thinking.

Mostly I thought about Holly.

On Monday—only three *real* days from now—I would start my cross-country ride. I was really looking forward to that and, of course, seeing Holly at the end. If I went home now, the weekend would be over with more quickly. But there were all those things you had to do before you left on a vacation, and having majored in Procrastination and Sloth, I hadn't attended to the first of them yet.

One of these things was to let my mother, Mrs. Rose Miller Leventhal, know what I was planning to do.

So tell me, Jackie, why are you going to Cedars Sinai?

That's Cedar Rapids, Ma.

All the way from California you'll ride your bicycle?

It'll be fine, Ma, I promise.

Oy, *don't do it, Jackie; you know I'll worry sick!*

I decided to get back on the Ultimate Bike Path.

Muriel, Walt, & Company had made it to the top but were now off their bikes, drinking water, gasping for breath, and sharing their near-death experiences. When I passed, Muriel waved and (I swear) did a bump-and-grind. Wonderful to know I had that effect on older women.

The Stuart Mesa hill was devoid of humanity as, riding down into a headwind, I pedaled furiously to make up the difference. At thirty-two mph I shifted into the Vurdabrok Gear and . . .

. . . well, by this time you ought to know.

I already had a plan: either Ralph Ralph's portal of light or a Gorbachev birthmark, whichever came first. With, of course, the option of choosing any gate that happened to reach out and grab me, as was sometimes their wont. Having so solid a plan my time on the *mhuva lun gallee* should have been minimal, right?

So naturally I began with an endless run of the iridescent snowmen, broken occasionally by an isosceles triangle. And none of *them* were inclined to offer an invitation. For a while I pedaled in what I called blur-speed; but they still dominated after I slowed down.

Come to think of it, the only time I'd tried one of the snowmen was on that little jaunt to Vulvan. Never even had a chance to look around. Maybe I should just concede and . . .

The snowmen were gone, just like that. A random pattern followed, every kind of gate imaginable . . . *except* a Gorbachev birthmark. I kept on riding, but to tell the truth, it was starting to get annoying.

Then, finally, a Gorby! It wasn't pulling me or anything, but that didn't matter. I penetrated its lemon-yellow mist . . .

◆　◆　◆

. . . and shifted down just in time to start a sneezing fit. Twelve in a row, far from my own world's record. Still, I disintegrated three heavy-duty Kleenex before it was over, which is when I looked around.

Maybe I would have been better off to keep sneezing.

I was on some desolate, boulder-strewn plain. The ground was the color of the dregs in the basket of your coffee maker, and smelled worse. Or maybe it was the air that stank, because the "air" was visible in all its yellowish-brownness, and you could rub it between your fingers. Gnarly trees were nightmares from the land of Oz. Compared to this place Areelkrokka was a garden spot, and Los Angeles would have made you want to suck in a deep breath and sing "Rocky Mountain High." No wonder I'd gone off on a sneezing jag! Uh-uh, this place wouldn't do at all. Class M it might be, but an unhealthy one. Quick decision: I'm outta here.

Visibility was not great in this muck. I could barely make out something looming in one direction, but I assumed it was a mountain range, so I started off that way. First I tied a handkerchief over my face to try to filter out some of this crap; looked like I was ready to hold up the Wells Fargo stage.

Actually, I was hoping that some bottomless pit or chasm would appear before I got there. After all, I was an old pro at free-fall now. But I was pedaling hard, and the mountains were looming larger, so either way I should've been out of this armpit of a place real soon.

Wrong-o. The ground began to shake, and I weaved from side to side, which at twenty-two mph was kind of hairy. I didn't get thrown this time; braking quickly, I leaped off the bike and tried to get a grip on what was happening.

The yucky earth was rising and falling in mounds of between four and five feet, but only in my immediate sphere, almost as if I'd been singled out for the honor of having seismic activity under my bike shoes. I staggered toward where it looked safer, but it seemed to follow. At least the ground wasn't opening up.

The ground opened up.

Not right below me, but a couple of yards away, close enough to send me scrambling atop a nearby boulder, which appeared to be stable. A second rift appeared, then a third, as I leaned down to haul up the Nishiki.

That was when the first of the whatevers appeared.

The whatever resembled a squid's tentacle, most of it as

thick as a telephone pole. On one side, probably its underbelly, there were these red, fleshy sucker-things, really gross-looking. Its end tapered down to a leathery bird's head, sort of like an eagle, with mean eyes and a clattering beak.

More of them started popping out of the openings in the ground. Fortunately none rose any higher than a yard or so.

Unfortunately, in my awkward position I wasn't able to pull the bike up quickly enough. One of the whatevers coiled itself around the frame; another grabbed the rear tire in its beak. I not only lost the tug-of-war but nearly got separated from my sanctuary. A nasty neb nearly nabbed me, but I dodged it and clambered to the top of the rock.

My beautiful and highly useful Nishiki was pulled under the roiling earth.

A few whatevers clattered around the boulder for a few seconds, then withdrew into the ground, which became still.

Oh, great, was this a way to ruin my day, or what! How in hell was I going to retrieve my bike? Let those things take *me* down there? Yeah, right.

Now then, Miller, let's not even *start* with the negative shit. Step one, get off the rock.

I got off the rock.

Steps two to five, take two to five steps and see if anything down below gets all excited.

I took the steps but didn't feel the earth move under my feet, or see the sky come tumblin' down.

Apologies to Carole King.

So now what, start digging? Jump up and down and yell *hey squid-things you took my nishiki and I'm really pissed off*? Maybe there was another kind of opening, like a big prairie dog burrow or a foxhole. Yeah, I couldn't wait to find one and climb down.

Scratching my name with a sharp stone on the boulder, I started exploring the immediate area. Each time upon returning to the spot I widened my circle, but everything was the same. If those whatevers did emerge from the ground it was through holes of their own making, and only when they felt like it.

Then, on a wider swing, I came across a path. A rough one, but definitely formed by the passage of footprints, wheel ruts, and animal tracks. No one was around, but at least there was hope of finding a person (or wanna-be person) who might be able to give me some kind of idea what I was up against below the surface of this polluted place.

I made an arrow out of stones and aimed it at the starting point, then explored the path for a hundred yards in each direction. Nothing. None of the tracks seemed fresh, either, though not being an eagle scout or a card-carrying Sierra Club member, I couldn't say for sure. The foul haze was still too thick to let me see very far; a city or town half a mile away would have gone unnoticed.

I covered the same ground twice, mostly to keep myself busy and not dwell on the deep shit I was in. It was before starting out a third time that I saw the animal.

The thing was snuffling around some rocks just off the path, stopping every so often to squirt an abbreviated stream. It was small, white, and fluffy, and from the rear looked like your ordinary pedigreed poodle. But its head, disproportionately large, was something else. It had a silvery, flowing mane and a face like a lion, though one that looked like someone had caved it in with a sledgehammer. The nose was flat, the eyes wide and bloodshot. Its curled-back lips revealed mostly broken teeth, except for two long, parallel incisors that could have been tusks. Assuming its temperament matched its appearance . . . I had a problem here.

Even though it was aware of my presence, the animal took its own sweet time about whatever it was going to do to me. Silent, it did the snuffle-squirt thing a few more times, then walked toward me slowly. It wasn't making any kind of sound. Who knows, maybe the thing was friendly . . . but it sure *looked* pissed off, and I gave that image priority as I backed away.

"Nice . . . thing," I said kind of stupidly. "Good doggy. Why don't you run off now, see if you can find a bone or something? Say, isn't that your mate calling? I . . ."

Maybe it was what I said, or how it sounded coming through the handkerchief around my face. Whatever; the poodle-thing reared, did a back-flip, and glared even more malevolently at me (if that was possible). Its mouth opened wide; I expected to hear a roar that would have shamed anything MGM had to offer.

"*Yip yip nyaah,*" it said rather weakly.

Then it ran toward me, and I knew it wasn't interested in playing fetch. Uttering a string of *yip yip nyaah*s it came in low and went for my ankle. I did this sort of spastic marionette dance to keep it at bay. Surprisingly its movements weren't that quick, and I had no trouble avoiding it . . . at first.

"Hey, knock it off!" I exclaimed, pulling down the mask in the hope of scaring it away. But that seemed to antagonize it even more. "Come on, before I turn you into—*ow!*"

Those incisors had punctured my left ankle, only because I'd stumbled and practically shoved it in the thing's face. Not deep, but it hurt like hell.

Now guess who was pissed off! Winding up in my best imitation of Rolf Benirschke, I kicked the little bugger through imaginary uprights about twenty yards away. It didn't squeal, but a subsequent string of *yip yip nyaah*s rose a full octave. It landed hard, and I was sure I'd taken the steam out of it.

Nope. It scrambled to its feet and started back for more.

That was when I noticed the gypsy woman fifteen yards away.

Yeah, an old gypsy woman, I swear. Smallish lady with a babushka and big dangly earrings and a serious expression. Behind her was a tired-looking old horse, and behind the horse an even tireder-looking old buggy with wobbly wheels.

The most noticeable thing was a gun the gypsy woman held. It was one of those old blunderbusses with a cavernous barrel. When she first raised it, I thought I was dead. My hand reached for the Bukko. But she twisted it around toward the poodle-thing, and with hardly any time to aim she pulled the trigger. The ensuing echoes of the explosion sounded like the last ten minutes of any Rambo movie. And you should have seen the projectile that came out of the gun! That's right, you could *see* the "bullet," which was about the size of a Scud missile. Hell of a thing to fire at that little animal. I figured it would be blown into nine thousand woolly pieces, but do you know what happened? This was weird. The poodle-thing *absorbed* the ball, and it began a sort of dance while changing from white to a glowing fluorescent pink. It turned three other colors, becoming brighter, until with a final *yip yip nyaah* it winked out of existence.

Sure, I was taken aback, but it didn't seem to faze the old gypsy woman in the least; or her horse, for that matter. Laying the blunderbuss down on the buggy seat, she led the horse to where I stood. Her expression did not change.

"You are wery lucky, yunk man," she said in a thick accent,

each word drawn out and deliberate. "Had I not destroyt the padoodle, it vould have bitten you."

"Yeah, thanks, I . . . the *what*?"

"Dot terrible creature, the padoodle. You know vot they say: 'Whoever is bitten by a padoodle and lives, becomes a padoodle himself.'"

There was something familiar about this gypsy woman; there was something familiar about what she just said . . . Yeah, I got it! This was Madame Maria Ouspenskaya, a great Russian actress who, near the end of her career, played this very role in the Wolfman movies of the forties. In the real world she'd been dead for decades, but the Ultimate Bike Path had a way of sending you to surprising places, didn't it. Okay, I'll go along.

"Don't you mean, 'Whoever is bitten by a *werewolf* and lives, becomes a werewolf himself'?" I asked.

"A verevolf?" she said. "Vot's a verevolf?"

"A verevolf . . . I mean, a werewolf is—*whoa! Jee-zis, you gotta be kidding!*"

"Vot's the matter?"

"I *was* bitten by the . . . padoodle!" I showed her my ankle. "See? It's only a little bite . . ."

She jumped back, startled, and made a sign that might have been a cross, except it had too many points. *"Oy wey!"* she cried. (Oy *wey*?) "You really vere bitten!"

"Yeah; uh, listen, Madame Ous—"

"Maleva is my name."

"Right, Maleva. Am I really in trouble here? I mean, was that little bugger rabid or something?"

She got even more solemn-looking, if that was possible, rolled back her eyes and recited from memory:

> *"Even a man who is pure in heart*
> *and says his prayers by night,*
> *may become a padoodle when the padoodlebane blooms,*
> *and the autumn half-moon is bright."*

The *half*-moon? "So, I *do* have a problem. Can you help me?"

"I can't, but I vill send you to somevun who can."

"That vould . . . would be appreciated. I'll go anywhere to save myself from being turned into a padoodle." (Do you think I was buying any of this?) "But I have a more immediate problem here."

"Vot's dat?"

I told her about what happened to the Nishiki. She jumped back again and made that same weird sign. There were too many points for even a Star of David.

"So you see, I have to get it back," I concluded.

"*Oy wey,* you are one cursed dude." (I *swear* that's what she said.)

"Right; uh, you can help me with this problem, can't you?"

"You say it vas right over dere?"

"Yes, about fifty yards."

"Your—vot did you call dat ting?"

"My bicycle."

"Yes, your votever is no longer anywhere in the wicinity."

No longer in the wicinity! Now I *definitely* didn't like the sound of those words. "What is that supposed to mean?"

"Your . . . votever was taken by the muunastrebors," she said (I think!). "Dey roam everyvere across the land. It vas only chance dat put them here. The muunastrebors alvays return to vhere they come from, vhich is around the Castle Frankenstein."

The Castle Frankenstein, of *course*! "So that's where I must go to find my bicycle?"

"Yes, and also to rid yourself of the padoodle's curse."

"Oh, right, forgot about that."

"The good Dr. Frankenstein is the only vun who can do this," she added.

"Great. How far is the castle?"

"About tventy kilometers."

Hey, not bad, twelve miles or so. "How do I get there?"

"I am going in the opposite direction, or I vould take you dere myself. Follow this path, and vhen it ends at a vider road, turn left. It has many tvists and turns, but vill ewentually lead you to Castle Frankenstein. Just be varned, the vay is not alvays an easy vun."

How come I knew that? "Yeah, well, thank you, Maleva."

She shoved a trembling finger in my face. "Bevare, yunk man, bevare the half-moon."

"Oh, for sure, I vill bevare," I told her solemnly.

This seemed to satisfy Maleva. I helped her atop her tired old buggy, and she called a command to her tired old horse, which started off along the road. A minute later the gypsy woman had disappeared into the smog.

CHAPTER 8

Dr. Who?

Now really, the aforementioned scene required more than a modicum of assimilation before I took even a single step in *any* direction. So I stood there awhile, and *assimilate* is exactly what I did.

Okay, this is what had gone down: An old gypsy woman named Maleva—*the same gypsy woman who had first advised Larry Talbot of his new lycanthropic tendencies in a movie from about half a century ago*—had just saved me from a killer padoodle. At the same time she had said that I, poor innocent Jack Miller, now bore the creature's curse. Yeah, and freeing myself of the curse necessitated a visit to (deep breath) *Dr. Frankenstein's castle,* which was twenty . . . uh, twenty kilometers away. And just by the merest of coincidences that was where my Nishiki was being taken by these humongous squid-thing whatevers called muunastrebors. One trip solves both problems, right?

Right. That's why I stayed in the same spot for a good five minutes after the whole tired old entourage disappeared.

The first decision I arrived at was that this curse-of-the-padoodle business was horse hockey. Forget about that (I think). I mean, it was only two tiny punctures, and they hardly bled at all. Next, did those mindless whatevers really possess a homing instinct? I don't know, but I wasn't going to trek twelve miles without expending all other possibilities.

Which, frankly, seemed to be diddly. But in spite of that I finally got moving; *not* in the direction Maleva had told me to go, but back to the rock with my name on it. I know, she'd said my Nishiki was no longer in the wicinity; still, I wasn't going to be convinced until I'd at least given it one more try.

Remember what I said before about jumping up and down and screaming? That's what I did now, all the time thinking how ridiculous I must have looked. If the whatevers were around I had to somehow attract them, although what I would do when they got here was something I hadn't considered. You know what would have been nice? One of those thumper things, like they used in *Dune* to attract the worms. Well, tough; I had to make do. But I sure as hell stayed close to the rock.

Yeah, you guessed it; nothing happened. I was still having trouble with the concept that the muunastrebors were headed for home, but I had to admit they were migratory. The squid-things—*and* my Nishiki—were definitely no longer in the wicinity.

Reluctantly I admitted that the old gypsy woman knew what she was talking about. I went back to the rutted path and with a shrug set off along it. Now I haven't been giving you a play-by-play of this, but ever since I'd pulled down my handkerchief to yell at the padoodle I had been sneezing regularly. Not in endless jags, but one or two a minute. And coughing, too. I mean, this place was vile! Sure, I'd covered up again after the gypsy left, for whatever good that did. The handkerchief probably looked like a cigarette filter saturated with tar and nicotine and all the other shit smokers suck into their lungs.

The first ray of hope on this trek was that after half a mile the yellowish-brown haze began to dissipate. What had been a bloodred sun now lightened to a sort of pale ochre, and soon the sky was no different from the one that hovered above Newark, New Jersey, on an average day. Not having sneezed or coughed for a while, I undid the handkerchief. Whoa, gross! Worse than a filter.

Pretty soon I came to the road that the gypsy woman had foretold, and I turned left. It was wider, as advertised, but just as rutted, not anything you'd want to run your Hyundai over at speeds in excess of seven mph. Nor could I see a soul upon it, even with the increased visibility.

The road twisted and turned a lot, also as advertised. Four or five miles distant were the foothills of a mountain range, which meant that the road would either be skirting the base or splitting a pass. In either case it would be nightfall by the time I got to the mountains, because the dingy sun was on its way down, and moving steadily. The prospect of a night in this place did not thrill me.

Bevare the half-moon, yunk man.

Oh, come on, Miller, you'd already decided that . . .

Someone was coming toward me on the road.

The figure was a quarter mile ahead and I couldn't make out

any details, other than being fairly sure it was a man. We both kept right on walking, and soon I could see him better.

It was definitely a man, fiftyish, wearing a baggy brown suit and carrying a large wooden cross (I swear) over one shoulder, like a sentry with a rifle. Studying me as intently as he was, he stumbled a couple of times. Soon, at ten yards away, I recognized him. It was . . .

Peter Cushing.

That's right, the British actor who in his career must have played in about three thousand movies (nowhere near the record of an American actor named Whit Bissell, who honest-to-God had a small role in every movie ever made). He played Dr. Who in the BBC series, and Tarkin in *Star Wars,* and appeared endlessly in the Hammer Films horror flicks of the fifties and sixties, many in the role of Dr. Frankenstein.

Frankenstein!

Had the mountain come to Mohammed? Was I finally having a spot of good luck, some *nachis* (hard *ch*), as my mother, Mrs. Rose Miller Leventhal, was wont to call it? Maybe; but in my usual cautious mode I decided to reserve judgment until I came face-to-face with the guy.

At five yards away Cushing/Who/Frankenstein stopped and regarded me curiously. I suddenly became self-conscious about my bright spandex wardrobe, the bike shoes, and the Padres hat on my head (my helmet was secured—still, I hoped—to the rack on my Nishiki). Must've struck him as weird. But I don't think that's what was on his mind as, now approaching slowly, he hoisted the cross above his head. The descending sun behind him cast a shadow on me. I grinned stupidly. He shook the cross, and the shadow danced. This time I shrugged.

After a few seconds Cushing/Who/Frankenstein seemed to be satisfied. Laying the cross back over his shoulder, he pointed up the road behind me.

"You don't want to be going that way," he said.

"I'm not," I replied, "I was going this—"

"You don't want to be going that way!" he repeated, more insistently.

O-kay. "Uh, no. I don't, thank you. Why's that?"

"Soon the night will come, and Castle Dracula is not far. It is then that the creatures of darkness awaken."

Uh-huh, Castle Dracula. No time for this. "Listen, speaking of castles, I was just on my way to see you."

"To see *me*?" He was surprised, and pleased.

"Yes; you *are* Dr. Frankenstein, aren't you?"

Now he wasn't pleased anymore. "You mistake me for Dr. *Frankenstein*?" he exclaimed. "That madman?" For a moment I thought he was going to impale me on the cross.

"Oh, sorry," I told him, acting really appalled at my ignorance. "Are you Dr. Who?"

"Who?" he asked.

"Dr. Who."

"Who?"

"Uh, never mind. Just *who* are you?"

"Who?"

"No, really!"

"I am Van Helsing, *who* else?"

Professor Van Helsing, of course! With all these clues, how could I not have known? Peter Cushing *had* played the vampire hunter to Christopher Lee's Dracula in some of the Hammer movies, though not nearly as many times as he had been Frankenstein. Maybe that was his favorite role. Whatever.

Squinting at him I said, "Oh, yes, it *is* you. Couldn't see without my glasses."

He nodded. "Yes, understandable. Well, time's a-wasting, and I have important work to do. If you insist upon seeing that fool Frankenstein, just follow this road through the pass. You'll come upon his castle soon enough. Just, uh, be careful getting there, young man."

The vay is not alvays an easy vun. Yeah, I knew that, but I thanked him anyway, then said, "You be careful too."

He whipped open each side of his jacket, like a guy in an alley trying to sell you a hot Rolex watch. There were jewel-encrusted crucifixes and Stars of David galore. Van Helsing the vampire hunter wasn't taking any chances. He started to walk away, then turned and looked at me again.

"Two things you must be warned about, young man," he said.

"What's that?"

He pointed ahead of him. "You don't want to be going that way."

"Yes, thank you. What was the second thing?"

"At all cost, do not get bitten by a padoodle!" This time he left.

Shit, why did he have to say that!

CHAPTER 9

What's in There?

The encounter with Cushing/Van Helsing/Whoever had not made my day. Not that anything else had from the moment I'd turned up here in wherever-I-was. But now this new warning had gone a long way in convincing me that what I'd been denying was true: I really *was* carrying the curse of the padoodle!

How about some melodramatics: the *Curse* of the *Padoodle*. Wouldn't a horror movie with a title like that just chill you to the marrow of your bones?

Okay, maybe I wasn't in major deep shit yet. Seems to me that, back home, the moon was in its full phase right now. If the same was true here, no problem. Sure, Lon Chaney Jr., Michael Landon, Oliver Reed, and guys like that might be in trouble, but *I* would be fine.

It wasn't going to be long before I found out. The sun was beyond the mountains, and by my guess there were maybe ninety minutes of daylight left. Actually, within a few minutes of resuming my trek I thought I'd overestimated that time, for it seemed to be growing dark all of a sudden. But that was because of the clouds now rolling in rapidly below the sorta-blue sky, gray, ominous things that seemed to say *think we're gonna rain on your already shitty parade jack.* Yeah, great. On the other hand, if it kept the moon hidden all night, maybe I could justify being dumped on.

Well, guess what, *nachis!* The clouds remained but there was no rain, lightning, thunder, nothing. The air even seemed a little less foul. Within an hour I was well along the mountain pass, the rutted road climbing steadily, but not radically. Nor had I run into anyone since my encounter with the vampire hunter.

It was just about then that I spotted the black lake.

Actually it was below me at the moment, the road having twisted its way to the summit of a knoll. Yeah, it really *was* black. I don't mean pollution-dingy black, but *black*. Prince William Sound black, nasty L.A. Raiders black. Kind of a striking body of water in a perverse way. I swear the whole thing looked flammable.

The lake filled a portion of an expansive meadow, and was ringed by cattails, tules, and stuff, none of which seemed to have any business growing out of that muck. Just before dropping down to skirt it I noticed that at the far end of the meadow a portion of the lake narrowed to an inlet, which split some low peaks. Maybe it wasn't a lake but a lagoon; an offshoot of a broad river, or even the sea.

So now I was walking along it, still amazed by the things growing there. Okay, but it sure as hell couldn't support any other kind of life.

Which, of course, is when the surface started churning five yards out.

A few seconds later the Gill Man bobbed up, pointed a webbed appendage at me, and started for shore.

I wasn't born yet when *Creature from the Black Lagoon* was in the theaters. But as a kid I used to watch the movie and its sequels on television, and I swear, the Gill Man scared the crap out of me! I had a plastic model kit of him. (Used to take it to school and freak out the girls, until this one in my class, Naomi Finkelstein, stomped it into a million pieces under her saddle shoes.) Even when I found out the creature was an actor named Ricou Browning in a zippered suit, I still believed that an encounter with him would result in the rending of my flesh and the consumption of my brain. Took me a while to get over that, too.

All of the aforementioned thoughts occurred over a period of time approximately seventeen hundredths of a second long, because I *was* about to have an encounter with the Gill Man. Ricou Browning or not, the thing that had just climbed from the ink-black lagoon and raised itself to its full height of six feet plenty was definitely in character. It had killed Richard Denning and others in the movie, and ripped off the face of Whit Bissell (see?), and now . . . *it was after me!*

Okay, so now I'm tearing ass along the road, which veered away from the edge of the lagoon. In case you didn't know, the soles of bike shoes were not made for running track, or even for short walks. Sort of reminds me of the shoes they put on dead people to make them look good in their coffins. While shiny on the surface, the soles of these corpse shoes were cardboard, because—after all—the wearer wasn't going anywhere.

Near-death experiences promote weird thoughts, don't they? I was running, the Gill Man was walking, but somehow he managed to stay the same distance behind me. Watch any horror movie with a stalker sequence and see if that isn't true. Well, at least he wasn't gaining, but one misstep on this lousy road and . . .

The creature had been making these grunting, hissing noises the whole time, but they soon changed into a steady asthmatic wheeze. Turning, I saw that he had stopped. Webbed hands on his *knees,* he was gasping. Well, he was a *Gill* Man, and he couldn't be out of the water too long, right? What luck! Throwing me a gesture that was either a show of respect or the bird, he staggered back toward the lagoon.

But we really had come a far distance from the water, and he was still ten yards away when he fell to the ground. From the way his lizard body was heaving I didn't think he was going to make it. Now, considering he would've probably had me for dinner, I shouldn't have cared if he croaked. Not so, because the Gill Man was a legend, a bona fide member of the Monster Hall of Fame, and I hated to see him go like this. I even thought about giving him a hand back to the lagoon.

Which was when the surface churned again, and this time the Swamp Thing climbed out. He splashed water on the Gill Man's scaly body, then carried him to the lagoon. Before disappearing below he smiled at me and made a thumbs-up sign, which I returned.

Interesting encounter, I thought, standing there. Then I turned and walked away, because I had promises to keep and miles to go and all that stuff, and it was really truly starting to get dark. The road began to twist again, and the black lagoon fell from sight.

Here's something I hadn't considered until now: At night, with ominous clouds filling the sky, walking through a mountain pass, *it was dark!* The road became treacherous, and based on recent history it was creepy not knowing what might jump out of the shadows and grab me.

And there was always the curse of the padoodle . . .

But nary a star was visible above, not for the subsequent hour or so that I trudged on. Good, keep it that way; one less worry. Even if the worst came to pass, what harm could I do up here in the middle of nowhere, with no one around for a zillion miles?

A village appeared on the road ahead.

No, I don't mean *appeared* like it was Brigadoon or something. I'd just come around the base of an outcropping when I saw it, or at least the light from its many torches. Not too far ahead, either. Maybe the natives could tell me how close I was to Frankenstein's castle . . . assuming they were friendly. If not, a hasty adieu would be in order.

Small, tidy-looking wooden cottages lined both sides of the road, like so many gingerbread houses. Larger buildings in the "center" of town might have been restaurants, inns, or shops. The townspeople, who really didn't begin popping out of the shadows until I neared the hub, were a sullen-looking bunch, all dressed in peasants' garb. Some carried torches, others walking sticks, so I suppose you could say they were armed. I tried nodding, smiling, and tipping my Padres cap a lot; to tell the truth, I don't think they were impressed.

"We don't like strangers here," one guy said.

"Yes, you'd best keep moving on," a woman added.

Now the first thing was, they didn't say this in a menacing sort of way, but rather timidly. And second, all of them kept casting furtive, twitchy glances over their shoulders, sort of like Dr. Richard Kimble in *The Fugitive* looking for Inspector Gerard on his ass. It made you nervous just watching them.

"Well, hello to all of you too," I replied. "Actually, I had only planned to pass through, but to be honest, I'm hungry and tired. Can you help me?"

That was all true, by the way. My stomach was grumbling and my feet were killing me. A chance to stop would be welcome. The townspeople, momentarily confused, glanced at one another (in-between their furtive over-the-shoulder stuff, of course), then looked at me again.

"There's no room at the inn," the first guy said. (Jesus, did I look like Mary and Joseph?) "Isn't that right, Hans?"

"Indeed, Horst, we are all booked up," Hans replied. "What about food at the restaurant, Helga?"

"No food, no food," Helga said. "Helmut, am I right in saying that?"

"Oh, yes, certainly," Helmut said. "But we can confirm it with Heidi."

"Heidi is visiting Hiroshi," Horst said. (Hiroshi?) "But I think Hilda—"

"All right, listen," I interrupted. "You made your point.

Fine, I won't stay. But do me two favors. At least fix me up with a sandwich, a bag of Fritos, and a diet Mountain Dew, or whatever, to take along.''

"Can't do that," said Hans. (Or maybe it was Helmut, or . . . Hooever!) "No food, remember?"

"Oh, right," I said wryly.

"What was the second favor?" Helga asked.

"Tell me how far I am from Castle Frankenstein."

Hoo boy, did this set them off! Chattering noisily they backed away, wagging fingers in my direction while still glancing over their shoulders.

"Why do you want to know that?" Horst finally asked.

"I, uh, need to recover something that belongs to me."

"And nothing else?" Helga asked suspiciously.

"No, that's it." Did you *really* think I was going to get into that with them? I didn't like the look of those walking sticks.

Horst nodded, apparently satisfied, and said, "It is not far, only three miles, but the way is dangerous, and you must be very careful."

Hadn't I heard variations on that same theme before? "Yeah, well, thanks for . . . whatever," I said disgustedly.

"Are you leaving now?" Helga (no, Hilda . . . I think) asked hopefully.

"Yeah, I suppose. You sure you don't even have a Butter-fingers bar around, or a Nestlé Crunch?" They shook their heads. "Okay then, I'm outta—"

Now wait a minute, hold the phone! I suddenly realized there were stars in the sky, visible through holes in the clouds. The edges of these clouds were well defined in the glow of the moon behind them. They drifted rapidly, more and more stars being revealed. The townspeople also shot glances skyward, in addition to all their other jerky movements. I had a hunch they were curious about my sudden interest in celestial bodies.

The moon *had* to be full; I mean, the glow behind the clouds was bright. The rift grew wider, and the edge of the moon appeared. I held my breath. Was this dramatic, or what! Most of it was revealed, until nary a cloud impeded my view of . . .

. . . the *half*-moon.

The first impulse I felt was to peel off all my clothes, which I did, everything but my Padres hat.

Next was to clutch my face in my hands, because I felt like

I was on fire. I was sure my skin looked as though I'd been basking in the glow of a Death Valley summer sun for twelve hours.

"See, he's turning into a padoodle!" Hans or Horst or Helmut cried. "He bears the curse!"

I started to tell him how much bullshit that was, but the only thing that came out was *"Yip yip nyaah."*

This sent them scattering to the four winds and evoked a chorus of slamming doors. Not that I paid any attention to it, because—after all—*I was turning into a padoodle!* Something was taking over my brain; I felt myself being pushed back, back, by some giant invisible hand, until what little remained of my consciousness was tucked into some dark, remote corner. *Yip yip nyaah* sounded endlessly through this place. I could see around me, but in a weird way, like my eyes were distant windows on a towering wall. When I tilted my (its?) head to glance down at my body I saw tufts of white hair springing up like hyperactive cotton balls. The paws had already formed. I tried to scream *Merde!* but couldn't hear a thing over the echoes of *yip yip nyaah.*

There was never an old gypsy woman around when you really needed one!

The ensuing minutes, or hours—or whatever—were pretty weird. I was running around a lot, changing directions as often as a reeling drunk. Many times, through the distant oval windows, I could see the bright half-moon, always coincident with a plaintive *yip yip nyaah,* like I (it) was baying at the blasted thing. I was most worried about what would happen when it ran into other people, not being especially fond of murder and such. But word had spread through the village, for I encountered only one man, standing in front of a cottage. He escaped inside, slamming the door behind him about half a second before my (its) claws raked deep furrows in the wood.

One thing I remember vividly about that night was taking a leak on every rock, tree, hitching post, you-name-it, that I passed. Now there was something to put in your memoirs.

Have you stopped to consider the ludicrousness of a six-foot padoodle in a Padres cap?

Along with my desire not to slaughter anyone, my other fervent hope for the night was to not come across a mirror. Really, I didn't want to see what I looked like.

So there I was, roaming the countryside, not causing any

havoc, futilely chasing an occasional rabbit or field mouse. The half-moon floated toward the mountains, and I hoped it would be over soon. Then, as my consciousness dwindled farther, I ran into another person. It was Lon Chaney Jr., or Larry Talbot, I suppose. He wasn't frightened by the padoodle; on the contrary, he was pointing at me and laughing his ass off, snorting so hard that his booger problem was out of control. I figured the padoodle would turn him into *pâté*, but it (I) just turned and hurried off. Professional courtesy or something.

How rude of him! I thought. Maybe *I'll* come back at the *full* moon and laugh *my* ass off in his furry face.

Yeah, right.

From somewhere up ahead I heard a sound; vague, but sort of familiar. I saw a cottage in the light of the half-moon, and as I came nearer I recognized the sound as the bleating of sheep. There was a corral behind the cottage. I stood on the bottom fence rail and peered over at five or six of the woolly little guys, all huddled up and scared shitless in a corner. The ensuing *yip yip nyaah* from my (its) throat had a nasty ring to it.

Uh-uh, this was too much! Whatever was going to happen, I didn't want to know. As the padoodle hopped the fence I let go the last thread of awareness, and there was a peaceful sort of emptiness that plummeted me into nothing . . .

CHAPTER 10

A *Long* Mile

It had to be early morning, because the sun wasn't too high up. The air was yucky again, not like when I'd first arrived, but bad enough.

I was observing all this while lying supine on a smelly bed of straw. My eyelids had just fluttered open; the first thing I observed (after the sun and sky) was that I was *me* again. Hands were hands, feet were feet, et cetera. Next, I was aware of sheep standing calmly around me, like I was part of the furniture. This was a good sign; I mean, wouldn't they have been pissed if I'd eaten one of their kinfolk? I looked around the corral for a carcass, checked my personage for blood; nope, nothing. Maybe the half-moon had gone down in time, or maybe padoodles had no taste for mutton. Whatever. The bottom line was, on my first night as a padoodle the curse had not affected anyone but me, except for perhaps giving the townspeople a bad dream or two.

The townspeople: They were lined along the railing: Hans and Helga and Horst and Heidi and Helmut and Hilda and Hiroshi (*he* was easy to identify) and a Hole Hell of a lot of others, still darting nervous glances all around. Standing slowly, I noticed that Hilda (I think) was holding my clothes. Right, I was naked as a day-old rat! I whipped off the Padres cap and covered up my privates, which seemed stupid, considering they'd all been staring at me since daybreak. Seeing my discomfort Hilda tossed me the bundle, and I dressed quickly.

"Now do you understand why we don't like strangers?" Hans asked admoningly. "No matter how nice they are, it seems they all bear one curse or another."

"Fortunately you wrought no havoc," Helga said. (*Whew!*)

"If so, we would have had to fire a gold bullet through your heart or drive a stake through your brain, or whatever the curse requires." (Double *whew!*)

"Yeah, well, thanks," I told them.

"Now then, you *must* leave our village," Horst said firmly.

"We know what you are now, and if you choose to stay we may not be able to restrain ourselves from whipping your ass and chopping you into small pieces for the cormorants and snapping turtles to feed on." (I almost tapped the UT6 in my neck after that last bit of bullshit!)

"Uh, right, thank you. Well, like I said last night, I'm outta here."

"If on your way back you bring a certificate of de-cursing signed by Dr. Frankenstein himself," Hiroshi said, "perhaps we'll be more hospitable."

You know, they actually didn't seem like a bad bunch of folks, just nervous. I could sense that they felt sorry for me. Helga, who was really sad-faced, held out a paper sack.

"Here, I found a bit of food for you," she said.

"Thank you." I smiled at her, and she blushed.

"You may have this, too," Hilda said, handing me another sack.

"And I brought you wine." Horst gave me a quart-sized skin.

"Me too," Helmut said.

The bottom line was, I left the village with two sacks of food, three skins of wine, a walking stick, and a fist-sized rock with red letters painted on it that said, *Souvenir of the Place You Just Came From* (now *there* was something really useful). Again dat ole refrain, *the vay is not alvays an easy vun,* was called after me.

Let me ruminate on that for a moment: I'd already covered about nine of the alleged twelve miles, and so far what was the big deal? Van Helsing the vampire hunter, although weird, was one of the good guys. The Gill Man could have caused bodily harm, but he was easy to outdistance. Lon Chaney Jr. was around, but harmless for at least another week. So with only three miles left to Castle Frankenstein, I wasn't too bent out of shape.

Would that I could know what was yet . . .

But first things first. To say I was hungry would have rendered me the perpetrator of a gross understatement. Besides, not having eaten since . . . whenever, I must have expended a lot of calories during my padoodlistic meanderings of the night just passed. In deference to the townspeople and their paranoia I left the village quickly, stopping as soon as I was out of sight. Picked a nice place, too, a grove of sorta-eucalyptus trees surrounding an idyllic pond. The water was neither black nor tidi-bowl-colored, but normal. No matter, I wasn't about to drink it, despite an overwhelming thirst.

Accordingly I squeezed half a skin of wine into my mouth, not something you'd normally do on an empty stomach, but I didn't care. To tell the truth, this "wine" wasn't anything like a ten-year-old chardonnay; more like week-old, watered-down prune juice with a slight bouquet of Mr. Clean. Anyway, it was wet and did the trick.

Helga's sack held a stale roll and a long, thick piece of wurst. Hilda's sack held a stale roll and a long, thick piece of wurst. The piece of wurst in Helga's sack was very tasty; in fact, it was the best wurst I'd ever eaten. On the other hand, the wurst from Hilda's sack was terrible. Without a doubt it was the . . .

Go ahead, you finish it.

Anyway, I ate everything in both sacks and washed it down with the other half skin of "wine." As I was finishing, an angelic-faced little girl of about six approached the far side of the pond. She was holding hands with the Frankenstein monster (Karloff's version, definitely *not* Christopher Lee's), who had this shit-eating grin on his stitched-up face. They dropped to their knees side by side and started throwing flowers atop the surface of the water. The monster thought this was really cool.

"Hey, kid," I called, "you don't really want to do that."

The little angel stuck out her tongue and said, "Eat shit and die."

The monster jerked up its middle finger and said, *"Mlooorg brabblag."*

Yeah, well, the two of you have a nice day! They resumed tossing the flowers, and I got ready to leave. But as per the script they ran out of flowers, and the monster got all teary-eyed, because he liked watching pretty things float. Now, this is the scene they *censored* in the 1931 movie, later restored on videocassette. The monster picks up the kid and heaves her into the water, where she's supposed to flounder and drown. But not this time. I reached in and dragged her to safety.

"See, I told you!" I said. "Little girls shouldn't play with monsters. If I hadn't been here you could've—"

Doing her best impression of the Trevi fountain, the brat

spewed a quart of water in my face. She kicked me in both shins, then backed away a few yards as I hopped around in pain.

"Tear his arms off!" she cried to the monster. "Rip off his scrotum!"

"Dooooong makkkaaa," the monster said menacingly, starting toward me.

All right, the hell with it! Let him drown the little shit next time. Grabbing my walking stick I exited stage right . . . *in haste.*

Moments later I was back on the rutted road that, a hundred yards farther along, narrowed as two sheer-walled cliffs on either side thrust themselves toward each other. At the same time an incredibly dense fog dropped down, filling the narrow rift and limiting visibility to ten feet . . . enough to see what was now on the road behind me.

A tall, spectral figure with seaweed and slime and shit dripping from it and eyes that glowed like burning coals. In its *hand* it held a nasty-looking gaff. It was the leprous Blake, and behind him the rest of his pissed-off crew from the *Elizabeth Dane,* the vessel sunk by the founding fathers of Antonio Bay, California, over a century ago. They were back, as usual, for their own brand of vengeance.

Gads, did these guys give me the willies!

"Jaaaa-c-c-kk," Blake called in a gurgling voice, the gaff swinging like a pendulum as he and his crew shuffled toward me.

Did you know that Mach one *could* be achieved on land without the aid of a vehicle?

Sure, I could've run into a stone wall, but the risk was worth taking. The road immediately widened, and the fog (excuse me, *The Fog*) lifted, and there was nothing on my ass.

But there was someone on the road ahead of me.

Freddy Krueger.

He was sitting on a rock next to an elm tree, grinning that burnt-flesh grin of his. "Where ya going, fuckerrr?" he crooned.

You know, this was starting to get annoying! Glaring at him, I said, "I'm not sure any of what's happening to me is real, but one thing I know is, *you're* not. You're just a nightmare, a rotten dream, probably the result of wine that tastes like prune juice mixed with Mr. Clean . . . !"

"Have it your way, fuckerrr," he said, and sliced off his chin with one of the finger-knives. I wasn't impressed. He scraped them on the rock, raising a shower of sparks, then carved the elm into sixteen million Diamond round toothpicks.

That impressed the hell out of me.

Finger-knives waving like the baton of some demented conductor, Freddy Krueger tried to block my path. I put a move on him that would have made Eric Dickerson envious, then achieved Mach one point five in short order.

"Pleasant dreams, fuckerrrrrr," I heard Freddy say from a long way behind.

It took a few moments for my legs to obey the *Stop!* command from my brain. Panting like an out-of-shape executive after his first date with Jane Fonda, I sat down on a patch of grass to catch my breath.

The vay is not alvays an easy vun. Yeah, well, apparently the vay vas bottom-heavy with all kinds of bullshit in the last three miles. And by my estimate—*even* surpassing the speed of sound—I still had about two and a half of it to go. Swell.

I hadn't noticed the storage shed on the grass behind me until now. That's because I don't think it was there before. I say storage shed due to its size; actually in design it looked more like a doghouse.

Biggg mother of a doghouse.

A deep rumbling sounded from within, and Cujo lumbered out.

Not big-dumb-sweet Cujo who licked you with a tongue the size of a Persian rug, but mean-son-of-a-bitch Cujo *after* the rabid bat had bitten him, with all the drool and shit dripping from his jowls.

The way he licked his chops when he looked at me gave off the message *oboyoboy lunchtime for doggy!*

At Mach one point seven zero I thought for sure I'd leave the monster in the lurch (where exactly *is* the lurch?), but he cranked up to Mach one point sixty-nine and managed to stay at my heels for one hell of a long time. I was about to discard the walking stick, which was slowing me down, when something else caught the crazed cur's curiosity, and he veered off. I spent the next seventy-four miles screeching to a halt . . . which probably meant that I'd come another quarter-mile or so.

No stopping now. The cliffs had fallen back, but trees rimmed both sides of the road and were real dense. I stayed in the middle, for whatever good that would do. The problem was, you never knew when anyone or any*thing* was going to appear.

Im-Ho-Tep, the mummy, was suddenly strolling alongside me, like he'd been there for a long time.

Scared the living crapola out of me!

Reacting too quickly, I fell on my butt and nearly impaled myself on the walking stick. I scrambled to my feet and back-pedaled a couple of yards, then stopped and held the stick out in front of me . . . like I was a bad-assed ninja or something. Im-Ho-Tep, swathed in those layers of shredded bandages, stopped and tossed me a military-style salute.

"How are you doing, Jack?" he asked in a raspy voice, as dust flew out of a hole where his mouth should have been.

"Not great, to tell the truth," I replied wryly.

The mummy nodded; lint rained down on the road. "Yes, the last three miles to Dr. Frankenstein's castle are a real bitch." (I *swear* that's what he said!)

"How'd you know where I was going?" I asked suspiciously. "Come to think of it, how'd you know my name?"

Ignoring my questions, Im-Ho-Tep said, "Listen, Jack, would you mind if I walked with you a ways? We so seldom see visitors of your caliber around here."

Hey, an observant mummy! Still, I cocked a dubious eye. "You won't eat my brains or anything?"

"Breasts of Isis, no!" he chuckled, which spewed more dust out. "We mummies are so misunderstood, and all because we're the walking corpses of those who died three thousand years ago!"

Yeah, well . . . He fell into step, and we continued along the tree-lined road. The dust and lint rising from him almost made me sneeze, but that wouldn't have been polite, so I held it in.

"Jack, may I ask you something?" he said, after a while.

"What's that?"

"Folks around here don't take to me all that well. Do you think there's an image problem?"

Hoo boy! "Yeah, could be. Have you considered your wardrobe? Some new duds can work wonders for a guy."

"What an excellent idea!" Im-Ho-Tep exclaimed, engulfing me in a cloud of dust.

"But clothes alone aren't enough," I went on. (Do you *believe* what I was saying here?) "How about getting a job, or starting a business? Folks look up to a successful mum . . . man."

He was ecstatic. "Jack, I can't thank you enough. Here, shake!"

I took his hand. Part of it crumbled in mine. *Eeeyooo!*

Anyway, the road went on to the base of some hills, where you had to turn either left or right. "Which way?" I asked, and Im-Ho-Tep pointed to the left. I squinted in that direction for a couple of seconds, then turned and said, "Are you sure . . . ?"

But Im-Ho-Tep, the mummy, was gone. Swell.

Guess what, the sun was already high in the sulfurous sky. All of the aforementioned crap had consumed a considerable portion of the day, although it hardly seemed possible. I had to get my ass in gear and find Castle Frankenstein, or else . . .

You know.

So what next? How about boulders, four- to five-feet-high, with television antennae sticking out of them? Nope, didn't make any sense to me, either, at least not immediately.

Until I saw Horace Pinker coming after me.

In case you didn't know (unfortunately, I did) Horace Pinker was the *big*, extremely bad-assed TV repairman/serial killer in Wes Craven's film *Shocker*. After murdering half the known population of North America he is given the electric chair, but his evil essence survives and carries out new atrocities by entering other bodies. Eventually, once again in his old form, he pops into people's homes . . . through the television, for crying out loud!

Which *wasn't* what he was doing now.

What he *was* doing now—in the flesh—was bearing down on my butt with a knife that was about the size of whatever Alexander used to cut the Gordian knot. Here was one wacko that, for a change, wasn't grinning at me, but sneering.

"Hey, Jack!" he exclaimed in a sandpapery voice. "Know what I'm gonna do with this toothpick? First I'm gonna carve both your buns into small, wormlike pieces and use them to bait my hooks when I go fishing in the piranha pool. Then I'm gonna shove your mutilated ass below the waterline and see how much more of it they can chew off before you start screaming in agony." (Now you know and I know *that* wouldn't take long.) "Next, I'm gonna make a perfect replica of the Venus de Milo. Finally, I'm gonna shorten your legs so you can get in cheap to the kiddy matinee on Saturday mornings. Doesn't that sound great?''

Yeah, as great as bubonic plague. You're right, I should have achieved Mach Two in a flash. I don't know why I couldn't; maybe it was being tired, or maybe this creep was scaring me more than the rest, or maybe a combination of the above. Whatever. I seemed to stagger in slow motion past the antenna-bearing rocks, while Horace, swinging that knife in a nasty whistling way, kept on my ass.

Fifty yards down the road I ran past a little old man, who I recognized as Edmund Gwenn. Now you might remember him as the delightful Kris Kringle in the equally delightful *Miracle on 34th Street*, from back in the forties. So what business did he have being in this weird place? In 1954, near the end of his career, he played Dr. Medford in the movie *Them!* (their exclamation point), which had to do with ants in the New Mexico desert mutating into giants as a result of atomic bomb testing. He was the one who warned everybody of impending doom. Yeah, I guess he qualified.

Waving frantically as I stumbled by, Dr. Medford shouted, ''Get the antennae! Get the antennae!''

''Huh? What?'' I said dumbly.

''Get the antennae!'' he repeated. ''He's helpless without them!''

He was gesturing toward the boulders. Oh, now I got it! Still on the move I swung the knobby end of the walking stick at the television antennae, snapping three of them and bending a fourth. Immediately I heard this crackling sound from behind. When I turned, there was Horace beginning to break up in a shimmer of silvery static. It looked like he was halfway through the process of being beamed aboard the *Enterprise* (the old one). His head was still whole, and man, did he look *extra* pissed off!

''Motherfucker!'' he growled. ''You know what else I'm gonna do to you?''

He told me, but I don't think I'll repeat it, because it was worse than before, and I resolved myself to try to forget it. The worst part was, I believed he could carry out those threats, because . . . he was beginning to re-form. *Oh, shit!*

''Get the other antennae!'' Gwenn/Medford shouted. ''Get the other antennae!''

Yeah, of course! Overcoming a momentary torpor I began

leveling television antennae on both sides, like a lumberjack gone berserk. Horace Pinker shimmered violently, then faded into cathode ray purgatory with a final hiss of static, his expletives echoing for a few moments after that.

I turned to offer profuse thanks to my savior, but with a final tip of his hat he was already disappearing beyond some boulders. Trying to catch my breath I stayed riveted to that spot, and ten seconds later I heard what sounded like . . . jingle bells, I swear!

And afterward a faint echo, something like *"Ho ho ho."*

I watched the foul sky and didn't see anything take off; but do you think . . . ?

Naaaah.

I set off again, and the antenna-bearing boulders fell from sight. Was the universe about ready to give me a break? It seemed so, because I walked for about fifteen minutes through the increasingly smoggy mountain pass without a single noteworthy thing happening . . .

. . . until Kevin McCarthy staggered up the road toward me.

He was Dr. Miles Bennell of Santa Mira, California, all wild-eyed and disheveled, like he'd become *after* he found out that body snatchers had invaded and that life on Earth as we'd known it was about to end. Pretty bent out of shape, I'd say.

"They're here already, they're here!" he screamed, arms waving frantically. "You're next! *You're next!*"

"Yo, how's it going?" I called out cheerfully. (Thought I'd try to loosen him up.)

He stopped a couple of yards away and regarded me with a look that one might have reserved for studying a bowl of pus. Waving a trembling finger he said warily, "How do I know you're not one of *them*?"

"Go ahead, try me. Tell me a sad story and make me cry. Or crack a few good jokes and see what happens."

He pondered this for a moment, then said, "Why did the chicken cross the road? To get to the other side. Take my wife, please! You know why Helen Keller's leg was yellow? Her dog was blind, too."

I looked at him with a screwed-up face. "None of *that* is funny."

He sighed deeply, relieved. "If you were one of *them*, you'd have probably faked laughing. Okay, you can be trusted. But can you help me?"

"Sorry, I have some heavy problems of my own at the moment. But I know someone who can."

"You do?"

"Just keep stagger . . . running along this road for a while. For sure you'll be picked up and taken to a hospital. The tall, balding doctor—Mel Cooley from *The Dick Van Dyke Show*? Forget him, he'll think you're full of shit. But the other guy, Whit Bissell (see?). He'll believe your story."

"Are you sure of that?" McCarthy/Bennell asked dubiously.

"Absolutely," I assured him. "Especially after the first load of beef and pea pods from a traffic accident arrives at the emergency room."

He nodded crazily and hurried off. For quite a while after I heard echoes of "They're here already! You're next!" bouncing off the rock facings. You know, I always felt sorry for that poor guy. I mean, twenty-two years later he was still running around San Francisco and shouting the same thing in the remake of the movie. At least in that version he gets hit by a car and put out of his misery.

Anyway, you know I wasn't pulling his chain; I really *did* have problems here. And to compound them, the ochre sun was already on its way down. *So fast, why so fast!* I kept thinking, which was an exercise in futility. I *had* to get to Castle Frankenstein, and I had to get there *soon*; a good possibility, I believed, if the road stayed as clear as it now was.

For the longest time it snaked between towering cliffs. I was really moving now, and even though I could never see around the next bend, I expected the castle to pop up soon. A good thing was that the yellowish-brown smog began to dissipate, and at one point you could just about take a deep breath without gagging.

An almost spectral silence was soon broken by the murmur of voices. I'm not sure how, but I thought it was coming from behind. I stopped, listened; yeah, it was. Weird. Aside from rocks and gnarly tree trunks, I hadn't seen anything for a while.

So with paranoiac caution I inched my way back about twenty yards along the base of the curving cliff. The voices grew louder, and I soon discovered to whom they belonged.

It was Helga and Horst and Heidi and Hans and Hilda and so on and so on . . .

I was at the edge of the same village where I'd spent the previous night as a padoodle.

There was a message I wanted to whisper softly into the ear of the universe.

SHI-I-I-I-I-T!

CHAPTER 11

I Brake for Muunastrebors

So what happened? I don't know, you tell me! Had I spent the whole day going around in a big-assed circle? Or had I just been spinning my wheels while all the craziness was allegedly going on around me?

Who cared?

The bottom line was, I had wound up back on square one, and Castle Frankenstein was nowhere in the immediate wicinity, and it was going to get dark soon, which meant I would turn into a padoodle and probably perpetrate some nasty things, unless these people wasted me with a stake or a bullet of precious metal, which they'd advised me in no uncertain terms they would do.

The temptation to rub the Bukko and leave this all behind was growing strong.

But what if couldn't shake the curse? Would I be destined to wander the streets of Del Mar and San Diego in the form of a padoodle every half-moon, until some cop blew me away? Granted, there was probably *someone* in southern California equipped to cure me; but did I dare take that chance? I didn't think so. Dr. Frankenstein was still my best bet, I believed.

So how did I deal with this latest frustration? How did I handle the crisis?

Yeah, I freaked. I turned and ran along the road in the direction I'd just come from, mouthing a bunch of unclean words. Almost immediately the road branched off in two directions (don't ask me, it hadn't before). I didn't care, so I took the left fork, and pretty soon I was descending a slope into a rather anemic-looking valley, which is when I finally slowed down.

Walking and panting on the valley floor now, it occurred to me that I was in one of those bad news/good news/bad news situations. The bad news was that the sun, dipping toward the horizon, wasn't going to be around much longer. The good news was that the sky ahead was filled with ugly dark storm clouds, and they were being blown this way at cartoon speed, and with any luck they would stay all night. But the other bad news was that, considering all the thunder already crashing and lightning streaking, this storm was shaping up to be a doozy. So even if I didn't turn into a padoodle, I could just as easily drown in the ensuing flash flood.

Hey Old Guys, are you getting all this?

Then, on the side of a hill two hundred yards away, I saw the wide mouth of a cave. Thankyewwww.

I started running as the first raindrops fell. But at thirty yards I had to stop, because that was when this giant disembodied eyeball floated out of the cave.

"What are you doing here?" the giant disembodied eyeball asked in a feminine voice.

Hey, I knew what this was! Back in 1953 there was this great movie, *It Came From Outer Space*, scripted by, would you believe, Ray Bradbury. It was shown in 3D, so that when eyeballs and other creepy stuff came out of the screen, you wet your pants. Anyway, it was about these aliens who land in the Arizona desert because their spaceship needs a lube job or something, and once they get it fixed, they're outta here. They have to make duplicates of local yokels from a nearby town to bring them stuff, which is about all the "bad" they do. This was in contrast to most of the 1950s sci-fi flicks, where the aliens always wanted to invade Earth and suck out our brains.

"Did you not understand me?" the giant disembodied eyeball said.

"Oh, sorry. I just wanted in out of the rain. Looks like a bad storm."

"Yes, I know. We created it."

"You did?"

"Uh-huh, to keep the local yokels away. We must repair our ship." (See? I was right.) "But we can stop the storm until you reach your destination."

"Oh, no, don't do that!" I exclaimed.

She/it asked me why, and I told her/it. "That's understandable. Very well, it will continue to storm all night, and in the morning you'll be able to see Castle Frankenstein from here. Now, come inside."

"Hey, thanks."

I followed the giant disembodied eyeball out of what was now a downpour and into the cave. Two small disembodied eyeballs were puttering (or something) around a flying saucer.

"Attention, pupils," the giant disembodied eyeball said, "we have a guest. Uh, what is your name?"

"Jack."

"Yes, of course. I am Iris, and my pupils are Fovea and Retina."

There were greetings all around, and then Fovea (I think) said, "We can *see* the problem with the ship, Boss."

"Yes," Retina agreed, "we've been *eyeballing* it for some time now."

"It's just that we weren't able to see *eye to eye* on what was wrong," Fovea added.

"Don't jest with me, pupils," Iris said pissedly. "I'm in a vitreous humor tonight."

"What a shame," Retina mused, "since only a while ago you were in an aqueous humor."

(Is all of this too cornea, or what?)

"Just keep working," Iris ordered. "Jack, I must help my pupils now."

"That's fine, I'll curl up in a corner and catch some Zs. Uh, unless you have something to eat."

"Yes, we are well provisioned."

Iris floated over a big box with a hinged top. I flipped it open. There were eight compartments, each containing live things with many legs or no legs that crawled or slithered or writhed or hopped or hissed or spewed slime or . . . *eeeeyoooo!*

I closed the box. "Guess I wasn't as hungry as I thought."

Iris went to work. I lay down, my stomach growling like Papa Bear after Mama Bear told him, "Not tonight, I just started my period," and slept the sleep of the dead.

In the morning the giant disembodied eyeball, both small disembodied eyeballs, the box of creepy-crawlies, the flying saucer—and the cave—were all gone.

No, nothing should have surprised me anymore, but it was still weird. I was sprawled in a field covered with these skinny, brownish-orange weeds. The ground was dry and brittle, which seemed odd, considering how much it had rained last night . . .

It *had*, hadn't it?

Well, whatever. I looked around, noting that, despite the

sulfurous air, visibility wasn't too bad. Based on what Iris had said, Castle Frankenstein should have been somewhere in the area.

Yeah, there it was, beyond the foothills across the valley, with some tall peaks looming above it. I'm assuming that's what it was, because there was nothing else in sight. Would've been nice if Iris had left a note (now there was a stupid thought), or maybe an arrow pointing that way. No matter; I started off.

After yesterday, nothing would have surprised me. But *nothing* was exactly what happened, and in a short time I was halfway there. Then, I came across a path that wound through a pine forest in the foothills, and at times I lost sight of the castle, and *that* made me nervous.

Oh, no, guess what, that damn village again! There might've been a few more houses and shops, and the immediate surroundings were a bit different, but it *was* that village, no doubt. And the people in the square definitely were, among others, Heidi and Helmut and Hilda and Horst and so on.

Well, tough, I wasn't about to lose more time bypassing the village, not with the castle so close. I walked through warily, prepared to fend off any crap that flew my way.

But you know, the townspeople were all pretty nice, I swear! They smiled at me, nodded; men tipped their hats, women did these nifty little curtsies.

"Glad to see you again," Horst said.

"You've almost made it," Helmut added.

"Won't you stop for a little schnapps and wurst?" Hilda asked.

Let's see, was hers the best or the . . . ? "No thanks, gotta keep moving." Yeah, I was really hungry, but I wasn't stupid.

"Dr. Frankenstein will be able to help you," Hiroshi said.

"Have a nice day!" they all called after me. *Oh, come on!*

At the far end of the village was this one isolated brick building. A sign in front read GOLDSTADT MEDICAL COLLEGE. There didn't seem to be anyone around at first; then I noticed a figure skulking on the side.

It was Dwight Frye.

Not in his role as Renfield, the bug-eating wacko from the 1931 *Dracula,* but the hunchbacked Fritz from *Frankenstein* of the same year. I was getting closer to the castle.

After glancing around furtively for a moment (I was either

the Invisible Man to him, or he just didn't give a shit), Fritz opened the window and climbed in. It was evident what he was up to, but I decided to have a look anyway.

The room was full of corpses on slabs, skeletons dangling from ropes, and shelves crammed with preserved organs of every kind floating in fat jars. One in particular resembled that crockful of pickled eggs (*eeeyooo!*) you see on the counter of your local convenience store. I didn't want to *know* what it was! Fritz had skulked his way to a shelf that was separate from the others, and held only three jars. He took off the one labeled NORMAL BRAIN.

"Hey, glad to see you got it right," I called from the window, unable to resist the impulse.

Naturally I scared the bejesus out of the little guy. The jar fell to the floor, shattering into a thousand pieces and carving up the brain. Fritz stamped his feet and nearly slipped in the goo.

"Ooo, my master will be so angry!" he cried. "He will whip me for sure! Why did you do that?"

"Whoops, sorry," I told him, but you know, it *was* the proper scenario. "What will you do now?"

He pointed at the second jar, which was marked ABNORMAL BRAIN. "Take this one, I suppose. I can peel off the label so my master won't know."

"Not a good idea," I said. Okay, why *not* mess with the scenario? "Try the other one."

The third jar on the shelf was labeled ASSHOLE BRAIN. Now *that* sounded interesting. Fritz took it down, removed the label, and hurried to the window.

"Here, hold this," he said, "and don't drop it!"

He climbed out and took the jar back. "Can I follow you to the castle?" I asked.

The look he gave me relayed the message *up yours jack,* but he said, "I must first see if the coast is clear. Wait here."

He hurried to the back of the building, made another stay-put gesture, then was gone.

A minute later, standing in the same spot with a finger up my kazoo, I realized he wasn't coming back. The little shithead!

Who needed him anyway? I got back on the road, and soon the village was gone from sight.

Again.

The road sloped upward briefly, then leveled over a rocky

plateau. Castle Frankenstein was half a mile ahead. Really. It was. Honest. No, I wasn't dubious.

A wagon drawn by a pathetic-looking old nag was approaching from the direction of the castle. The guy on the jockey box gave me a nod but kept right on truckin'. I had the impression he was in a hurry to get somewhere . . . or maybe it was *away* from something. When he passed I noticed a bumper sticker on the back of the wagon. It said I BRAKE FOR MUUNAS-TREBORS.

Huh?

Anyway, the wagon and the nag and the guy all passed beyond the ridge and out of sight. I continued along the path, which narrowed to a cracked ribbon of little more than two yards. Also, the rocks and brittle shrubs that had lined both sides fell behind, the terrain looking more like a desert, except the sand had this weird bluish tinge. And jeez, was it quiet! I'm talking the proverbial *deathly stillness* or *vacuumlike silence*. It was really starting to give me the willies.

Then, a big mound of sand grew, and guess what popped out. (I BRAKE FOR MUUNASTREBORS?)

It happened five yards ahead of me, about half that distance off the left side of the road. The leathery bird head of the squid-thing emerged like a cannon shot, then its body, with all those gross, undulating red suckers. But unlike my first encounter with them, *all* of the whatever—over twenty feet of it—rose above the sand. It bent into the shape of a boomerang and seemed to hover motionlessly for a second. Then, beak first, it hit the sand on the other side of the path, burrowing through it as easily as if it were diving into water. Before it disappeared completely I had a look at its "tail," something like black metal pincers that opened and shut spastically. *Real* nasty-looking.

Just after that a second muunastrebor did the same thing, this time behind me. Then a third, ahead, closer than the first two. And the worst part was, this one noticed me! Its beady eyes looked me over, and its beak clattered a Morse code message that said *do you know how thoroughly we masticate our food jack?*

Strange thing: With these humongous whatevers hitting the ground, you'd have thought it would feel like what we Californians call the Big One. But there was no rumbling, no nothing.

Until one of the muunastrebors undershot its target and landed on the path.

Now *that* jarred my teeth, took my legs out from under me, and left a rather long, two-inch-wide crack down the middle. I scrambled up quickly, walking stick poised, figuring it was going to attack. But it slithered (or something) off the road and was quickly gone under the blue sand.

Castle Frankenstein now loomed barely a quarter mile ahead. But the next hundred or so yards of the path was flanked by sand, and I started having a bad feeling about my prospective passage. I moved quickly but held off going into overdrive, because caution, not speed, seemed more expedient.

Most of the leaping muunastrebors achieved their objective; but this one—definitely *not* the Greg Louganis of squid-things—landed beak first on the path and had to pry itself loose. I, of course, had been knocked on my ass a couple of yards away and had to duck its flailing, clattering pincers. That was the closest call. Well, at least the end was in sight.

One of them leaped into the air with my Nishiki trailing behind.

It held my bike around the frame with those damn pincers. I couldn't tell what condition the Nishiki was in, because I only saw it for a couple of seconds from fifteen yards away. But I didn't care; I knew what had to be done next.

Yeah, you guessed it: If the whatever came up once it would probably come up again. All I had to do was wait out the other jumping monsters, then hope it emerged near enough for me to wrestle the bike away before it disappeared.

Simple, huh?

So there I stood, flitting around like Muhammad Ali in his prime, walking stick at the ready, Nishiki-less muunastrebors leaping all around me. I did my own hopping when a couple landed on the path, and I managed to keep my feet. Two *long* minutes of this craziness passed before I saw my bike again. This time the squid-thing emerged from the opposite side of the road, ten yards away, still too far for me to do anything about it.

But maybe there was a pattern here. I moved five yards closer and concentrated on the side of the path where I first saw my bike appear. Yeah, I still had to watch out for the others, but so far so good.

Then I got to thinking, did I *really* want to run blindly across the blue sand in pursuit of my Nishiki? I mean, look how easily these things went under. Granted, they might have weighed about four tons each, but still . . . So I took that souvenir rock given to me by the villagers and tossed it on the sand. Guess what, it sank like an anvil in paint thinner.

Okay, maybe it wasn't my best idea of the day, but I didn't have anything better. I waited, and it wasn't long before I knew I'd been right about one thing. The whatever with my Nishiki emerged less than a yard off the path where I was standing. It wasn't too high above me when it jackknifed, and I knew it would barely clear the path, which was good, except that the whiplash might drive the bike against the hard earth, and *that* was bad.

Ignoring anything and everything else I kept my eyes glued to the plummeting Nishiki as I sidled across the path. I was almost more right than I'd figured, the thing missing the path by little more than the width of its body. Fortunately the tail wasn't swaying too wildly; but its descent was swift, and I wasn't going to have a whole lot of time to pull this off.

Discarding the walking stick, I planted my feet firmly and waited. When the bike was in front of my face, I grabbed both tires. Now, this was the hairy part. Knowing the thing's momentum to be considerable, and assuming its hold on the frame to be strong, I would have to establish one hell of a grip, or at least be able to let it go before *I* was pulled under.

I braced myself in the best tradition of those grunting Olympic weightlifters.

The bike slipped so easily out of the grasp of the pincers that both it and me rolled crazily to the other side of the path . . . and off. It sank; I half sank, but with one hand was able to hold on to the edge of the path. It seemed like I was dangling off a cliff. Precarious as hell, but I was somehow able to drag both me and the Nishiki up to solid ground, where I lay panting for a moment.

(*No, Jack, a highly accelerated heartbeat is not necessarily a precursor to a coronary.*)

But no time for that, because the offending squid-thing, deprived of its toy, poked its head up, and did it look pissed! Not waiting to find out what its next move was, I started running with my bike that, as far as I could tell, was none the worse for wear. Good deal. I jumped on the seat, pedaling slowly at first until the chain, which had been off a couple of gears, slipped into place.

That was when I tore ass out of there, leaving behind the one who most desired a gobbet of my flesh. Ducking under flying muunastrebors, weaving around those on the path and bracing against seismic thuds, I headed for Castle Frankenstein, and the awful sandbox was soon behind me.

CHAPTER 12

It's Alive!

Okay, no bull, the front door of Castle Frankenstein was now barely fifty yards away. I kept my eyes glued to it (did you ever consider what it might feel like to have your eyes glued to *anything*?) just to make sure it wasn't going to wink out on me or whatever. Like I really could've prevented it, right? But I didn't think that was going to happen.

Honest.

Another thing about those last fifty yards was that I had to walk them. The narrow path was steep, which I could have handled on the bike, but twisty, which made it harder. And worse, it was strewn with debris, pitted with craters, I mean *really* messed up. You would have thought that no humans had walked it in a very long time.

Maybe none had.

The main door of Castle Frankenstein finally loomed before me. One step led up to the door. Only problem was, the one step was ten feet high. Great.

But it always helps to get the whole picture, doesn't it? Continuing around one corner I came across four steps leading up to the entrance. They were still spaced pretty far apart, but I managed, even carrying the Nishiki. No way was I leaving it down there. As long as I was in wherever-the-hell-I-was, my bike was going to be at my side.

The door *was* big, as assumed, though not huge enough to make me feel like the Incredible Shrinking Dude. It was made of roughly textured wood and might have once been painted but was now a nondescript, faded hue of brown-orange-gray-whatever. The walls into which it was deeply set were fabricated of mortared stones, covered in places by something green and mossy, like the steps I'd climbed.

Well, I had to get this over with. I didn't see a doorbell, but there was this great big lion's-head knocker at eye level. For a moment I thought it had changed into Leo G. Carroll with a toothache; but no, the face snarling at me was that of a lion. Definitely. A squashed, tusky . . .

. . . padoodle's face. Oh, great, I really needed this!

Shutting my eyes, I drove the knocker against the door a whole bunch of times.

So I thought.

Deep within the castle there were no pounding noises, but instead some words from an old rock-and-roll song: "Let me in, wee-oop." They echoed until I let go of the knocker.

Half a minute later the door creaked open. I'm talking *Inner Sanctum* creaking here, worse than chalk on a blackboard. Unconsciously I took a couple of steps back, which nearly put me off the edge of the high step. Now *that* would have been brilliant.

The door was half-open when the creaking finally stopped (thank Crom) and Fritz slipped out. "Ooo, it's you again," he said, none too happily. "What do you want?"

"Yeah, nice to see you too," I told him dryly. "And by the way, thanks for leaving me behind."

"You're welcome."

"Right. Look, I need to see Dr. Frankenstein real quick—"

"You came at a bad time," he interrupted. "The doctor is at a critical point of his experiment. See!"

He pointed at the sky, which had begun to darken. Gloomy clouds were rolling in from different directions (huh?), thunder rumbled, and spastically zigzagging streaks of lightning looked like a San Diego Chargers' preseason practice.

"So you'll have to come back another time," Fritz went on, starting to close the door (that damn creaking again!). "Maybe tomorrow."

Hey, no way! Another night of padoodlistic activities was not penciled in my Day-Timer. I leaned my back against the portal. Fritz was no match for me.

"I have to see him now," I said firmly. "Take me with you. If you don't, then the next time I see the doctor I'll tell him that you switched brains."

Was I a prick, or what! Who cares? It worked.

"Oh, very well," Fritz grumbled, opening the door again (my teeth, my spine!). "Just you mind yourself in my master's presence. He's a busy man and has no time for idiots."

Yo' momma, Fritz. He waved me impatiently into a dark corridor and pushed the door closed (shit!). I followed him a short distance to the foot of an extremely narrow stairwell, one which quickly disappeared as it spiraled upward. To climb it I would have to move sideways. No way would the Nishiki fit.

"You'll have to leave that here," the little guy said.

"But I can't—" I began.

"Fritz!" a voice from above bellowed. *"Where are you?"*

"My master!" Fritz exclaimed. "I must go."

He started up. I glanced down the corridor. There was this big suit of armor standing against the wall a few yards away. I checked it out. Rock-solid. I chained the Nishiki to a leg.

"Keep an eye on it for me," I said, patting the suit of armor on the shoulder.

"I'll do my best, sir," the suit of armor replied.

I got the hell away from there fast.

You have no idea how quickly you can go up spiraling stairs sideways when motivated. Even so, I never did overtake Fritz. The little sucker must've done this a thousand times.

After a distance of what seemed the equivalent of the summit of Mt. Whitney I came to the top of the stairs. No corridor here, just a direct route into the la*bor*atory (that's British style, accent on the second of *five* syllables) of the brilliant but obsessed Dr. Henry Frankenstein (as played by Colin Clive, which I'd already figured would be the case).

Yeah, it was just like the great old Universal Studios set, with all the electrical conductors and switches, man-made lightning crackling and sparking through the vast chamber, the gauges, the bubbling beakers and bunsen burners, the whole nine yards. And in the middle of it, swathed in rags atop a table, was the figure of a man, a *very* large man. At the moment Fritz and his wild-eyed boss were strapping the body down.

"You there!" Frankenstein called, not looking up.

"Who, me?" I asked.

"Yes, yes. I'll tend to you later. Just keep your arse (that's what he said!) out of my way!"

Yeah, well, you have a nice day too, Doc. I stood there and watched as they finished with the body, then scurried about the la*bor*atory, bumping into each other no less than three times before getting to where they wanted to be.

Outside, the storm raged. You could see streaks of lightning through the skylight directly above the table where the lifeless creature lay. Dr. Frankenstein, looking up from the switches of this one huge machine, was nearly foaming with glee.

"It's time, Fritz, it's time!" he cried. "Raise him up!"

The bent servant had both hands on a wheel, which was connected by a heavy chain to a series of pulleys. He began turning it, and with a groan of protest the table was lifted off the floor. It rose halfway to the skylight, Fritz straining and turning red, Frankenstein grinning and rubbing his hands together. It would've been nice if he'd helped the little guy, but he didn't give a shit.

When the table was just below the ceiling, Frankenstein finally started being useful. He threw a switch, and the skylight opened. Sheets of water immediately poured in and doused the white-frocked looney, but he didn't seem to care. Grabbing another switch (with wet hands??!!) as the table rose above the roof, he threw it with what seemed undue effort. There was a loud humming noise, and the electricity that danced between the poles grew brighter, more frenetic. I took a couple of steps back.

In the sky the lightning streaked like a son-of-a-gun.

One of the bolts hit the table (I think).

Now it seemed like the electrified gremlin from the second movie of the same name was darting crazily about the laboratory. I ducked back down the stairwell a few steps (what a chickenshit) and peered around the curving wall. Somehow, the doctor and his assistant survived being fried. The only real damage was some broken glass, including the empty jar in which Fritz had brought the brain.

The ASSHOLE BRAIN.

The same brain in the soon-not-to-be-dormant creature above.

Did I really want to see this?

The electrified gremlin faded into a wall socket. Above, the sky cleared. Frankenstein, now laughing like Myrna Turner on *The Odd Couple,* threw the switch the other way, while Fritz lowered the table to the floor. Soon the three of us surrounded the table, the others closer than I was.

The bandaged body lay motionless.

You could feel the tension in the la*bor*atory. Frankenstein looked to be on the verge of a seizure. Fritz was frothing freely in frantic frustration.

The creature with the asshole brain sneezed.

Scared the shit out of me. The others jumped, too, but for joy, as the creature's left hand jerked up, then reached under the bandages that engulfed its head. When it came out, boogers were hanging off two fingers. It discarded these on the floor with a backhanded flip.

"It's alive!" Dr. Henry Frankenstein cried. "It's alive!"

"Ooo, Master, you did good," Fritz said.

"It's alive!"

"Excuse me, Doc," I said, "but I have this problem—"

"It's alive!" he shrieked, pumping my hand.

"Yeah, great, but you see—"

The creature began to mumble something. "Later, later," Frankenstein said. "I must see what happens here."

He and Fritz undid the straps. Still mumbling, the creature sat up. I finally realized it was talking that way because of the bandages. The creature did, too, because it reached up and pulled them back.

Its stitched-up face looked like a cross between the old Boris Karloff monster and John Candy when he played Uncle Buck. With a spastic scowl he threw the bandages to the floor.

"Jesus H. Christ on a pogo stick!" he exclaimed in a Maxwell Smart voice. "Those things were a pain in the ass!" He climbed wobbily off the table, reached behind him, and started scratching inside his crack. "And speaking of 'pain in the ass,' God, my hemorrhoids are fucking killing me!"

"It's alive!" Frankenstein cried.

"What'd you expect, making me lie on that morgue slab the whole damn time," he said, pulling the hand out and using it to pick his nose. "You got hemorrhoids like mine, the size of fucking Ping-Pong balls, you don't wanna be on your ass too much, know what I mean?" He cut loose a loud, staccatolike fart.

"It's alive!" Frankenstein cried again.

Yeah, I thought, what a blessing to the world.

The asshole creature sneezed again. Half of it landed on Fritz; he wiped the other half on the sleeve of a tunic they had dressed him in.

"Must be getting a fucking cold," he said. "Hey, stick around, I'll give it to you." He thought that was funny and smiled as he cut another fart. "Christ, it's so dark in here I thought I was going blind!"

"It's alive!"

"Speaking of *blind,* you know what Jesus' first miracle was? He made a lame man blind. You know how Helen Keller met

her husband? On a blind date. You know what her parents did
to her for swearing? Washed her hands with soap. Oh, shit, this
is great stuff!''

Thus spake the creature with the ASSHOLE BRAIN.

''*It's—!*''

''Okay, stuff that!'' I told Frankenstein, kind of pissedly.
''You can carry on your half of this deeply insightful conversation later, but right now I need help.''

The scientist's eyes unglazed, and he looked me over. ''Oh,
of course, where are my manners?''

''Beats the pus out of me,'' the asshole creature said, then
pointed at my face. ''Gotta be Jewish with a beak like that!
Hey, know why Jews have big noses? Because air is free. This
Jew with an erection walked into a wall, right? He broke his
nose!''

''You asshole!'' I exclaimed.

''Ooo, I thought you weren't going to tell,'' Fritz said.

''Tell what? It's obvious he's a jerk-off.''

''Speaking of jerking off,'' the asshole creature said, ''this
Polack had a penis transplant, but his hand rejected it. You
know why Dr Pepper comes in a bottle? Because his wife is
dead.''

Frankenstein got between us and told the creature, ''I must
help this man. You settle down and behave yourself, and we'll
talk later. Fritz will bring you something to eat.''

The creature farted again and said, ''Got any horny women
around this dump? I need a drink, too. Women and booze. The
perfect woman is crotch-high, toothless, and has a flat head so
you can sit your drink.''

''Ooo, I should have taken the ABNORMAL BRAIN,'' Fritz said.

''What was that?'' Frankenstein asked.

''Nothing, Master, nothing.''

''Come along then,'' the scientist told me, grabbing my arm.
''What seems to be your problem?''

When we were across the la*bora*tory, far away from the
asshole creature, I said, ''I was bitten by a padoodle and now
bear its curse.''

I expected him to jump back, look agog, make a sign,
something; but he just waited calmly, like I was going to tell
him more.

''Is that it?'' he finally asked.

''What do you mean, *is that it*?'' I replied indignantly.

"Oh, I wasn't implying that bearing the curse of the padoodle is not a big deal. But it's a simple thing to take care of. Here."

He reached into the pocket of his lab coat and pulled out a flat plastic case, like what women keep their makeup in. Sure enough, when he snapped it open there were eight little compartments, containing what I swear were different colors of eye shadow.

"What's that?" I asked.

He pondered the contents, ignoring me. "Let's see, padoodle, padoodle . . . padoodle! Yes, that's it for sure. Hold out your right hand, palm down, and try not to move it."

"Is this going to hurt?" I asked wimpily.

"Of course not; it's just rather . . . ah, surprising."

I did what he said. He took a little dauber and picked up some of the "eye shadow," a pale green. Not very much of it, either. He put a tiny dot on my hand, just above the middle knuckle, then stepped back. I wasn't thrilled about the "stepping back" part.

Suddenly the spot began to glow like burning phosphorous. Frankenstein turned his face away and gestured for me to do the same. I did, reluctantly. If this was going to burn a hole through my hand, I at least wanted to keep an eye on it.

Oh, yeah, did I really?

It didn't hurt at all, like he'd said, but after growing gradually in intensity it flared brilliantly for a second, then faded. The green spot on the back of my hand was gone; I suppose the stuff was absorbed into the skin.

"That's it?" I asked, rubbing the hand dubiously.

"Yes, yes, you're cured," he replied impatiently, snapping open a pocket watch. "Fritz will give you a certificate of de-cursing on your way out. Now, if you'll excuse me, I must get—"

"Master!" Fritz interrupted as he ran toward us. "Ooo, Master, we have a problem. From the tower window I see villagers coming toward the castle, and they seem a bit ruffled!"

The asshole creature, behind Fritz, moved awkwardly but steadily across the laboratory. Every pair of stiff-legged, clunky monster steps was followed by a long, gliding strut.

"Ruffled, my pink ass!" the creature said as he clunk-clunk-strutted to a stop. "Those fuckers look pissed! But hey, they got *women* in their ranks, you know? Let's invite 'em up for a party. A little healthy bodice-ripping might be—''

"How close are they?" Frankenstein asked his servant.

"Ooo, Master, they are so close that—''

The sounds of "Let me in, wee-oop" echoed through the vast building; the villagers were at the knocker on the front door. Frankenstein scowled and shrugged.

"Ah, if it isn't one thing with those morons, it's another! I suppose we must find out what they want.'' He pointed a warning finger at the creature. "You stay here, I mean it.''

"Sure, Doc, whatever you say.'' He tried a wink, failed miserably. "Listen, I saw this one in a red dirndl . . . a little on the chunky side, but big bazooms. I'm talking *big!* That's the way I like 'em. Why don't you see if . . .''

While he was flapping his gums, Frankenstein pulled out the eye shadow case again. He daubed up this bright blue shade and spread it on the creature's hand. Almost instantly there was a brilliant flash, and the asshole creature, in the middle of a lurid description of what he would do with the girl in the red dirndl, crumpled to the floor. Frankenstein put the case back in his pocket.

"Did you put him to sleep?" I asked.

"Oh, no, he's dead,'' the scientist replied. "Dead as a doornail.''

Dead? I was incredulous about two things: First, that he was carrying such deadly stuff in his pocket. Second, that he'd worked so hard to create the creature—asshole or not—and now destroyed it just like that. I asked him about the latter.

"It's no big deal,'' he said. "I can restore its life with another of the colors whenever I wish.''

Yeah, tell me another story! "If that's true, why didn't you skip all those pyrotechnics and use that stuff to bring him to life before?''

"Because the creature was new, made up of many different parts, so the 'pyrotechnics,' as you call them, were necessary the first time. But now that it has known its own life—''

"Let me in, wee-oop" began resounding again after a few seconds of silence. The villagers were really hammering on the padoodle-head knocker. Frankenstein hurried to the stairs, then Fritz, with me bringing up the rear, though not before stopping to grab an oil can off a shelf. The descent was dizzying. When we reached the bottom (yeah, the suit of armor had done a good job watching my bike), Fritz squeezed past the scientist to open the front door. I did, too, and before the little guy could put a hand on the doorknob I'd saturated all the hinges. It swung open easily (and quietly), nearly knocking him on his butt.

Villagers with torches (don't ask me why, it was daylight) were everywhere. Among those on the doorstep was Horst (or maybe it was Helmut; no, I'm sure it was Horst). In his arms was the little girl I'd first seen by the pond with the monster. She sure as hell looked dead. But you know, I didn't think the villagers looked ruffled, or pissed, or anything else in that vein. Weird.

"Dr. Frankenstein, one of your monsters has drowned my little Maria!" Horst shouted.

"I'm so sorry," Frankenstein said. "If you wish, I'll turn the monster over to you so that you may destroy it."

"*Destroy* it?" Helga exclaimed. "We wish to throw a party in its honor for getting rid of the miserable little brat!"

The villagers began cheering and waving their torches; even Horst looked happy. Dr. Frankenstein was relieved. The hunchbacked Fritz danced around gaily. It was shaping up to be one hell of a party.

But wait a minute, this was bullshit! All these people whooping it up over a dead kid. Okay, she was obnoxious, but *come on!* And there was something else I suddenly thought of . . .

Dr. Frankenstein was looking over the festive throng when I slipped up behind him. Before he knew what was happening I had eased the eye shadow case out of his pocket and put some distance between us. He started toward me, but I held the case behind my ear, ready to throw it like a football. That stopped him.

"What are you doing?" he cried. "You don't know how dangerous—"

"Which one is it?" I interrupted.

"Which one what?"

"The one that restores life."

"You don't want to do that!"

"Tell me."

He looked frantic. "Truly, you don't—"

"I'll snap open the case and splatter the whole thing on your lab coat. Ought to be fun watching what all of them together will do to your body—"

"It's the pink one!" he blurted. "The . . . pink one . . ."

I opened the case, shook the dauber, and touched it to the pink square, picking up a very small amount. Frankenstein watched me but didn't say anything, so I figured I was doing it right. As Horst chatted with Hiroshi over his shoulder, I made a pink dot on the back of poor little Maria's hand. I then returned the case to the scientist, making a mental note to ask if he was interested in marketing the concept.

The ensuing pink flash occurred within three seconds. Considering this was life-giving stuff, the intensity of the flash was rather subdued when compared to other ones. But it did catch the attention of the villagers, whose heads turned to the girl.

Maria's eyes snapped open so fast, it scared the shit out of me. The first thing she did was cough up a gallon of water and three minnows.

The second thing she did was poke two fingers in her father's eyes, like Moe does to Curly.

Yelping, Horst dropped the kid, but she landed catlike on her feet. The villagers were murmuring; Fritz was saying something to his master that might have been about how much more of an asshole I was than their creature, but I couldn't be sure.

Maria, a minnow slithering down her frock, looked at me and grinned. "Hey, if it isn't the peckerwood from over by the pond," she said. "Thought your guts would've been spread all the way to Hell's highway and back by now."

You know, when this kid got older she'd make a perfect mate for the creature upstairs. But this wasn't the time for matchmaking, because the brat ran toward me, and even knowing what was coming I wasn't quick enough to stop her. She got my left shin with one of her nasty shoes, and the other while I was hopping around. Then, as hyper as someone who'd just received an intravenous overdose of Hersheys, she ran shrieking and babbling among the villagers, kicking some, biting others, tripping a couple of old ladies. She popped the bodice of one woman, whose ponderous breasts did their impression of a double dribble (the asshole creature would've loved that).

The villagers, as one, turned toward me. Their silent looks could not be interpreted as *hey thanks a million jack.*

"I told you not to do it," Frankenstein said.

God, I hate I-told-you-sos!

One villager's suggestion won unanimous approval: "Let's see how many torches we can fit in his various orifices!"

Fortunately they took a few seconds to whip themselves up into the proverbial frenzy, and my hosts, unwilling as they might be, were able to whisk me back inside the castle. Frankenstein shut the door, and Fritz slid a heavy bolt into place . . . an instant before they started pounding on the other side.

"Hey, thanks for saving my . . . arse," I told the scientist.

"Oh, it's not saved yet. You can't stay here. If they try hard enough, they'll get in."

"But what'll I do?"

"Fritz will show you the secret passage. You won't avoid them, but you should be able to outrun the dolts. And it will get them away from here. Now go; you've been quite a bother."

I was going to thank him again (really), but he disappeared up those crazy stairs. The villagers continued to pound at the door, loud "Let me in, wee-oops" echoing through the corridor. I wondered if they were using Maria as a battering ram. Fritz, looking rather put out, grabbed the sleeve of my jersey.

"I'll show you to the passage now," he grumbled.

"Not until I get my bike," I told him.

"Very well; it's on the way. Hurry!"

We ran along the corridor. I knelt by the suit of armor to undo the chain.

"I hope you're pleased with my performance, sir," the suit of armor said.

"Oh, yes, great job. Here, you've earned this." I left him the oil can.

"My favorite brand! Thank you, sir."

Always glad to make a suit of armor's day.

Anyway, Fritz led me to this cleverly concealed trapdoor, and we descended into a *really* dark, *really* smelly tunnel, or cave, or something. Water was dripping, and slime was running down walls, and . . . You don't want to know. Sufficed to say, I followed him for what seemed ten minutes, struggling with the Nishiki the whole way, until we came to *another* cleverly concealed trapdoor, which put me outside, halfway down the twisty part of the road.

"Good riddance," Fritz muttered, when me and the bike were out, "and don't come back."

"Wait a minute, what about my certificate of de-cursing . . ."
But he slammed the trapdoor, and you couldn't even tell where
the seams were.

Frankenstein had been right about one thing: I wasn't
going to avoid a confrontation with the villagers. This portion
of the path was in plain view of where they were massing
above, looking for my blood. Still, with most of them intent on
the castle there might have been a slim chance of escaping
detection, had one of them not glanced in my direction. Yeah,
you guessed it: sweet little Maria.

"Hey, there goes the dipshit now!" she screamed, managing
to get their attention. "Let's tear 'im up!"

A Stephen King character once said something about dead
sometimes being better. In Maria's case . . . *how true!*

Nishiki, do your stuff! With torch-bearing villagers on my
tail, with muunastrebor-squid-thing-whatevers leaping above a
path that often felt as if it ran down the middle of the San
Andreas Fault, I bid a hearty *guten tag* to Castle Frankenstein
and the carefree inhabitants who dwelt within its sphere.

CHAPTER 13

Let's *Do* It

Fritz was climbing into the window of the GOLDSTADT MEDICAL COLLEGE when I rode past at approximately the speed of light. I don't have a clue how he got there ahead of me; didn't give a shit, either.

The little Bavarian village was deserted; naturally, with everyone in hot pursuit of me. Strings of wurst hung in the window of one shop; pastries were on display in another. They were tempting, and by now I was starving, but *no way* was I stopping.

Actually, for my purposes I was traveling the wrong way. The mountain range was behind me. Find a good steep path, or a cliff I could jump off, and I was outta here, back on the Ultimate Bike Path, halfway home, or wherever I wanted to go. But I really wanted to put some distance between me and this place, and I figured that, with the Nishiki, I could eat up the miles of the valley floor. The mountains on the other side would suit me just fine.

But a couple of miles across the rugged landscape, I suddenly became aware of some things. In the first place it had been a long and trying day, and I was beat. Also, because it *had* been a long day, the sun was about ready to go down, and this route, mildly hazardous in the daylight, would be murder in the dark.

And then there was something else on my brain . . .

Okay, so Dr. Frankenstein had put a spot of eye shadow on my hand and proclaimed me cured, even though I departed without my certificate of de-cursing. But after my experience of two nights before, the thought of turning into a padoodle was unbearable. What if he'd messed up and given me something to prevent goiter? What if he was pulling my chain? I mean, he was *not* your average stable person. And considering how clear the sky was, the half-moon (or something fairly close) was bound to appear soon.

As I continued along, giving serious thought to chaining

myself to a tree, a building popped up. Some vaguely familiar landmarks indicated this to be the previous site of the cave with the disembodied eyeballs. But now there was a four-story structure standing in the same spot. It reminded me of a Ramada Inn, but funkier, built from a weird combination of Italian terrazzo tile and redwood, with—get this—a pyramid roof. A sign on top, done in olde English letters, read IM-HO-TEP INN. I'll be damned! There was a nearly full parking lot in front of the main entrance, which seemed strange, considering the fact that no roads led to the building. Pedaling closer I was able to identify the vehicles parked there as BMWs, Mercedes, Lexus LS400s, even a couple of Jags. A blue, battered Toyota Celica stood out in this crowd like a sore thumb.

The sun was way beyond the mountains. It seemed my destiny to stop for the night at the IM-HO-TEP INN. I rode up to the entrance, where a uniformed doorman eyed me disdainfully.

"Here for a room, sir?" he asked.

"Yep, that's right."

"May I see to it that your . . . vehicle is properly parked?"

"Sorry, it comes with me."

"Very good, sir."

He was going to open the door just barely wide enough for me and the Nishiki to squeeze through, until two people emerged from the lobby, which prompted him to swing it all the way. The man and woman, thirty-something yuppie-style *beautiful people*, looked me over with even more disgust than the doorman as they passed. I have to admit I wasn't quite at my fashionable best, but *give me a break!*

"An asshole," the male yuppie muttered.

"I can't imagine anyone who would *do* lunch with him," the female yuppie said.

Yeah, well, both *yo' mommas!* The doorman was amused by this. But I turned the tables on him by slipping into the lobby before he could shut the door on me.

The plushy carpeted lobby was absolutely crawling with thirty-something yuppie-style *beautiful people*. Refrains of *doing* lunch and *doing* tennis and the like filled the air. Also, the word *asshole* must have been echoing, I heard it so many times. But I forged on to the front desk, where . . .

Im-Ho-Tep, dressed in a crewneck Hugo Boss sweater,

Barry Bricken cotton twill trousers, and Gucci loafers—all of this over his bandages—greeted me.

"Jack! Great to see you again," he rasped, trying not to notice the dirt streaks left by my tires on his carpet.

"So, Im-Ho-Tep Inn, huh? Good going." I waved an arm around the lobby. "Impressive looking place."

"Thank you. After our chat I decided you were right, so here it is!"

A female yuppie in tennis short-shorts, with legs-to-die-for, waved a racquet in our direction as she passed and said. "Hi, Immie, let's *do* lunch tomorrow. Who's the asshole?"

Immie thought that was funny; I didn't.

"Anyway," he went on, "looks like you could use a room for the night, and a square meal."

"You got that right."

"Actually, we're booked solid. But I always save one room for special occasions, and I can't think of one more special than having you as a guest. It's yours, Jack . . . no charge. After all, I owe you one."

"Thanks. Uh, question: Do you know if there's a storm scheduled for tonight?"

"No; in fact it's supposed to be clear . . ." He chuckled. "You're worried about turning into a padoodle. Weren't you successful with Dr. Frankenstein?"

A male yuppie walked by. "Immie, why don't you have your people call my people and we'll *do* breakfast some time next week? Who's the asshole?"

"I did find him," I told the mummy, "and he allegedly cured me, but . . ."

He understood. "You won't believe it until it's put to the test. Leave your bike here and stand on that spot."

Im-Ho-Tep indicated an embroidered likeness of King Tut in the carpet across the lobby. After what I'd been through I was reluctant to abandon the bike, but I did, figuring that I'd at least be able to keep an eye on it. The mummy followed me but continued on to a wall, where he drew back a heavy red drape. A high window revealed the sky, much darker than it had been a few minutes earlier.

"Don't move now, Jack," he said, going over to what looked like a switch box. "That's important."

Before I could reply he did something with the box, and a big metal cage dropped from the ceiling, engulfing me. A yard in either direction and I would have been crushed, or impaled. It settled to the floor gently, but let me tell you, it was *solid*. I tried rattling the bars; they wouldn't budge.

"Hey, what's going on here!" I exclaimed, even though I knew the answer. It was for my own protection, and the protection of others.

"It's for your own protection, Jack, and the protection of others," the mummy said. "Be patient, the moon should be rising shortly."

Naturally the yuppies thought my predicament was funny. They said all kinds of smart-assed things, but it was this one guy's "Hey, fella, let's *do* jail," that really pissed me off. I tried to ignore them . . . unsuccessfully.

Then, the moon rose over the mountains, looking just as perfectly halved as it had two nights earlier. I squeezed the bars so tightly that my knuckles whitened. The yuppies backed away; so did Im-Ho-Tep.

The half-moon kept climbing until it was totally revealed.

Nothing happened.

Immie waited a couple of minutes more, then raised the cage. The yuppies resumed their commentary, but at the moment I was too relieved to let it bother me.

"See, no problem," my host said. "That man may be mad, but he does good work. Now, let's get you a key. If you want to eat before you go upstairs, you'll find some great food in Mummy's Kitchen."

"Thanks, but I'd like to go to my room. Can you have something sent up?"

"Oh, of course!"

While he was getting me the key, a male yuppie and a female yuppie walked by. "Yes, we must definitely *do* water polo next week," the male yuppie told the female yuppie. "Oh look, I wonder who the asshole is."

All right, bullshit and a half! You can only take so much, you know. I put a fist into the yuppie's jaw, and he went down like he'd been shot. A small crowd gathered as the female yuppie knelt at his side.

"Does anyone here *do* first aid?" she asked, pouring a bottle of Perrier on his face.

Im-Ho-Tep handed me the key; I headed for the elevator fast.

Actually, my act of macho stupidity seemed to turn on some

of the female yuppies. They smiled at me suggestively; a few ran tongues across expensively tinted lips. But besides being dead-tired I was also an accounted-for man, so I passed them by and rode up.

I assumed that room 407 would be on the fourth floor; I assumed correctly. The interior was okay, neither the Beverly Hilton nor the Armpit Arms. Big soft bed, which was nice.

The oddest thing about the room was that there were all these safes against the walls; nine of them, to be exact. Moslers, Sentries, all makes and models. Weird. I mean, how many valuables could anyone have to lock up?

Figuring that it would take a while for room service to get there, I grabbed a shower. Despite being pooped I was feeling pretty good, now that I knew for sure I was finished with this padoodle business. I washed my clothes and hung them up to dry, then wrapped a towel around me when I heard a knock on the front door.

The bellman was Laurence Olivier, at the moment playing what I assumed was a Venetian gondolier; thin black mustache, slicked-back black hair, flouncy colorful clothes, all of it. He wheeled a cartful of food in, then walked over to the nearest wall and pointed at a Mosler.

"Is it a-safe?" he asked.

"Yes, it's a safe," I said.

He went on to the next one, a Sentry. "Is it a-safe?"

"Yes, it's a safe."

This went on for five safes, until I got tired of it. "Listen, why don't you—?" I began.

He reached in his pocket and pulled out something long, skinny, and metallic. Yeah, it was one of those nasty pick-things you hate to see the dentist grab when you're sitting helpless in his chair, all that shit stuffed in your mouth. "Is it a-safe?" he asked.

"Yes, it's a safe."

We did all nine, and he finally put the pick away. I gave him a five-buck tip and sent him on his merry way, double-locking the door after him. Then, after consuming nearly everything on the cart, I either fell asleep or lost consciousness.

When I awakened in the morning, the IM-HO-TEP INN was gone.

No parking lot full of trendy cars, no yuppies *doing* anything, no room 407 with all the safes.

I was on the dusty floor of the valley, naked as a jaybird. (How naked *is* a jaybird, really? For that matter, what the hell is a jaybird?) The Nishiki was there, and my clothes; that's all.

Really weird.

I got dressed, rode to the other side of the valley, and found the steepest negotiable path possible. Not long after I was . . .

. . . back on the Ultimate Bike Path, just barely missing one of the walls because of entering at so severe an angle.

You know, it was good to see the familiar tunnel again. Earlier, I had been positive about heading straight back to Camp Pendleton, then home, for a long dose of reality time, a dose that would include my cross-country ride to Cedar Rapids. Now, pedaling along the *mhuva lun gallee* with a decent night's sleep behind me, I began to rethink the plan. Maybe another brief excursion or two before packing it in, because I wasn't going to be back this way for a while.

Okay, so I stayed on the Path, and for the longest time no particular gate lured me, which was fine. I continued to look for the glowing portal that would lead me back to Ralph Ralph, but you can guess the outcome of that. No problem, because I was fine, and before long I was bound to be summoned by a Florida gate, or a black circle with bread slicers, or an Elmer Fudd. Anything this time but a Gorbachev birthmark . . .

Up ahead, clicking Daisy Duck shoes against the sides of a go-thing, was a Vulvan. Now it might have been Hormona, but I wasn't about to assume that just yet. On my visit to Vulvan (I didn't share *too* much of that with you, did I?) I discovered that *all* feline females looked pretty much alike . . . yeah, gorgeous! For that matter so did the male Toms, or whatever you wanted to call them. It took a lot of asking before I found the one I was after, although *any* of the Reproductors . . . never mind.

Pulling up alongside the go-thing I smiled and said, "Hi there, my name is Jack." (Yep, she had those same incredible indigo eyes-to-die-for.)

The cat-woman glanced at me and made that nifty L-shaped bow, then snapped up. "For economy's sake you may call me Utera," she said.

Right. "Uh, is it reasonable to assume that you're a Reproductor?"

She showed a hint of surprise. "Yes, how could you know?"

"Just a lucky—"

Her body suddenly stiffened. The killer aroma engulfed me as she ran her tongue across fiery lips. Utera was about to invigorate herself.

I took two deep breaths, then got the hell out of there at blur-speed.

Scenario: Study Group Old Guys watching Jack Miller search frantically for the portal back to Camp Pendleton.

Study Group Old Guy #1: "That was quite an adventure from which Jack just returned."

Study Group Old Guy #3: "Yes, I agree. Your faith in him is justified."

Study Group Old Guy #4: "But why are his activities so frantic at this time?"

My Old Guy: "He is trying to get back from where he left to resume what he refers to as reality time."

Study Group Old Guy #2: "He has returned many times before, but never like that."

My Old Guy (smiles, which puzzles the others): "He is anxious to begin this reality time and be united with his female. I'll explain it to you in detail later, but it seems like we have lost him for a while." (Sticks finger in ear.). "He is what his species calls . . . horny."

CHAPTER 14

Distasteful Doses of Reality

Remember that story I told you about the aardvark with the clock in its belly? Yeah, the blue door back to the Stuart Mesa hill again decided to be elusive . . . which, I'm sure, initially had to do with the fact that I didn't get down out of blur-speed. At least it tired me somewhat, got my libido out of overdrive. Big deal.

But even after slowing down I couldn't find the blasted thing. Here's what was weird: Usually, when that gate did not appear for a stretch, you wouldn't see *any* similar blue doors back to our world, past, present, or otherwise. Not so this time, because for a while the whole right wall of the *mhuva lun gallee* was dominated by them . . . every one *but* mine. A contradiction, one which, in my present state of mind, was driving me nuts!

Naturally, as always, it appeared—on the *left* wall, amid what had been a long run of isosceles triangles and iridescent snowmen. I came close to passing the blasted thing by, but compensated my angle enough to burst through dead-center . . .

. . . and hurtle down the rest of the hill, as deserted as when I'd left it, a zillion years and a microsecond ago.

By eleven-fifteen A.M. on Friday I was back in my Del Mar condo. Glad to be there, too.

That's what I thought.

It was the start of a weekend that—ultimately—I would work hard at forgetting.

Distasteful Dose of Reality #1: There was a message on my machine from Izzy McCarthy, agent nonpareil. It seems there had been a big upheaval in my publisher's editorial department. Now, similar upheavals in the publishing business occur about as often as you brush your teeth, so it wasn't a major shock. But the bottom line was, those who had thought highly of Jack Miller and his brilliant works were outta there. For the moment everything was on hold, including the contracts for *Wasp Women of Naheedi* and the sequel to *Tree Men of Quazzak*. More than likely, Izzy believed, the new editors would go ahead with them. After all, the honcho there had always been fond of my stuff. Still . . .

Now, there was an *up* side to this. In the publishing business editors *do* resurface, oftentimes at houses better than the one they left. So down the road there was a chance at an in with some biggie or other. Nonetheless, Izzy's message didn't make my day.

I spent the rest of the afternoon and evening with my trusty legal pad writing down all that had happened to me along (and off) the Ultimate Bike Path, from little (big!) Harlan on. No way was I going to try to remember it a month or so from now. Actually it was a hell of a lot, and I'd just gotten past my meeting with Horace Pinker when I found myself too tired to do any more. At least I still had Saturday and Sunday.

Distasteful Dose of Reality #2: On Saturday morning, as I lay in bed contemplating how to tell my mother, Mrs. Rose Miller Leventhal, first about Holly, second about my bike trip to Iowa, I got a phone call from Chainsaw Leventhal.

My mother was in the hospital.

Now you've got to understand, in all my three-plus decades of existence my mother has *never* been a patient in a hospital. She hates them. Doctors, yes; oh, she'll definitely go to a doctor's office. She is a horn of plenty when it comes to aches and pains and stuff, and has probably sat in the waiting room of every specialist in South Florida. One doctor commissioned a statue of her to grace the lawn of his West Palm Beach clinic; another immortalized her name on the license plate of his Mercedes 300SE. No problem with doctors, but *never* hospitals.

Chainsaw couldn't tell me much, which was frustrating. He had just gotten a call from Sadie Melman, my mother's best friend, who was with her when whatever happened happened. Sadie is one of the most emotional people on the planet. She's in the *Guinness Book* for usage of the word *oy* and has been known to cry during cat food commercials, so no wonder Chainsaw was in the dark. He was on his way there now and would call me as soon as he knew something.

Okay, with all I have to say about her, she's still my mother and I love her and I worry about her. The first thing you figure is that she's fallen victim to the Big One. (In the retiree haven of Florida the Big One is infinitely different from its namesake in California.) How bad was it? Did someone nearby know CPR? (Not Sadie Melman, for sure, she was probably too busy screaming *oy!*) Was she . . . ?

Half an hour later, as I was giving serious thought to calling my travel agent and having her check the schedule of the day's flights into Fort Lauderdale, I got another phone call . . . from my mother. Yeah, she was fine, but *hoo boy,* was she pissed at Sadie, and especially at Chainsaw for calling me unnecessarily and *giving me aggravation* (her words).

What happened was this: She and Sadie were having bagels and coffee in their favorite restaurant. On her way back from the ladies' room my mother slipped on a piece of lox inadvertently spat out by a two-year-old in a high chair. She chipped a bone in her ankle and hit her head on the edge of a table as she fell, which caused a slight concussion. With Sadie's screams of *oy!* resounding through the restaurant a couple of men carried her next door to the emergency room of the hospital. In Florida there's either a hospital or some other medical building on every corner. She was not thrilled to find out where she was, and with it now being over she was going to have Chainsaw drive her home. *Don't worry, Jackie, I'm fine, what's a little more pain? I'll call you in two weeks around.*

Okay, at least that turned out all right. Now, I didn't say a word to her about Holly or the trip. I could always tell her tomorrow, after things settled down there . . .

On the other hand, in *two weeks around* I could always call her from Nebraska, or wherever-the-hell I was at that time, when most of it was over. Was that the coward's way out, or what?

I went back to the legal pad and stayed there for a few hours. Tomorrow I would look at the route to Iowa, highlighted on one of those trip-things from AAA, though for the most part I'd already consigned it to memory. Remember, a cross-country trip was something I'd wanted to do for a long time.

I was supposed to call Holly that evening. Naturally I was surprised when she called me in the middle of the afternoon.

Distasteful Dose of Reality #3: Okay, bottom line first, then I'll try to sort it out . . . our relationship was suddenly on hold.

In a way it was Paula Kaufman all over again, but not quite, because I'd never come *close* to feeling about Paula what I felt about Holly Dragonette.

Shit.

The similarity had to do, of course, with an old boyfriend. In Holly's case it was a guy she'd known most of her life. She'd told me about him and assured me it was over.

Right.

They had grown together through their adult years . . . to a point. Although educated, this guy suffered from a typical Midwest mental anomaly of not being able to see the sky beyond the horizon of corn. Holly had been content with that until the past few years, when she'd at first questioned it, then found it loathsome.

Her decision to move to California, made nearly a year ago, had opened the rift between them. She had wanted him to come along, but it was a nonnegotiable issue on his part. All his pleading, cajoling, threatening, whatever, had made it worse. They broke up . . . for good, she believed.

But now the poor distraught guy (read: codependent asshole) was ready to chuck the husks and give the Golden State a try, if that's what it would take to keep her. He'd already put some feelers out in the way of résumés while she was gone. Yeah, he was serious.

So what about us? I'd asked. What about all the things that were said? Oh, she meant them, she'd assured me. But ours was so new, and the other had been a lifetime; hard to break away from something like that. She had been looking forward to the growth of our relationship, and still was, and really didn't think she'd change her mind regarding Mr. Cedar Rapids.

But . . .

She needed *time to think,* a chance to *clear out her head,* finish up the *old business* once and for all. It's me, Jack, not you, and I'm sorry, and I care deeply for you, and I'll talk to you soon.

Yeah, well, I'm sorry too.

An accounted-for man, isn't that what I said I was?

Those yuppie females would have come up to my safe room. Utera the Vulvan would have been pleased to let me invigorate her.

Maybe all of that would be better, because relationships can hurt.

An accounted-for man . . .

What kind of shit was I thinking?

Crazy shit, because that's how I felt.

Relationships *can* hurt.

Maybe Holly Dragonette wasn't Melvin Butterwood's great-whatever-grandmother.

Then again, maybe she was.

Relationships *can* . . .

Well, *shit happens,* and one of the ways I've always dealt with shit happening was to dive into my writing.

An accounted-for . . .

I had plenty left to write about my recent excursion, significant things about muunastrebors and padoodle curses and Freddy Krueger and creatures with ASSHOLE BRAINS and such. It would take me at least until tomorrow morning.

Then, I would be back on the Ultimate Bike Path for a *long* time. Enough distasteful doses of reality.

Relationships . . .

CHAPTER 15

The He-Whos

No way was I going to do it again. *Absolutely* no way was I going to do it again.

Remember the time I left for the Ultimate Bike Path without being sure the Old Guys were watching? Well, not only wasn't I going to leave from *anywhere* else except the Starting Point on Camp Pendleton, but I wasn't about to budge from the lone eucalyptus without some acknowledgment of my journey's undertaking. I may have been despondent, but I wasn't stupid.

I'd been sending vibes during my drive up the freeway, but so far no response. With me allegedly going to Iowa they could have abandoned their study indefinitely. Perhaps another project warranted their attention, the mating habits of lice or something. In any case there I stood, off to the side of Stuart Mesa Road, trying to look like I was doing something, with lots of other riders (this being a late Sunday morning) asking me if I needed help. Just maybe, if it hadn't been so busy, I might have jumped up and down and yelled *hey old guys my girl's done left me but instead of booze or drugs I want to drown my sorrows on the ultimate bike path*. Uh-uh, I couldn't.

About the time I had some slight inclination to disregard my former vows and head down the hill, my Old Guy came riding up on his Schwinn. I must say, from a distance I didn't think it was him, because he was handling the bike skillfully. He knew it, too, as evidenced by his happy grin.

When he raised one hand to wave at me, he nearly went over on his head. Oh, well.

"Halloo, Jack," he said. "I didn't—*owww!*"

He had finally learned how to use the kickstand, but this time he put it down on top of his foot. I moved his bike aside. "Are you all right?" I asked.

"Yes, quite, thank you. But why are you here? We thought you were anxious to be with your female. Since your return yesterday we have embarked on another project, the reproductive instincts of bloodworms that have been exposed to high levels of radiation.'' (See? I told you it was something like that.)

Actually, I wasn't in the mood for talking about my problems. I offered him an explanation in general terms. He listened intently, scratched his head, nearly stuck a finger in his ear.

''I've been absorbing some of your world's literature and film on the subject of *love*,'' he said. ''Rather curious how much of it there is. Your species is so preoccupied with . . . Ah, but even though I don't understand, I know it's troubling you. Perhaps another time you'll explain it to me. For now, return to the *mhuva lun gallee* if you wish. I'll be observing you, and I'm sure the others will join me soon. So far our project has proven uninteresting, for you see, when two exposed bloodworms perform the act of reproduction they always burst together, whereas when one is exposed and the other normal—''

''Thanks for sharing that,'' I interrupted. ''Right now I'm outta here.''

''Good luck, Jack,'' he called, but I was already over the rim, and I pumped hard to reach the speed I wanted fast . . .

. . . so that my too-real world was behind, and I was engulfed by the mystery of the Ultimate Bike Path's rust-red walls.

I wanted to race at blur-speed, and then again I didn't. I wanted to find a gate to get lost in real quick, and then again I didn't. In other words, I didn't know *what* in hell I wanted, I was so screwed up.

Almost immediately a lengthy run of Bart Simpson heads appeared, dominating both walls. Now, as much as I wanted to learn more about the Afterwards, this was not the time. So of necessity I went into blur-speed for a long time, until their presence was little more than sporadic.

Whatever the speed, I did not see another rider for the longest time. That was okay; after all, I was depressed and feeling sorry for myself and didn't feel like *any* company, human, subhuman, or otherwise.

Then, I started thinking how nice it might be to run into a Vulvan.

Hormona, or Utera, or any Vulvan of the female persuasion who had the need to be invigorated.

All of a sudden I had a better perspective of what *I* needed at the moment.

So naturally, not a single feline female pounding the sides of a go-thing with Daisy Duck shoes appeared on the Path. But the first rider I overtook was rather interesting. You know those FAT people that make the *Guinness Book*? The ones who can't fit through doors, and get buried in piano crates, that sort of thing? Imagine taking one, spinning it in a blender for seven seconds, microwaving it for fifteen, then putting it in a huge Corning Ware server that moved along on top of four bowling balls. *That's* what was now riding alongside me, smiling (I think) with enormous, fiery-red "lips."

"Hey, big boy, wanna mess around?" the mass of mutilated flesh said, a huge Jabba the Hutt tongue emerging from its "mouth" and moving like a windshield wiper across its . . . whatever.

I got outta there *faster* than fast.

Utilizing a brief burst of blur-speed, I was able to stifle the gag reflex. When I finally slowed down it was in time to be confronted with something new and unexpected . . .

A fork in the Ultimate Bike Path.

Oh, great, decisions; *that* I didn't need. The Old Guy had never said a word about the *mhuva lun gallee* splitting in two directions. Maybe the intrepid Vurdabrok, with all the time he put in exploring the thing, had never come across this. Hey, yeah, I was breaking new ground! Should I be excited, or scared shitless?

Whatever; I had about one point four seconds to make my choice, because even at cruising speed . . . there they were. I started *eenie meenie,* and on *minie* found myself entering the left fork. Not even time for *moe.*

Well, nothing looked different. A random pattern of gates that had existed for a while continued, then changed into a nearly unbroken run of iridescent snowmen with the laser needles.

Yeah, snowmen.

One of which was the doorway to Vulvan.

Oh, please, if there *is* some Greater Power: I must admit that I don't regularly attend the church of my choice, but on the whole I'm a good person, and that should count for something, so even though you may have a lot more significant things to

do, you might consider that *this* good person is in extreme
need, and . . .

Nope, no yellow ribbon (it *was* still tied on, wasn't it?), and
even at a speed that I called *nearly falling over* there wasn't any
way I could count to seventy-three thousand four hundred and
ninety-two.

Ooo, *frustration!*

Well, ribbon or not it was time to make something happen.
I angled toward the next snowman on the left wall, burst
through . . .

. . . and braked to a stop rather effortlessly as I shifted
down from the Vurdabrok Gear.

The place where I stood was not just flat, but *flat*. Absolutely
nothing resembling a mountain range, or even a hill, in *any*
direction. The sky was sort of amber, with a distant white sun
that nonetheless generated sufficient heat for this world to be a
bit on the warm side. The peppery-white "sand" below me
was tightly packed, more like sandstone. It was cracked in
places, but nothing significant. Not a single growth of any kind
was evident.

On the whole this place was pretty boring.

Yeah, but I couldn't get out of here yet. Without a hill to ride
down or a chasm to leap into, I was stuck. Even on an easy
surface like this there was no way I could hit the necessary
speed, not in high gear. So, looks like I was back on the road
again.

I started pedaling in a direction that I hoped was west,
toward the setting sun. Wrong-o, I was headed east, and the sun
was still climbing, and it was getting uncomfortable. Great, I
needed this! It had taken at least half an hour to realize that fact,
and I still couldn't see anything but flatness ahead.

Then, finally, something that had a shape! Before long I
realized what it was I rode toward: a forest of immensely tall
but skinny trees, all packed tightly together. Their middle
branches were full with broad, greenish-brown leaves, but
those on top were practically denuded. Really weird-looking.

You would have thought the ground would change, start
looking more fertile the closer I got to the trees. Uh-uh, the
sandstone floor remained constant right up to the edge of these
wood giants. I paused there for a moment, then pedaled into the
dense forest.

Oh, yeah, I do mean *dense.* I'm talking barely-able-to-fit-the-bike-through dense, the trunks of the weird trees being so close together. I stayed on the bike but had to move *real* slow; walking alongside it would have actually been harder. At least there was no ground cover, just that same sandstone floor. Small consolation, since it felt like I wasn't getting anywhere.

Then, just to piss me off, there suddenly *was* ground cover. The sandstone floor darkened, and pretty soon there was this short purple grass, which quickly became long purple grass, and now I *had* to get off the bike seat. I still couldn't walk alongside it, so what I had to do was straddle the top tube, which got to be annoying. My progress could have been measured in centimeters.

About the time I was giving serious thought to retracing my steps and trying to circumvent the forest, the blasted thing came to an end. Or, at least, there was a break in it, because the trees began again across a clearing of purple grass, by my guess about a quarter mile away. To the north, not far, were these knobby knolls, a bunch of them, all about the same size. Not impressive, nor helpful, but at least it was something other than *flat.* I angled toward them.

I had set my sights on this one in particular, slightly higher than the rest. Scaling it was easy, the coarse blades of the purple grass providing good traction. Standing on top I surveyed the clearing.

Smoke was curling in the air from a village or something, about two miles south. Funny, I hadn't noticed the smoke before. Well, a village normally meant people, and assuming these weren't headhunter types who liked to cut off your testicles, shrink them down and wear them as hair ornaments, they might be able to steer me toward the nearest earthquake fault or mountain range.

Who knows, maybe the customs of these people included offering their women to a stranger.

I rode down the knoll and pedaled toward the village. A mile away I came across the start—or the end—of a rock-strewn dirt trail that had been cut through the grass about a yard wide and lined with stones. Emerging from the village this seemed to be the proverbial road-leading-nowhere. There weren't any tracks on it that I could see. I slowed down.

The village consisted of over fifty wood-and-brick cabins

scattered on both sides of the road, which had widened. But while their locations were haphazard, their construction was definitely not. They were of *identical* size and shape. Each had a narrow chimney atop a severely sloping roof, and two tiny windows flanking a narrow door, which you approached by climbing two wide steps.

There wasn't a soul around, not even in a big corral to the west of town, where a herd of green llama-things grazed. No communal cooking fires, no nothing. The smoke I'd seen rose from most of the chimneys, the strands intertwining high above. Couldn't imagine these people being cold on a day like . . . no, wait a minute, it *was* kind of brisk here; probably had been ever since the forest, but I just hadn't noticed it.

After I'd walked past the first dozen or so cabins, I realized that there *was* a difference between them. Wood plaques hung above the doors, with "letters" scrawled on them. Their color and shape were indescribable; they looked like something an eighteen-month-old would make if you told him to write his name with a quill pen, dipped in a mixture of Log Cabin syrup and Dentu-Creme. From where I stood they meant nothing.

I hadn't mentioned this, but back when the Old Guy replaced that defective translator with the UT6, he clued me in on its attributes. One thing it did was to translate any world's *written* language by touching the page, sign, whatever, the words were on. Sounded weird, but . . .

I touched the first plaque, and guess what, it worked! The squiggles transformed into He-Who-Is-Less-Than-Nobody. Now there seemed to be a bunch of those. Another couple read He-Who-Is-Nobody. Farther along I found He-Who-Is-Almost-Somebody, but I passed it up for He-Who-Is-Somebody. I mean, if this was the best they had, why not go for it?

Sure a lot of He-Whos around here, but so far not a single She-Who.

So just as I was about to knock on his door, He-Who-Is-Somebody emerged. He was short, chubby, and wore a monk's cowl, his head set so far back in the hood that I could barely make out his face. I smiled and held up a sixties peace sign, hoping not to scare the guy into sounding an alarm or something.

"Hey, how's it going?" I said. "Maybe you can tell me—"

A stubby pink hand popped out of a huge sleeve, and I was

motioned to silence. The guy then reached up to his hood and flipped it off.

I was looking at a bald caricature of the old Communist boss himself, Nikita Khrushchev.

The most significant feature on this guy's round, puffy face was an enormous pair of lips. They had a bluish tinge, the kind you would see on someone who was suffocating, or already dead. But this fellow's eyes were alert.

"Yeah, nice to see you," I said, which sounded stupid. "All I wanted to know was—"

Again that *shut your face pal* gesture. His lips parted, and I thought he was going to speak, but you know what?

After he peeled back a layer of gross, fleshy lips I saw his mouth, which was zippered shut.

I swear, like on a fly or the back of a dress! The zipper's teeth gave him a Skeletor look. If this guy *was* a monk, keeping a vow of silence shouldn't be too hard.

As I pondered on the weird sight, the guy raised a stubby finger and pointed in the direction of the dwellings at the far end of town. I assumed he was advising me where to go, but I couldn't tell if he meant one in particular. Before I could ask he pulled up his hood and walked off.

Other cowled figures began popping out of their cabins. Outwardly they looked identical. One of them, a He-Who-Is-Less-Than-Nobody, lowered his hood when I passed. Surprise, a mini-Khrushchev, just like the first guy; even had the zippered mouth. He was no help, nor were the next four peas-in-a-pod. Just what *did* rank buy you in this burg?

The cabins toward the south edge of town were more tightly bunched together than anywhere else. I walked past He-Who-We-Are-Not-Sure-Of and He-Who-Does-Not-Have-A-Prayer, then He-Who-Keeps-On-Trying-But-Failing. The next one was He-Who-Bakes-The-Bread-For-Us-All (sounded pretty important), then He-Who-Feeds-And-Tends-To-The-Skukkos, which must've been what they called those green llama-things. Yeah, for sure, because the resident of the next cabin was He-Who-Shovels-The-Dung-Of-The-Skukkos-And-Molds-It-Into-Fuel-Balls. Was this poor guy lower than He-Who-Is-Less-Than-Nobody, or what?

Anyway, I was running out of cabins fast, and the next one, He-Who-Does-Penance-For-Having-Thoughts-Of-A-Carnal-Nature, was *not* going to solve my problem . . . although I gotta say, this He-Who sounded like an okay guy. Still in all, the end cabin *had* to be what the first mini-Khrushchev meant, its occupant being He-Who-Answers-Stupid-Questions-Asked-By-Strangers. Yeah, I'd say that was pretty straightforward.

Before I could knock on the door the guy came out; they all seemed to do that. He threw back his hood, and for a moment I thought he was my late Uncle Benny. But then, everyone used to say Benny looked like Nikita Khrushchev, so I guess that made sense.

"Hi there," I said, "I'm obviously a stranger in these parts, and I have some stu—some questions. I was hoping you could help me."

Uncle Benny looked me up and down, then folded back his fleshy lips (God, I hated that!). His mouth was like all the others, but with a sort of ceremonial flicking of the right wrist he unzipped it, then exercised his gums briefly, as though it had been a while since he'd last spoken. That didn't surprise me.

"Peace be with you, Brother Stranger," he said. "I am Brother Ignatius of the Order of Demakk, entitled He-Who-Answers-Stupid-Questions-Asked-By-Strangers. Now, let me recite to you the rest of our Order. There is, first and foremost, Brother Axel, entitled He-Who-Is-Much-Much-More-Than-Somebody." (So, He-Who-Is-Somebody was really nobody after all.) "After that we have Brother—"

"Yeah, that's all great," I interrupted, "but can we skip right to the questions at hand?"

Brother Ignatius scowled at me. "Because you are a stranger I will overlook the sacrilege one time. But do not interfere with the Recitation of the Order again, lest you risk the standard consequence."

"Which is?"

"The severing of the middle finger on your right hand."

Oh, right, no way! I wasn't fond of any form of *severing,* and besides, the digit in question would undoubtedly see plenty of action on freeways and such in the future. I gave Brother Ignatius my undivided attention.

Let me tell you, that was one shitload of He-Whos I had to hear recited! There must've been cabins I hadn't yet seen, because I swear he rattled off at least a hundred. But finally he was done.

"Yes, now what can I help you with?" he asked.

"First question," I told him, "what is this place?"

"You are in Celibattown," he replied, rather reverently.

Yeah, I should've known that right off. *Celibattown,* for chrissake! *This* is where a man in my present state winds up. My apologies to the universe, but . . . *you didn't hear me so well this time!*

"Okay, next question," I said. "I need to know—"

"I am Brother Ignatius of the Order of Demakk, entitled He-Who-Answers-Stupid-Questions-Asked-By-Strangers," he said again. (Oh, jeez!) "Now, let me recite to you the rest of our Order . . ."

Uh-huh, I had to listen to the whole blessed thing again, just to get another answer. I kept thinking, *Remember the finger, remember the finger.* It got me through.

"Yes, now what can I help you with?" he said again.

Make this good, Miller. "I need something deep to jump into, like a chasm, or something high to ride down, like the side of a mountain. Can you tell me what options I have?"

If my request puzzled Uncle Benny, he didn't show it. "No chasm or hole, nothing like that. But of course there are mountains. You can go to the Mountains of the East or the Mountains of the West."

Hey, imaginative names! Okay, think this out carefully, before you accidentally ask a question and get the guy started on the He-Whos again. I definitely would have preferred to know which of the two ranges was closer. But I'd come from the west, and there wasn't anything back there for a *long* way. So, eastward ho!

"Thank you," I said carefully.

Uncle Benny, aka Brother Ignatius aka He-Who-Answers-Stupid-Questions-Asked-By-Strangers, nodded curtly, zipped up, put his hood back on, and went inside. I would have left Celibattown then, but there was still one cabin that really intrigued me.

I knocked on the door of He-Who-Does-Penance-For-Having-Thoughts-Of-A-Carnal-Nature.

Just *who* or *what* did these monks of the Order of Demakk, dwelling here in Celibattown, have carnal thoughts about? *That* was the question interesting me as I watched the door open. It didn't occur to me that this guy had *not* anticipated my coming. Rather than step outside, he waved me in.

The stark, warm cabin contained little more than a table, chair, bookcase, and an uncomfortable-looking cot, where my host sat after waving me to a chair. I'm not sure what I was looking for, and I suddenly started feeling kind of dumb. I got up.

"Uh, listen," I said, "no sense taking up your time when you can't even—"

He gestured me to be quiet and flipped back the hood. Yeah, another mini-Khrushchev. When he peeled back his lips (*eeeyooo!*), I saw what looked like a small hole in the zipper.

"Yes, I can talk to you," he said in a garbled voice, sort of what you sound like when your mouth is stuffed with food. "Demakk knows I'm in enough trouble already, so what's a little more?"

Dang, I should've come to this guy first. Sure would've beat listening to a lot of He-Whos.

"Great. Well, hello, my name is Jack, and as you can probably figure out, I'm just passing through town."

"Peace be with you, Brother Jack. I am Brother Rockwell. What do you want to know?"

That's right, it wasn't the same prompt I'd gotten from Brother Ignatius, but still . . . "I wanted to find out which is closer, the Mountains of the East or the Mountains of the West."

"The Mountains of the West are *mmruuffa pwaakaluu*—" he began.

"Excuse me?"

He squeezed two fingers into the zipper hole and stretched it wider. *Grossed me out!* I wish he would've warned me.

"There, that's better," he said. "I try not to keep it too big, in case there is an inspection. As I was saying, the Mountains of the West are about one hundred miles away, and so are the Mountains of the East. But you definitely want the Mountains of the West."

"Why? Is it easier traveling there?"

"No, the forests and the *plakkablebbel*—"

"Huh?"

The hole had shrunk down again. He widened it. *Jeez, why didn't he just unzip the blasted thing?*

"What I was saying was that the forests and plains and such from here to either range are about the same."

"Then why do I *definitely* want the Mountains of the West?"

"Because"—he seemed reluctant to say it—"there are *women* in the Mountains of the East."

Oh, yeah, that was a real deterrent, huh? I suppose that, to these guys, it might've been.

Trying to be as nonchallenging as possible I said, "As you can see, Brother Rockwell, I'm not of your Order, or any other for that matter. So I don't think encountering women would—"

"You don't understand!" he exclaimed. "It is in the Mountains of the East that the Amazin women dwell!"

He didn't say *Amazon,* like the river, but *Amazin,* like *Those Amazin' Mets.* And there was a real shakiness in his voice when he said it.

"Just who are these Amazins?" I asked.

Whoops, wrong question! His body shook as badly as his voice; the hole in the zipper shrank, and he folded his lips back over the whole thing. Brother Rockwell might have been a transgressor, but he had his limitations.

Anyway, based on the fear in his voice, and the physical appearance of this world's males, I quickly formed a mental image of the women he referred to as Amazins. They were all about four feet eight, weighed in excess of two hundred fifty pounds, were hairy everywhere, especially on the tops of their enormous flat feet, and carried cudgels. I mean, why else would these guys choose monkhood? Mountains of the West, here I come!

"Well, I'm outta here," I told Brother Rockwell. "Thanks for the info. And sorry if I shook you up."

It didn't seem like I was destined to learn anything about his *thoughts of a carnal nature.* But as I started for the door he held up a hand for me to stop. He reached for his lips, and this time I did a thorough job examining his ceiling as he peeled them back. I figured he would be enlarging that hole again, but instead there was this chalk-on-the-blackboard sound as he unzipped his mouth.

"Oh, that feels good," he sighed, performing the same exercises as He-Who-Answers-Stupid-Questions-Asked-By-Strangers. "You said you're not of any Order. Is that the truth?"

Did he think I looked monkish, or what? "I kid you not, Brother Rockwell."

He went to each of the windows, peered out furtively, then turned to me. There was a sly little grin on his chubby face.

"I'm doing penance for thinking about the Amazin women."

"Oh?"

"Being a fine artist, I drew pictures of them. Brother Axel and the others found many, and they were destroyed. But I have more. Do you . . . want to see them?"

"For sure."

"You won't tell on me or anything?"

"Cross my heart and hope to die."

That seemed good enough for him, even though I don't think he knew what in hell I was talking about. He walked to a far corner of the room, knelt down, and began working a floorboard loose. His hands were shaking as he withdrew a dirty envelope.

"The Amazin women," he said with both reverence and fear.

Brother Rockwell had been right about one thing: He was an excellent artist.

Brother Stranger, aka Jack Miller, had been wrong about one thing: The Amazins were gorgeous.

I'm talking drop-dead, women-to-die-for, faces-and-bodies-that-launched-a-thousand-ships *gorgeous*.

The drawings he had made on thin, yellowish paper with some sort of charcoal depicted women that, normally, I might have believed could only have been summoned out of the deepest reaches of male fantasies. However, I had the feeling these monks of the Order of Demakk were not the most imaginative folks. What I was looking at here was *exactly* what Brother Rockwell had seen: exquisite, sensual faces, cascading locks of hair, lithe bodies clothed in skimpy animal skins, great breasts.

Yes, I was on my way to the Mountains of the East!

Something I'm sure Brother Rockwell sensed, because he looked at me incredulously. "You don't want to go that way," he said in a croaking voice.

"But why?" I asked. "Can't you tell me?"

Oh, hell, he freaked again! He zipped his mouth, folded the lips over, and this time covered his head with the hood. Taking back the pictures, he replaced them under the floorboard. He stayed on his knees, his back toward me, bowing and groveling and all that good stuff. It was definitely time to leave.

"Listen, Brother Rockwell," I called from the door. "If it makes you feel better, I'm on my way to the Mountains of the *West,* okay?"

He didn't turn around, but a hand came out of a sleeve, and he gave me a thumbs-up sign. At least I'd calmed the guy down, even though I didn't have a clue about what he was so afraid to tell me.

Anyway, I left the cabin of He-Who-Does-Penance-For-Having-Thoughts-Of-A-Carnal-Nature, determined to get out of Celibattown as quickly as possible. After being in the dark room the daylight momentarily blinded me, but it passed. A bunch of hooded figures were gathered around my Nishiki, which I'd left propped against the side of Brother Rockwell's place. They let me through, then watched as I squeezed some Gatorade out of my bike bottle.

Listening to my stomach grumble, it suddenly occurred to me how hungry I was. I'd pigged out on pizza and Häagen-Dazs Saturday night, one of the ways I dealt with distasteful doses of reality. But Saturday night was a long way behind me, and I didn't have as much as a stale granola bar in my bag.

"I don't suppose you have an Arby's or a Jack in the Box in this town?" I asked my spectators with a smile.

The hood of one was tossed off as the others turned toward him. Uncle Benny peeled back his lips, zipped open his mouth, and flapped his gums.

"Peace be with you, Brother Stranger. I am Brother Ignatius of the Order of Demakk, entitled He-Who-Answers-Stupid-Questions-Asked-By-Strangers. Now, let me recite to you the rest of our Order . . ."

Oh, shit!

CHAPTER 16

A Really Awful Night

You know, some good actually *did* come out of having to listen to the Recitation of the Order again. After it was done, and Brother Ignatius figured out that I was hungry, he led me over to the cabin of He-Who-Bakes-The-Bread-For-Us-All. Yeah, there was bread; great bread, too, like the sourdough you get in San Francisco. But this silent mini-Khrushchev made all kinds of great stuff, including a meat stew (probably out of those llama-things) that was outstanding. They might not've been the most personable hosts, but they sure fed me well.

I finally left Celibattown and headed down the road. My reason was that, in case He-Who-Does-Penance-For-Having-Thoughts-Of-A-Carnal-Nature was watching, I didn't want to freak him out by having him see me ride toward the east.

Come on, *you* know that's where I was going. I mean, you would not have *believed* the pictures of the Amazin women! Whatever the risk I was going to check it out for myself. At least I would be in the mountains, with some viable means of escaping this place.

The path wove between some knolls half a mile farther south; for the first time I could not see the town, or vice versa. I immediately turned eastward, sped across the plain, and penetrated the forest of weird, towering trees.

Once again my pace slowed to that of a slug.

But for a change I got lucky, because the long purple grass quickly became short purple grass, then no purple grass, and soon I emerged from the forest. I still couldn't see any mountains, the sandstone floor going on endlessly. No problem; I was well fed, eager to go, and could easily put a bunch of miles behind.

So of course, fifteen minutes later, my front tire went flat.

A nasty, four-inch-long nail had penetrated my Cycle Pro Mudslinger at a forty-five-degree angle. Yeah, a *nail* in the middle of this sandstone desert; probably the only one around for umpteen square miles, and I found it. Great. This was even harder than running into the Bush of Turttek.

Fixing it was not a major problem; I had a patch kit, a good Zefal pump, all of that. Still, it took a bit of time, and it was while working on it that I suddenly realized something: I was about to run out of daylight. The forest I'd recently passed through was still visible, and the setting sun was on top of it. Maybe half an hour before dark, not much more.

Okay, but the night still wasn't going to stop me. First, there would probably be some moonlight, and second, this was a clear plain, not much in the way of obstructions.

As long as I didn't run into any more nails.

With the offending fastener tucked in my seat bag, the tire patched, I started off again. As advertised, the sun set and the sky darkened with astonishing quickness. There were quite a few distant, twinkling stars but as yet no moon. This wasn't nearly as black as the infernal Pit of Perdition I'd once found myself in, but it was dark enough.

It wasn't much later when the Really Awful Night began.

Remember how warm it had once been? Then how it had cooled off when I went through the forest and stopped in Celibattown? Well, it was now downright *freezing!* And all I had to wear was my spandex; no sweatshirt, no nothing. Uh-uh, I was not thrilled about this. Sure, I could've pedaled like a madman, kept myself warm by burning calories. But no matter how clear it seemed to be ahead, I was still afraid of riding too fast into something I couldn't see. So I compromised with a brisk but cautious cadence, which did little to prevent my buns from turning blue.

And that was only the start of the Really Awful Night.

Aside from those green llama-things that the He-Whos called skukkos, I hadn't seen a living creature here. Not an insect, bird, or four-legged animal, neither on the sandstone plain nor—surprisingly—in the forest. *That* now changed rather suddenly.

There was first this slithering, hissing reptilian sound; loud, then louder. I slowed down and looked all around, because it was impossible to tell which direction it was coming from. It kept growing louder, as in *deafening.*

The shape that glided past on my left was about the size of an Amtrak baggage car.

I couldn't make out any features, it went by so fast. A

moment later another crossed in front of me. The hissing grew
louder still, like a thousand air brakes being released.

Something began to growl.

It was a deep, throaty rumbling, and I have to say, the
perpetrator sounded pissed! The longer it went on, the more I
realized I should have said perpetrators, plural. A whole bunch
of furry tan streaks they were, weaving amid the Amtraks.

Where in the hell did all these creatures come from? Up out
of the sandstone floor? Or was there a forest nearby? If so I had
a problem, because I had been counting on reaching some trees
so I could light a fire and thaw out. Well, maybe that would still
be okay, because if I could get a fire going before one of them
ate me it might drive them off, and . . .

Something *caw-cawed* above my head, and there was a loud
flapping of what I perceived were *very big* wings.

One of the Amtraks passed a yard in front of me.

The growls turned into roars.

Steely talons clattered out a message that said *skewered bike
rider will make a nutritious meal for the young in our nest.*

Was I in serious shit here, or *what!*

Scenario: Study Group Old Guys (dimly) watching Jack
Miller about to assist the animal population of some weird
world build strong, healthy bodies ten different ways.

Study Group Old Guy #2: "It appears we returned from our
bloodworm study just in time."

Study Group Old Guy #4: "Yes indeed. Your subject has
gotten himself into quite a dilemma."

My Old Guy: "This is true. I was giving thought to pulling
him out."

Study Group Old Guy #1: "Why don't you? It's hopeless."

Study Group Old Guy #3: "I agree. At any moment now he
will reach for the Bukko."

My Old Guy (smiling): "Jack has not let me down before.
Let us give him a few moments longer to see if he can extract
himself from this one."

I reached for the Bukko.

Like, what did you expect me to do? This may sound
melodramatic, but *Death was all around me.*

Before I could rub the coin, one of the Amtraks reared high
in my path. *Hoo boy!*

"Jeez, get the hell outta here!" I screamed, not having much time to carefully choose the last words that would come from my mouth on this particular plane of existence.

Hey, guess what, they must've been good words, because the Amtrak-whatever fell backward and slithered away, like it was scared. For that matter, all the other things around and above me retreated, and there was even a period of silence, which didn't last long. I didn't care, because for the time being I wasn't being threatened. I even eased my grip on the Bukko, but I didn't let it go.

The sound of my voice, that had to be it! Maybe they weren't used to hearing one, or maybe it was the intensity with which I'd let them have it. Whatever; it was my only weapon, and I decided to use it wisely and well.

Remember the speed I used on the Ultimate Bike Path, the one I called *nearly falling over*? That's how I pedaled now, wary of the creatures presently exhibiting so great an interest in my being. It was hard keeping an eye on all sides; but the buggers kept their distance, and I even made progress, though not much.

And don't forget, even with the adrenaline going I was still freezing my ass off.

Before long the slithering and hissing and growling and roaring and cawing and flapping grew louder. Not only were they starting to close in again, but I swear there were more of them. This time I wasn't going to let any of them get *that* close.

So what did I choose to scare the beasties with? A chorus of "Born to Be Wild." After all, there's not much difference between my singing voice and a scream of terror. It worked, too. They backed away, probably thinking it was one of the scariest sounds they'd ever heard.

Some music teacher had once kicked me out of the school chorus, saying the exact same thing.

Well, I soon had it down to an art. They stay back for about five minutes; I add some distance; they close in, I let fly with my impression of Aretha belting "R-E-S-P-E-C-T," or Ike and Tina doing "Proud Mary" nice and rough, or *anything* by the Four Seasons, which really sent the creatures into fits of fear.

I don't know how many hours I kept this up, or how many songs I went through. At some point hearing Frankie Valli made them bolder, probably because I'd overused it, especially "Big Girls Don't Cry-Yi-Yi." So I switched to a hodgepodge, everything from Tiny Tim's "Tiptoe Through the Tulips" to Pavarotti's "La Donna Mobile" to James Brown's "I Feel Good." *(Owwwoo!)* Tiny Tim gave me at least a ten-minute respite.

The moon never did come out, which was good, because I really didn't want to see what I was fending off with oldies, opera, and such. I kept at it, growing colder by the minute, and more tired from my efforts, not to mention the tension of this whole episode. When would it ever end?

So of course, a forest suddenly loomed above me. *Loomed,* hell, I nearly rode into one of the trees, because it was just *there.* And the cacophony rising from this forest made my entourage sound like the senior citizens' reading room at the public library. It was *awful!*

I got off the bike and gathered all the loose branches I could find. Fortunately they were as dry as a bone. Belting out "The Impossible Dream" to ward off my aggressors, I thought about doing the old Boy Scout thing to get the fire going. Aha, not necessary, because in my seat bag was a book of matches I'd once picked up at a Chinese restaurant, for lighting candles and incense. Fortunately I'd forgotten to take it out.

Now singing the *Brady Bunch* theme song (I was really getting desperate), I set the branches ablaze. With a final cry of *curse you jack* my entourage disappeared. I still never got a good look at any of them, but I didn't give a shit. All I cared about was getting warm, and I built up the fire accordingly.

Five minutes later I had forced the chill out of my bones.

Five minutes after that the cacophony of noise from the forest was silenced.

Ten minutes after that the sky grew light, and somewhere to the east the sun came up, and then it was warm at the edge of the forest, and I didn't need the fire anymore.

Well, at least the Really Awful Night was over.

CHAPTER 17

Follow the Orange Brick Road

Pardon my Ferengi, but this next stretch of forest really sucked the big one. It was longer than the first forest, and full of purple grass—and even greenish-yellow grass—from start to end. No narrow plain divided it, like the one where I'd found Celibat-town. I don't think anyone lived around here.

And to make matters worse, the caution I now exhibited while inching along bordered on paranoia. The animals that had bugged me last night must have surely emerged from the forest. Even though it was deathly quiet they still had to be somewhere, sleeping or whatever. Just what I would have needed, to step on the tail of some well-concealed beastie.

A last consideration about the forest: Make sure you're not in one when the sun goes down!

Which, considering its endlessness, had begun to worry me. But it finally did end, and the sun hadn't reached its zenith yet. Still plenty of time.

Eureka, I could see the Mountains of the East! Still distant, but there they were. I'm not sure if the sandstone plain now before me stretched all the way to them, but I didn't worry about it. I set off at a speed designed to leave a large number of miles behind me in the least possible time.

A couple of hours later the unbroken plain was broken in a major league way. Let's see, He-Who-Does-Penance-For-Having-Thoughts-Of-A-Carnal-Nature had mentioned forests and plains on my journey to the mountains.

He hadn't said anything about a river.

Some hummer of a river, too. Real wide, a bluish ground fog preventing me from seeing beyond the opposite shore. Swiftly flowing, choppy water, kind of muddy. I was of the opinion that it was really deep. And as far as what might be in it, I didn't want to guess . . . because I didn't want to *know*.

Oh, great. Maybe there was a bridge. Uh-huh, sure. I pedaled two miles downriver, returned to the starting point, and did the same thing upriver. If anything I swear it was wider.

Then, just as I was thinking that it might be necessary to find out how deep it was and what swam below, I came across something. It was a bell, the kind that called many *hongry pardners* in from fields and corrals for chow. I rang it a bunch of times, waited a while, then rang it again when nothing happened.

Oh, yeah, now something happened. The ground fog on the other side had become a river fog, wafting out to the center. I couldn't see anything yet, but I heard this creaking noise, slow and steady, growing louder. I'd definitely accomplished something with the bell, because a vessel that looked like a gondola soon emerged from the mist. The ferryman at the helm was . . .

. . . whoopee, another guy in a hooded robe.

But not stumpy, like the monks of the Order of Demakk. This one was tall, and lean, and his robe wasn't even the same color. I only hoped he was more communicative than the zippered denizens of Celibattown.

The closer he came, the more I thought there was something familiar about this ferryman. It didn't take long to figure out why.

"Hey, how goes it?" I called cheerily, after he had skillfully negotiated the gondola-thing into a niche along the bank. "Can you run me over to the other side?"

He stood there, not responding, not flipping off the hood. Peering into the darkness I could vaguely make out a face . . .

. . . a skeletal face.

A hand emerged from one of the enormous sleeves . . .

. . . a thin, skeletal hand.

Just like Charon, the ferryman of the River Styx, in the underworld of Greek mythology.

Oh, no, let's not and say we did.

The fingers of the hand clattered insistently. That's right, you have to pay this guy if you want him to do anything. (Or else what, he eats your brains? I don't know.) I dug in my bike bag, pulled out a quarter, and placed it in his *palm*. The fingers closed around it; he stuck it under the hood, and there was this grinding sound.

Phuutoo! The quarter came flying out; hit me square in the chest. Guess it wasn't good enough.

I tried a dollar bill. *Phuutoo!* It floated down all cut up. What did this guy want, anyway?

Trinkets. What was in my bag? A panda bear pin from the San Diego Zoo. Irresistible. *Phuutoo!*

Could it be this walking bone pile wanted something to eat? Okay, before I left Celibattown He-Who-Bakes-The-Bread-For-Us-All gave me a hunk of that great sourdough to take along. I handed a piece to the ferryman. The ensuing sound was awful, but at least it didn't come back. He motioned me into the boat.

The ride was weird; I mean, cutting across the strong flow of the river as if it wasn't there. Maybe it wasn't; I stopped trying to figure out most of this stuff a long time ago. The ferryman didn't say a word. Did you expect him to? Me neither.

We reached the other side. I picked up the bike and climbed out. The bony guy stayed in the boat. I tore off another piece of bread and offered it to him. What the hey, he'd done a good job, and it wasn't much of a price.

"Thanks a lot," I said. "Here, enjoy . . ."

The bleached hand emerged, but he did something else with it, rather than take the bread. If I didn't know better (maybe I didn't), I swear I'd just been flipped the bird by a robed skeleton. How rude! But then, maybe I had affronted him by offering more than was required. How the devil should I know?

Anyway, he ferried away, and I walked away, and that was that. I popped out of the blue mist, got on the bike, and rode off. That could've been worse, I suppose. Maybe a little *nachis* was in order for a change.

Nope, sorry, Jack-o. Another forest in my face after less than an hour of riding. Great.

Here's the problem: Let's assume that dusk on wherever-the-hell-I-was took place at six o'clock, PST. From the position of the sun it was about three-thirty. I had to be on the other side of this forest in under two and a half hours, or else . . . uh-uh, I didn't want to think about *or else*. Do I take the chance, or do I call it a day right here?

Two and a half hours wasted; *that* would drive me up a wall.

What the hell, I *plunged* into the foliage.

Now don't think I haven't been learning anything from the times I'd done this before. I'd not only perfected the art of little mincing steps as I straddled the top tube, but I'd also learned to move with the bend of the purple grass. This required a lot of zigging and zagging through the trees, but there was no resistance. As long as I wasn't changing direction too radically . . .

But in spite of this I was still surrounded by trees after what my body clock advised me was the passage of about two hours. Somewhere out there the sun was getting ready to go beddy-bye; somewhere in here big live nasty things would be thinking, *aha a snack so soon upon awakening.*

Thus mused the master of hindsight: *I definitely should've waited.*

I minced along quickly, hoping for any kind of a break, even a small clearing. Though still in the midst of the forest, at least I could get a fire going and move away from the trees.

Ha, break number one! Not a biggie, just a gradual change in the height of the purple grass, but that was a good omen. The trees even cooperated by spreading apart some more. Great; just a little farther and . . .

Nearby, something growled.

High in the trees, something *cawed.*

Had there been an Olympic event for the hundred-yard mince, I would've been bringin' home the gold.

I burst out of the forest just as the sun went down. My first impulse was to tear ass across the sandstone floor, but I controlled it and stopped at the edge.

Now, lest you wonder about whether I'd considered the possibility of spending another Really Awful Night, be assured I had. Knowing how cold it got, I'd scoured the forest for anything that could have been utilized as clothing. Nope, leaves and grass just wouldn't do, and I don't think one of the furry things would have parted with its coat, no matter how nicely I asked.

The next thing was wood, for fuel. I had knotted my jersey into a sling, and for the last hour or so I'd been picking up choice branches; not too many, because it had gotten heavy real quick. Now, at the edge, I gathered up all I could and heaved it out on the plain. Plenty of it, too.

It grew darker.

From deep in the forest the sound of something slithering over tall purple grass told me that the Amtrak would more than likely be arriving on schedule.

Fifty yards from the edge of the forest I formed a wide circle of wood around me and the Nishiki. It took everything I had.

I set the wood afire (which was easy, I'd learned last night), then raced back to the forest for whatever else I could carry before . . .

It grew *totally* dark.

Screaming out (in French, with no subtitles) the "Toreador Song" from *Carmen,* I dashed back to the ring of fire and leaped through the flames.

Yep, a whole bunch of Amtraks roared by shortly thereafter.

This wood burned slow and steady, which was good. I'd stayed near the forest figuring sooner or later I would have to get more, but from the way it looked, that wasn't going to happen for a while. Great, because I was beat. I sat down and dug out some of what He-Who-Bakes-The-Bread-For-Us-All gave me, but I didn't start eating until after I'd thrown a chorus of "Great Balls of Fire" into the night.

It was halfway through my meal that the rumbling growls joined the reptilian sounds of the baggage cars.

Even with the fire going I couldn't see any of the things, especially after rendering a medley of Little Richard's hits. Yeah, they were keeping their distance, but you know the game. I didn't have a prayer of getting any sleep, something I'd actually given a moment of serious thought to.

Maybe this night wasn't going to be Really Awful, but it *was* shaping up to be Kinda Shitty.

Then, the big flying things showed up, and you know what happened? The first ones there caught me between songs, and they dropped so low that the stirred-up air from the beating of their wings scattered my burning branches all over the place. Dang, I didn't need that! One of them set a furry creature afire, because its growling suddenly became a scream, and in its flight it nearly bowled me over. It was some sort of cat, and it smelled bad, which was the least of my problems.

All right, enough was enough! No way was I going to hang around; no way was I going to ride along at *nearly-falling-over* and have a sing-along. *No way! Forget it!*

Yeah, you're right, I was freaking, but it was my preroga- tive. My situation rated high in the *Best Times to Freak Out* manual. I hopped on the bike seat and pedaled ass out of there, screaming (for real) at the top of my lungs. *Hey, suckers, outta my way! Jack's comin' through!* Did I give a shit if I was eaten, or rent to shreds? *Naaah.*

Well, somehow yours truly, once again vying for the title of the universe's largest posterior orifice, managed to get through the whole thing unscathed. The first time I realized that I couldn't even hear the things anymore was shortly after I flipped over the handlebars of the Nishiki, which had stopped dead in sand. That's *sand*, not sandstone. I spat some of it out as I got up quickly, still afraid something would jump me. Uh-uh, all of that was far behind. It was quiet now.

But instinct kept *noodging* me to move on, so I did. No way could I pedal across this loose, lumpy sand pile, not even on the Nishiki, so I didn't try. Let me tell you, pushing the bike was no fun; even worse, at times the sand gave way so easily that I was afraid of being sucked under.

To say this world was starting to annoy me would definitely be an understatement.

After about two miles I was negotiating small dunes, which was even more of a pain. It was then, from a high point, that I spotted lights not too far ahead. From the way they stretched in a long, curving line it seemed as if they might be lampposts along a road or something. Though a little incredulous, I headed toward them.

But I hadn't quite gotten there yet when everything I'd been through in the past couple of days caught up to me, as though a big dark wave had broken over my head. So sayeth Cervantes, *Now blessings light on him that first invented this same sleep.*

Beasties or not, I stretched out alongside the Nishiki at the base of a dune.

The sun had just arisen when I opened my eyes. Was I refreshed, invigorated, ready to take on the world? Yeah, right. Another eight hours would have done me good; but what the hell, I'd gotten *some* sleep, and I hadn't been eaten, so life was okay. I dragged myself up and finished what little food I had left. Motivated by the thought that this was going to be an eventful day, I set off eastward again.

The *road* I'd seen was just that. It had been angling up from the southwest but now curved east at the point where I joined it. Farther along it headed east-northeast, but that was still on the way to the mountains, so it was okay.

Now get this: The road, about five feet wide, was paved with orange bricks. There were light poles, skinny things ten feet high and spaced wide apart on alternating sides. The light source was a fat candle encased in a glass globe, obviously what I'd seen last night. None of them were lit right now, which meant that someone had to come along to both light and extinguish them. No one was evident in either direction.

An *orange* brick road; why not? If a bunch of singing and dancing Munchkins suddenly popped out of the sand, I wouldn't have been surprised. Was I on my way to the Emerald City, or was it a different color? Was I off to see the Wizard, or the drop-dead-gorgeous Amazin women, as depicted by He-Who-Does-Penance-For-Having-Thoughts-Of-A-Carnal-Nature?

Was any one crazier than the other?

I got on the Nishiki, and we followed the orange brick road.

CHAPTER 18

Some Amazin Women

Within a few miles the orange brick road began climbing into the foothills. Okay, that made me feel better. There would be no more forests or stretches of sandstone plain, not even lumpy deserts. I could get back on the Ultimate Bike Path today . . . if that's what I wanted.

The road had so far been deserted, but now I came across a guy driving a creaky wooden cart, drawn by two or three of those green llama-things called skukkos. He would pull up alongside a light pole, stand on the cart and snuff the candle, then go on to the next one. You guessed it, he was dressed in a robe, a really tattered olive-drab garment. His hood was off; no, he didn't look like Khrushchev, or any other world leader past or present. Actually, his smooth, unlined face seemed unfinished, I guess, like an artist or someone was supposed to come along and put in the final details. He had hair, but it was white and wispy-thin. In spite of its color, I'm sure he wasn't old.

I approached slowly, not wanting to shake him up. With the Nishiki banging over the bricks he had to hear me coming. Yeah, he was watching, but there was no curiosity on his face. His lips were thin, unlike the monks of the Order of Demakk, and I don't think his mouth was zipped, but I wouldn't swear to it.

"Good morning," I said, doffing my cap with a flourish as I slowed.

He stared at me another second, then turned around, which I thought was rude. But do you know what was on the back of his head, just above the neck amid the wispy hair? This is gross. It was a *mouth,* with thick lips and a red tongue and . . . *eeeyooo!* The tongue was wagging as the lips parted slightly.

"You don't want to go that way," the mouth said.

"Why not?" I asked.

But it closed up, and the guy went on to snuff out another candle. Figuring it was useless to press him, I rode off.

Others began appearing. They were all unfinished males with mouths on the back of their heads, though in different places, including near the top, which *really* looked weird.

A second gross mouth told me, "You don't want to go that way."

A third gross mouth told me, "You don't want to go that way."

But none of the gross mouths would tell me *why* I didn't want to go that way. No matter, because I'm sure it had to do with the Amazin women, since the warning was the same one Brother Rockwell had given me. And I'd already resigned myself to meet the challenge, so no problem.

Right?

The first burg I passed through was half the size of Celibattown, and shabbier, and no one seemed to give a hoot that I was there, except for two more gross mouths, which issued the same warning. I rode out quickly, and pretty soon there were no more of those unfinished fellows.

But now there was an amalgam of robed figures along the orange brick road. Tall and emaciated guys, short and chubby, cowled and uncowled, walking or behind skukkos, and so on. A pathetic sampling of manhood, few little more than remotely interested in me or my strange conveyance. Yeah, again all men, not a single female in sight.

What was going on here?

A pinhead-sized mouth on a skinny guy with cauliflower ears said, "You don't want to go that way."

A long, razor-thin mouth on a stumpy guy with a skinny lick of hair like Alfalfa said, "You don't want to go that way."

And you know what, I was starting to believe it.

All this time the orange brick road had been climbing deeper into the foothills. I still couldn't use it for a return trip to the *mhuva lun gallee,* because it wasn't *that* steep. But the Mountains of the East were looming, and by getting off the road I could have found my way to a desirable hillside in little time.

Uh-uh. There's an old Yiddish proverb that says, *A man should live if only to satisfy his curiosity.* I went on.

Wasn't there another proverb about curiosity doing something nasty to a cat . . . ?

I passed through a few other towns and received a few other warnings from a few other weird mouths, though by this time

I really didn't care. The orange brick road had become congested, and I had to be careful weaving through a crush of robed guys.

Then, at the end of one town, I saw a woman.

A drop-dead-gorgeous woman.

The same kind of woman that He-Who-Does-Penance-For-Having-Thoughts-Of-A-Carnal-Nature has carnal thoughts about.

She was standing on a cart, flailing her arms and shouting orders at a bunch of subservient robed guys. I'd say she was an inch short of six feet in sandals with thin cross-straps that rose halfway to her knees. Her auburn hair ended at her buns. She wore a wraparound something-or-other that, despite being furry, was not bulky. Her *looong* legs emanated the message *we bet you're curious as to how many times we can wrap ourselves around you.* As for her face: Michelle Pfeiffer on her best day would have been envious.

Guess what, she wasn't the only female there.

I could only make out the tops of a couple of heads, what with all the people surrounding me. But I continued working my way forward, determined to have a closer look.

A vertical mouth on a rotund Mussolini look-alike said, "You really didn't want to come this way."

I had a hunch I'd arrived.

Soon I was ten feet away from the woman on the cart.

Our eyes met across the throng.

She smiled at me—I think—and made an insistent gesturing motion.

"You, get over here, now!" she shouted, causing many of the robed guys to cringe.

Hmm, kind of pushy, I thought. Waving a hand I said, "Sure; what'd you have in mind?"

I swear, you would've thought someone had just blown a fart in an elevator! The heretofore dull eyes of the men stared at me in disbelief; the woman-to-die-for on the cart turned about seven shades of red and shook her fists like a kid having a tantrum. It looked like she was going to explode.

"He *talked* to me!" she exclaimed. "The creature talked to me! I want him brought here, *now!*"

I figured all the robed guys would jump me, but they backed away. Two other women, one with jet-black hair, the other a blonde, appeared from behind the cart. Yeah, they were drop-dead-gorgeous too, but there was no time to enjoy it, because they were *pissed,* and they were coming after me!

"Outta my way!" I shouted at the robed guys as I hopped on the bike. Okay, I did my best to avoid hitting any as I started down the road, because a face does not look or feel well after being run over by mountain bike tires.

Then, someone was crossing with a llama-thing in tow, and when I swerved to avoid them my tires went out from under me.

I avoided hitting my head on the orange brick road, but the hard surface knocked the wind out of my lungs.

Two beautiful women fell on top of me. Nice thought under other circumstances. Not now.

They tied my wrists in back; they tied my ankles.

The blonde threw me over her shoulder like I was a small sack of potatoes.

Oh, did she smell good!

I was carried to the first Amazin, who had settled down but was still furious. She didn't have to say a word to the others; they knew what to do. I was carried to a large, deep cart, something like the one Averill used (oh, I hope not!), and tossed inside. Already half out of it, this didn't do me any good.

Nor did it do much for the guy on top of whom I fell.

There were actually five guys in the cart, something I ascertained only after I'd shaken off the grogginess. By that time the crunched one had already pushed me off.

"Are you okay?" I asked.

He said, "I suppose so. Nothing seems to be broken. But you ought to be more careful where you're thrown."

Yeah, right. Anyway, now that I could focus I noticed that the guys in here looked different than all the others I'd yet seen, more . . . normal. I hate to use that word, but it was true. They wore short pants and tunics, not robes, were of average to tall size and build, and had their fair share of hair on top. No zipped mouths, no *misplaced* mouths, as far as I could see.

Still, something wasn't right. Aside from the guy I'd fallen on they didn't look too bent out of shape, considering the circumstances. And now that my head had cleared totally I noticed that, unlike me, none of them were tied up. It was as though they were resigned to their fate.

"Yes," I told the first guy, "I'll definitely watch where I'm thrown next time. Listen, be a sport and untie me, okay?"

He put a hand to his mouth, appalled. "To ask me to do such a thing! Oh, without a doubt Beulah the Bimbo would have my womanmaker cut off for even *thinking* it!"

Beulah the *Bimbo,* that's what he said. At least, that's what came through the UT6, though for the first time since its installation I felt a twinge in my neck.

"Yeah, well, thanks for nothing," I said sourly. "What's a womanmaker?"

He pointed down into his shorts. "There is my woman-maker, that which—"

"Okay, I got it. Anyway, if you won't untie me, at least answer some questions."

The other guys, who had been placid, were now doing some silent *shushing,* shaky fingers at their mouths. They were trying—and failing miserably—to keep their eyes from looking up. I checked out what it was that interested them.

The woman with the jet-black hair—who looked like an even more sensual Gloria Estefan—was peering over the rim of the cart, scowling. The first guy, I swear, was ready to wet his shorts.

"I heard talking in here," the woman said menacingly. "If there is any more talking before we reach the city, I will cut off all your womanmakers and feed them to the skukkos. This is the word of Beulah the Bimbo."

Ow, the twinge! I glanced at the first guy as the other four turned their backs on us.

"You were right," I whispered, "Beulah is a bitch."

"Oh, that wasn't Beulah the Bimbo," he whispered back. "That was Tama the Trollop." (*Yow!*)

"Sorry, I should've known."

"Tama the Trollop is Beulah the Bimbo's right-hand woman," he went on, and I wish he hadn't, because the UT6 was malfunctioning like crazy. "She takes much pleasure in carrying out Beulah the Bimbo's orders. I will talk to you no more."

He really did clam up, even simulating the zipping of his lips (I don't know, maybe it was something they aspired to here). And considering how much of an attachment I had to my own womanmaker, I decided it would be best to do the same thing.

I did, however, have one word left to say. The cart, which I later found out was pulled by six skukkos, was jerked forward suddenly, and this time the first guy fell over on *me*. Yeah, it was a four-letter word, and it puzzled them.

So now we were moving, and the first thing I thought about was the fate of my bike. Being the novelty that it more than likely was, I felt certain the Amazin women would not have left it in that town. It was close by, for sure, in another cart, headed for the same place as me.

Keep thinking that way, Jack-o, and you'll be fine.

One thing for certain, we were headed *up*. The town where they captured me had been on a plateau, but within a few minutes of leaving my weight had shifted to the back, the cart tilting sharply. Outside, loud imprecations from an Amazin drove the skukkos. The native curses being weird, the UT6 was making me nuts. If . . . *when* I got back, replacing it would be the first order of business.

The bozos across from me had long since turned around and now contemplated either their bare feet, the sky above, or each other. Not so the first guy, who had managed to put eighteen inches between us in an effort not to lean on me when the cart tilted. I could sense his curiosity, even when he wasn't glancing at me. In spite of it I was able to keep my mouth shut.

But before long he couldn't stand it anymore. I had to tune in intently when he spoke, his voice being so low.

"In many ways you are like us nobodies, but then again you are not."

Like us *nobodies*? "What do you mean?"

"I was about to be put in here when you approached. The strange wheeled thing you pushed was not like anything I ever saw before. But that was nothing compared to . . ."

"What?"

This time his voice nearly rose above a whisper. "Talking back to Beulah the Bimbo! That is *never* done, not anywhere across Amazina, unless permission is granted."

Amazina; well, that made sense. You should've seen the other guys freak when they heard about my offense. It looked like they were mouthing a bunch of silent *oy*s. The picture in my mind about this place, which had long since begun to form, was becoming clearer.

"Where I come from, permission is not needed to speak to another. Men and women interact freely."

Now *that* set all of them off, even the first guy. Their eyes kept darting up, and I swear, you would've thought I had a communicable disease from the way they tried to blend into the walls of the cart.

Finally the first guy exclaimed, "You spoke the ancient forbidden word!" (*Forbidden* is what came out, but *jeez did it hurt!*) "We are nobodies, not . . ."

"Not what, *men*?" I said disdainfully.

Did they have a spaz, or what! Maybe I'd better cool it, I thought, before *they* deprived me of my womanmaker.

It took a while, but they finally settled down. The bozos went on contemplating their whatevers, but the first guy was still curious.

"Listen, uh . . ." I started to say. "What's your name, anyway?"

He looked at me strangely. "Nobodies are forbidden names, at least until after we have served Amazins well and are allowed to join an Order. Do *you* have one?"

"That's right; it's Jack."

He rolled it around on his tongue. "It's a good name."

"But how could you *not* have one? If someone was trying to get your attention in a crowd and called out 'Hey, you,' I don't think it would work."

"Us nobodies all have *designations*. I am Q734W29. These other nobodies are—"

"Yeah, well," I interrupted, "I'll stick with 'Hey, you.' It's easier." Right, I was contemptuous.

This made the first guy reflective for a minute. He finally said, rather hesitantly, "Jack, will you . . . give me a name?"

All right, Q734W29 had balls! The other guys, of course, went into convulsions. I thought a moment, then came up with Dirk Pitt, the oftentimes reluctant but always successful hero and all-around superstud from Clive Cussler's techno-thrillers.

Looking solemn and kingly I tapped the guy lightly on both shoulders and said, "I hereby dub thee *Dirk.*"

Wow, did he like that! Must've said it fifty times or more. The others got interested. After a hushed conference they turned to me.

"Please, we would also like names," one of them said.

Well, a short while after I was sitting across from four happy guys named Clint, Dustin, Harrison, and Sean. You don't need me to explain that.

After all the excitement had died down Dirk said, "Jack, will you speak more of your world, where women and—you know—interact?''

"Sure; but first it's your turn.''

He looked at the others; a round of nodding ensued. With the cart slanted sharply, wheels clattering on what I assumed was still the orange brick road, drop-dead-gorgeous women shouting at dray animals, I learned more of this weird place called Amazina.

CHAPTER 19

The Great City

Actually, my traveling companions were *not* fountains of information. Most of what I got came from Dirk and Sean. Harrison, although he tried, was the nitwit of the group. Clint and Dustin just clammed up; made me want to revoke their names.

As best I understood it, Amazina was their whole world. It existed within a bowl, surrounded by four mountain ranges. You already heard about the Mountains of the East and the Mountains of the West, so I'm sure you can guess the rest. Beyond these mountains, they believe, is a sort of Nothingness.

Women, of course, ran the show. Men were *nobodies,* their servants and slaves, a situation that had existed for ages, although the definition of *ages* was beyond Dirk and Sean. As boys (Dirk called them *wee nobodies*) they were "raised" on what I suppose you could call "farms" all across Amazina. At a certain time (late teens, which is how old these guys looked) they were brought to the Great City in the Mountains of the East to perform "various services" for Sharra the Slut, the queen, and her Amazins. They did not elaborate, but I think it was safe to assume one of these services had something to do with their womanmakers.

Later on, Sean said, after they'd performed their services well, the nobodies were "changed" and allowed to join an Order. They were seldom called again. He didn't elaborate on "changed," either, but that wasn't hard to figure out.

And that was it, a lot of unanswered questions . . . which would probably be answered before too long, whether I wanted to know or not. Did I really feel like going through with this?

Sharra the *Slut,* Beulah the *Bimbo,* Tama the *Trollop.* Yep, I guess so.

Anyway, I didn't have much choice. No matter how hard I tried there was no way I could undo the ropes. So to kill time I complied with Dirk's request to tell them of the strange land called southern California, where the sexes openly interacted. They all cringed whenever I said *man* or *male*; but hell, I'd cringed (or *twinged,* actually) over lots of words they'd said, so I wasn't feeling sorry for them.

I didn't say much, but you know, they listened intently to every word and pondered silently thereafter. Maybe I'm wrong, but I might've just planted some seeds of doubt over their dubious life-style.

My best guess was that at least three hours had passed since leaving the town. I was still wasting my time working on the ropes when the cart squealed to a stop. We were flat, I suddenly realized. When did that happen?

Beulah the Bimbo leaped into the cart, alighting like a cat in front of me. "Come on, out out out!" she exclaimed, sounding like a drill sergeant with a bunch of recruits on the first day of boot camp. "Move it quickly, lest your womanmakers be in jeopardy!"

Always with the womanmakers! Everyone scrambled to their feet. Beulah the Bimbo assisted us none-too-gently up to Tama the Trollop, who was just as rough. Jeez, were they strong!

Yeah, we were still on the orange brick road, but it was wider, and in better condition here, on a broad, fertile-looking plateau. I was dumped on my butt. Tama the Trollop produced a *big,* nasty-looking knife and held it between my legs. I got real nervous, until she cut the rope around my ankles. At least now I could walk, and I still had my womanmaker.

We were on the outskirts of the Great City, which was not especially *great*; but more on that later. The Amazins did not want skukkos trotting along the streets of their burg, taking dumps whenever nature so summoned them. This was the end of the line. Small work details of nobodies took our llama-things, as well as those from two other carts that had been in the procession. Yeah, all right, there was my Nishiki! It had been in the third cart but was now on its side in the middle of the orange brick road. A couple of other drop-dead-gorgeous women were studying it curiously.

Counting the five guys from my cart there was a total of thirteen nobodies (*not* including me). The subsequent march into the Great City took shape like this: Beulah the Bimbo and the blonde were at the head, followed by a single line of twelve nobodies, then me. Tama the Trollop and another woman parallelled the line, with two others close at my heels. The odd man out was assigned the task of wheeling my bike along the road, which he had trouble mastering. After it had fallen over on him twice Beulah assigned a second guy to assist him, and together they carried it, which made me feel better.

Okay, the Great City. The buildings were made out of reddish-brown adobe, or something like it. Most were a single story, some two, none higher. A few were warehouse size, others no bigger than a storage shed, with many variances in-between. There were hundreds of structures, the outermost of them reaching across the plateau nearly to the base of some craggy, awesome-looking cliffs. Narrow, graded paths ran off the orange brick road and twisted wildly between the buildings.

Glancing all around I could see where the skukkos were kept. Low fences surrounded lush grazing areas. There were also fields of wheat, and other crops, tended by lots of stooped nobodies. I caught a glimpse of a vineyard, and a couple of orchards, before one of the Amazins whacked me on the head with something that looked like a wooden ruler.

"Eyes straight ahead, creature," she warned, "or I'll cut off your womanmaker!"

Yeah, and I hope your makeup base contains itching powder.

We were in the city now, and there was a plethora of fantastic females. Now get this: no small girls, no old ladies, not even thirty- or forty-something types. These were *all* women-to-die-for, tall, ages eighteen to twenty-nine. An audition for Las Vegas showgirls probably looked like this.

Even so, drop-dead-gorgeous or not, these women had the same hard look about them that I'd noticed on Beulah the Bimbo and Tama the Trollop (I was beginning to wonder about those colorful appellations). Sure, it could've been for the benefit of the nobodies. But I don't think so, because they didn't even joke around with each other. Unless I missed my guess, these ladies were not very happy with their lives. Okay, so they didn't have a great time with guys; but hell, there wasn't even a major mall within miles of this place! So what *did* they do?

It was obvious how much in contempt the Amazins held the nobodies, because they ragged them all along the way. They did the same to me, too, but unlike Dirk and his pals, who stared at the bricks, I gave the ladies the evil eye, and that made them nervous, not to mention even more abusive. The one behind kept smacking me with the ruler, which finally pissed me off. I spun around and glared at her.

"Listen, sister, how'd you like to eat that thing?" I snapped.

She jumped back, stunned. The column stopped. Dirk, Sean, and the rest wished they were somewhere else. Beulah the Bimbo, pulling a knife from her belt, stormed to the rear.

"He spoke again!" she cried. "Never before has one of the creatures spoken back!"

"There's always a first time, right, sweetheart?" I said smart-assedly. At the risk of my womanmaker . . . was I on a roll here, or what!

Oh, was this a wild lady, flailing away with the knife! She almost decapitated the blonde, who had followed her. *"I'll cut it off!"* she shrieked. *"This time I swear—!"*

But the blonde grabbed her wrist and said, "Stay your hand. Is this not the kind of nobody Sharra the Slut has often spoken about?"

"Hannah the Harlot is right," Tama the Trollop said (*ow!*). "We should advise the queen and let her decide what to do."

Right on! I only hope Beulah the Bimbo agreed. Well, she bared her teeth, hissed like a steam engine, but finally waved the column on. While most of the nobodies still had their eyes on the road, Dirk was casting an occasional awed glance in my direction. Sean was, too, and even Clint.

One good thing was that the women along the orange brick road, having seen or heard about the incident, stopped bugging us. And don't think it went unnoticed by the nobodies.

By the way, the streets of the Great City were immaculately clean. Nobodies were sweeping and picking up specks of dust all over the place. We passed a bunch of them on our way to a main intersection, where we stopped. I was pulled out of the column; so were the guys with my bike. The rest of the nobodies, led by Hannah the Harlot, marched straight ahead. We turned down the road on the right.

"See ya, Dirk," I called cheerfully. "Sean, hang in there, dude. Clint—"

An open palm against the back of my head made bells ring and birdies sing. "Be silent," Tama the Trollop warned, "lest you discover that Beulah the Bimbo does not always obey the rules."

Agreed; let's not get her pissed. I kept my mouth shut, and the girls and me got along splendidly, until a couple of minutes

later, when the nasty lady yanked me in the direction of a small
adobe building.

"This is where you will rot, creature, until Sharra the Slut
decides what to do with you." She tested the edge of her knife.
"Be assured what *my* choice is. In the meantime . . ."

She waved over another woman, one who had not been part
of our group. If I didn't know better I would have sworn I'd
seen her face last week at the supermarket checkstand on the
cover·of *Mademoiselle*.

"This is Lenore the Lascivious," Beulah the Bimbo said.
"She is in charge of you for now. You'll find her temperament
on a par with mine, so you'd best not dick around."

That's what the UT6 said she said, but . . . *jeez, my neck!*
"Sure, whatever," I gasped.

"The creature *talked!*" Lenore the Lascivious exclaimed.

I was getting tired of this bullshit, you know? Fortunately I
was dealing from impunity, short-lived as it might be. Beulah
the Bimbo held off Lenore the Lascivious, while Tama the
Trollop pushed me into the building. The door was slammed
and bolted.

The room was small, its floor made of stone. Other than a
narrow cot there were no amenities. A tiny barred window was
up near the ceiling. Standing on the cot—which I'd first tested
gingerly—I was able to look outside.

Beulah the Bimbo and the rest of the original party were
gone. The nobodies had left my bike in front of the building.
Lenore the Lascivious was checking it out. I checked *her* out
for a few seconds, then sat down.

Okay, now what? Do I wait to find what Sharra the Slut has
in mind for me? As bad as these other ladies are, she could be
the definitive bitch. Maybe she'd want my womanmaker
ornamenting the flagpole on her roof. Uh-uh.

First matter of business: get my hands free. Easier said than
done. The walls, though rough, were flat. Aside from the cot
there were no other choices, and the edges on *it* were not
promising. But what the hell; I sat on the floor, pushed the rope
up against one of the legs, and began sawing away.

I'm not sure how much time passed. It was still light outside,
but I had no way of seeing the sun through the window. My
best guess was that most of the day had passed. At least one
night in the Great City seemed inevitable. Swell. But as long as
I was around to see the next sunrise, what the heck.

All this time I had been working on the ropes without any success that I was aware of. But now I heard a *twanging* sound as one of the strands unraveled. Yeah! I renewed my efforts; there was a second *twang,* a third, and the gap between my hands widened. A minute later the bonds were cut through completely.

Okay, what was the second matter of business? Get out of the cell, right. Hop on the bike, cruise down the orange brick road, return to the Ultimate Bike Path. Drop-dead-gorgeous or not, colorful appellations or not, these Amazins didn't share the same passions as the wonderful Vulvans, or Jack Miller, for that matter. So why bother?

But as you can imagine, accomplishing the aforementioned was not going to be easy. I couldn't break out; I'd have to be taken outside, then give it my best shot . . . my *only* shot, probably, before my womanmaker became part of some biological study.

While trying to decide what to do with the severed rope I heard voices. Before I could climb the cot to look out the window the bolt on the door was removed. I sat down on the floor, back against the wall, and waited.

The door was pushed open. Lenore the Lascivious and another woman, a stunning redhead, stormed in and took up positions on opposite sides. They were wielding these medieval pikes, rather ominous-looking weapons.

"Supplicate yourself, creature!" the redhead cried. "Supplicate yourself even lower than you already are in the glorious presence of Sharra the Slut, queen of Amazina!"

The woman who glided in was far and away beyond my humble abilities as a purveyor of words to describe. If the other women in this place were drop-dead-gorgeous, then Sharra the Slut was easily drop-dead-gorgeous-times-ten. Maybe more, yes. Her peppery-blond hair was not quite as long; she was not quite as tall. But everything about her was physical perfection, notably her sensual, fiery-red mouth. *Oh, please, Great Power, if I have to die someday, let me die kissing that mouth!*

And there was something else about Sharra the Slut, something different from every other Amazin I'd yet seen. Yeah, she was regal; you could tell that from the proud way she held her head, and from how the others looked humble in her presence. But what I sensed was the absence of that hard edge. I don't know, it was something I could sort of *feel.*

All of a sudden I felt more secure over the immediate future of my womanmaker.

"You were told to supplicate yourself in the presence of the queen!" the redhead warned. "Now do it!"

Not being able to take my eyes off Sharra the Slut, I hardly heard her. My mouth opened; you know what came out?

"Hey, how's it going?" I said dumbly.

The two angered guards would have impaled me on those nasty toothpicks, but the queen stepped forward and waved them back. "Leave us now, Lenore the Lascivious and Ruta the Raunchy," she said (*eeeee!*). "I will talk to the prisoner alone."

"Oh, but, Highness—!" Lenore the Lascivious started to say.

"I will be fine. Do as I tell you."

Uh-huh, they jumped at her words. Once they were outside, she shut the door and faced me. She didn't speak for a while, but studied me all over; *inside,* too, I swear.

Finally she said, "You don't have to keep pretending your hands are tied."

Okay, so much for my clever ruse. I showed her my hands as I threw the rope into a corner. She did not back away when I stood; still, I was compelled to say, "I won't try anything."

"Oh, I know you won't." She indicated the cot. "See if you can lift one end of that."

Now I knew the sucker was heavy, but honest, you would have thought it was bolted to the floor. After much grunting, gasping, and a red face I managed to get it a couple of inches up.

Waving me back, Sharra the Slut effortlessly lifted the cot to a nearly vertical position with one hand, then brought it down gently.

Maybe it was done with magnets like the sword in the stone at Disneyland, which a burly adult couldn't budge but a little kid could pull right out.

No, I didn't believe that.

"You have a name, don't you?" the queen said.

"Yes, it's Jack."

She absorbed that for a moment. "Jack. You are not of Amazina, Jack." It wasn't a question.

"No."

"Then you come from somewhere beyond the mountains." She almost betrayed her excitement.

"Yes, far beyond the mountains."

Sharra the Slut nodded. "I always believed there was something other than Nothingness beyond the mountains. It is not a view shared by my people." She looked me up and down. "You are not fearful of us?"

"No, not afraid, exactly. I don't like being a prisoner, though, having my life or my . . . womanmaker threatened."

She smiled. *Oh, God, a smile-to-absolutely-die-for!* She grew solemn quickly, but for that moment it had lit up her whole being, and it was incredible.

"So you do not fear women. That must mean, where you come from, women and . . . *men* communicate with each other, perhaps are even on equal ground." (She spoke the ancient forbidden word with as much difficulty as Dirk and the guys had hearing it.)

Well, I could've told her about our male-oriented society, about the women's movement, about how far they had come since the sixties but were still fighting all the bullshit conceived during centuries of repression and stereotyping. Naah; maybe after I got to know her better.

"Yes, that's right," I said simply.

The very thought would have rocked Beulah the Bimbo and the others to their heels. But like I told you, the queen of the Amazins was *very* different. She pondered for a while, her expression at first thoughtful, then changing into one that was, I perceived, laced with self-doubt, even sadness.

"I'm not sure if my people are happy," she finally said. "I don't know if we are living the fullest lives that we can."

"Are *you* happy, Sharra?" I asked.

Whoops, she turned queenly again. "My name is Sharra the *Slut,* and you will address me accordingly!"

But I didn't back down. "Sharra is a beautiful name all by itself, and does you proud."

Okay, she liked that. "You may call me Sharra. As to your question . . ."

"Yes?"

She was within herself again. "So many things—feelings—I cannot understand . . ." She turned and walked around the cell, then said, "Jack, I would ask something of you."

"Why not just command it?"

"No, I would rather you did it because you wanted to."

This was some woman in more ways than one. "In that case, I'll be happy to do whatever you ask."

"Let me show you what life is like in the Great City. Then you will be able to say what you think of it."

"Is that all? Sure, no problem." Actually, now that the pressure was off, I really was curious about this place.

"Very good. You'll remain here a moment until I've spoken to the others."

But she didn't leave, and as she continued to stare I began to wonder if there was something I was supposed to do. Then I remembered: she's a queen, right? Fine, but no way was I going to grovel. I tilted my head a few inches in one of those little Japanese bows. This made her happy, and she left.

Half a minute later a chastened Ruta the Raunchy, sans pike, opened the door and waved me out. I had been right about the time of day, because the sun was about to set. Sharra and Lenore the Lascivious—the latter also pikeless—were looking over the Nishiki.

"I was told that you *rode* on this thing," the queen said. "Will you show me how it's done?"

"Of course."

I stood the bike up and straddled it. Before I could start Sharra grabbed the handlebars firmly.

"Lest you consider trying to escape," she said, "there are women positioned all along the roads who will stop you."

"I had no intention of trying," I told her, which was true.

She eyed me for a moment, shrugged, then chanced a slight smile (*yeehah!*). "I knew that," she said. "I'm . . . sorry."

Saying *that* didn't come easily; it had probably been a long time. The others, I'm sure, were shocked out of their sandals, but they kept their mouths shut.

Anyway, with the queen of Amazina watching I rode my bike up and down the road, which attracted the attention of other drop-dead-gorgeous women. Sharra, impressed, requested a lesson. Hey, no problem! I made a minor adjustment in the height of the seat, then showed her how to get on and off, doing my best not to lay a finger on the royal personage. She was agile, and eager to imitate my efforts. After a couple of aborted attempts she got going with the help of a push from me. Soon she was a hundred yards down the road, and I doubt if she could've been any happier.

Let me tell you, my Nishiki never looked better with the pair of legs that now propelled it!

After a wide turn the queen pedaled back, and I held the bike while she got off. Nodding, she said, "It is wonderful. I would like my people to have a look. It will aid them in creating something similar."

"Sure," I replied, trying not to think of the crudeness of the only transportation I'd yet seen here.

"Thank you. It will be returned before long."

She ordered Lenore the Lascivious off with it. I asked her, "Are you ready to give me the grand tour?"

"No."

Say what? "But I thought you said—"

"In the first place it is nearly dark, not the best time to see the city. And second, it occurred to me that you have had a long and hard day. I would say you look worse than week-old-crud-warmed-over, and . . . Jack, what's wrong with your neck?"

"It's . . . nothing," I assured her through clenched teeth.

"Therefore," she went on, "you'll accept my hospitality for the night. Quarters are being prepared for you, and refreshments will be brought. Ruta the . . . Ruta will show you there. Consider yourself my guest, Jack. I'll come by in the morning."

The queen of Amazina walked off, which warranted *all* my attention for as long as I could see her. My nursemaid, the lovely Ruta, shook her head over this unprecedented change in policy. But while she didn't try to be nice, at least she didn't give me any crap while leading me along the curving side streets of the Great City.

A nifty room had been fixed up for me, with plenty to eat and drink. Among the victuals was a great wine and a dish that looked like short ribs. With nightfall it had grown cold, which made the pile of furs on the futon-type bed all the nicer.

My choice would not have been to eat alone.

My choice would definitely not have been to sleep alone.

Sharra would have been top seed, *every other* Amazin a close second. But none came a-knockin' at my door.

What the hell. I was well fed, and comfortable, and there was always tomorrow. I fell asleep thinking nice thoughts.

CHAPTER 20

The Main Function

Ruta the Raunchy was standing outside my adobe abode the next morning. I don't think she was there to guard me, just keep an eye on things. This time I could look out a normal window, one without bars. Ruta noticed me watching her; I smiled and waved, but she didn't respond. Wow, were these ladies uptight!

I must've slept like a dead man, because last night's leftovers had been taken away, and a whole new round of food and drink was there. I had another good meal, contemplating the fact that Sharra would soon be by. Not a bad way to start the day.

For people who could do little better than archaic transportation, they had managed to come up with indoor plumbing. Among other things I was able to take a shower in the adjoining bathroom. My clothes had been washed last night, and were dry.

Sharra showed up shortly after. Would you believe, the queen of Amazina actually *knocked* on my door?

"I hope the accommodations were satisfactory," she said.

"Yeah, great. So was the food."

"On my way here I inquired about your . . . bike. My people are not done with it yet. They are not too imaginative. On the other hand they are quite imitative, so it is likely they will come up with something. Either way you'll have it back by the afternoon."

"Good."

She looked at me sheepishly. "I must admit, I had another ride on it. Riding the bike is . . ."

"Fun?"

She got regal again and said, "Yes, that's it. Come, and I will show you the Great City."

Ruta the Raunchy was conspicuous by her absence. In fact, few Amazins were afoot at the moment. Sharra was going it alone. She had confidence in her ability to take me if I tried anything.

She had every reason to feel so cocksure.

It was while walking toward some of the larger buildings that many Amazin women began to appear on the street. It made sense, because by this time word had spread regarding the queen's interest in this strange nobody. And speaking of nobodies, it was toward their "quarters" that we were headed, according to Sharra. They turned out to be large barracks, each nobody—each *man*—occupying a small cubicle with the sparsest of amenities.

"These are similar to their quarters in other places across Amazina, where they are grown from wee nobodies," Sharra explained. "It makes their transition to the Great City easier."

"Really conducive to individuality," I muttered, expecting to piss the queen off. But she remained silent, thoughtful.

I saw rooms where men were taught reading and writing, even art, enough to render them useful to the Amazins and provide them with some skills for the time after, when they joined an Order. Dirk and Sean were in one of these rooms, and both noticed me. I gave them an *everything's cool* sign, and you know, there was hope on their faces, a far cry from the contented bovine look on the rest.

"So you keep them here," I said, "but you put them to work all over the city?"

"Yes, tending our streets, working in the factories, the fields, and the orchards. But sooner or later each is called upon to perform the main function."

"The . . . main function?" I think we were getting around to the womanmaker business, don't you? "So you take them to bed with you, right?"

The expression on the queen's face was similar to one you might make when driving past a manure truck. "Take them to . . . What kind of idea is this?"

Now *I* was confused. "Okay, why don't you show me this main function?"

She nodded, and we went on to another part of the Great City, skipping what I believe were factories and residences and such. Again, scores of drop-dead-gorgeous women watched us pass; but you know, I was becoming de-sensitized to it, especially considering the cold aura that surrounded them. Something about this place was definitely off-center.

"A question, Your Highness," I said.

"Ask it."

"I haven't seen any kids . . . uh, small girls around, or older women, for that matter. What's the story?"

It took her a moment to understand. "Wee women are raised elsewhere, until they have come of age. Elders—those who have reached thirty years—are sent to special places here in the mountains to live out their lives. The Great City is only for those of our ilk."

Yeah, the *ilk* of being gorgeous and between eighteen and twenty-nine, like I said before. I didn't even want to *know* what they did with ugly little girls. Probably had a *special place* for them, too. I was beginning to like this burg less and less. Still, Sharra wasn't relating this to me with pride. It was kind of mechanical, like old programming.

A divergent thought: Let me find a retirement village of thirty-something women who had once been of the Great City ilk, and I could be *very* satisfied.

"See, this is one of the places where the main function is performed," Sharra said.

The building she indicated was one of those 'tweeners. On one end a short line of men disappeared inside a door. They were casually watched by an Amazin who might've been Tama the Trollop, but I wasn't sure. There was a second door farther along, and at the moment two men were emerging. Each had a dreamy expression on his face. A scowling woman pointed them in the proper direction. They walked as if they were drunk.

"It is here that the womanmaker fluid is acquired," Sharra said. (*Womanmaker fluid*; yeah, you guessed it, a pain in the neck!) "Would you like to see?"

Semen; she meant semen, of course. But . . . *acquired*? "Yes, I would."

Well, I went in while the queen waited, and I came out fast, which must've surprised her no less than the pale, dumb-founded expression on my face.

You probably got it figured out, so no need to get descriptive. The acquisition of womanmaker fluid by the Amazin women had *nothing* to do with physical contact.

"Is it clear to you now?" Sharra asked.

"Oh, right . . . clear," I said vaguely. "Then you . . . ?"

"What?"

"You do it by artificial insemination? By *injecting* the womanmaker fluid?"

She was a bit confused but said, "Yes, of course. Is there any other way?"

Wow, how long had *this* been going on! "Oh, most assuredly."

Sharra nodded. "I had thought there might be. You will show me."

Oh, thank you thank you thank you thank you, Great Power! Jack Miller, author, lecturer, explorer along the Ultimate Bike Path, swears his eternal devotion!

"Listen, Sharra, how about we go back to your place?" I said, working hard to be cool.

"We can't do it here?" she asked.

Right, I struggled with a straight face. "Trust me, it'll be better there."

"We'll go then."

"But first I'd like to get something out of my bike bag."

"Very well; it's not far."

On my way there, though, I saw something that nearly took the starch out of my . . . sails. There was another building where I at first thought the main function was being performed. But the guys going in seemed older, and the one I saw coming out at the other end was garbed in a robe that was the same color as the monks of the Order of Demakk. He flipped his hood back, and yep, another mini-Krushchev with a zippered mouth.

"This nobody, having served us well, has been *changed,* and can enjoy the rest of his life thusly," Sharra explained matter-of-factly.

"I'm sorry," I said angrily, "but *that* is not a nice thing you're doing to him, or any of them!"

She didn't act like I'd affronted her. "I . . . don't understand. This is the way it has always been."

The way it has always been. *Dat ole debbil programming* again. "They don't like it, you know."

Uh-oh, queenly again. "That is not true!" she snapped.

"Yes it is," I said, and told her about the subconscious part that had caused so many to warn me against coming to the Mountains of the East. It made her thoughtful.

Anyway, you know what Sharra did? She ordered all *changing* stopped until she had time to do more thinking. That made me feel better. And do you know what she told me then?

"They can all be changed back to the way they were. We have that ability."

Now *that* made me feel wonderful. The starch was back in my sails. We continued on.

As advertised, the place where they were studying my bike wasn't too far away. A Christie Brinkley clone in a tight fur garment was wheeling it outside.

"A prototype is being completed at this moment, Highness," she said, "so we are done with it."

"It is too bad we cannot both ride upon your bike," Sharra said.

"But we *can*," I told her.

She was puzzled. "How is this possible?"

Straddling the top tube I said, "Get on the seat, but keep your legs out away from the bike."

"What will I hold on to?" she asked, quite innocently.

Okay, I could've told her to grab the bottom of the seat, or the carrier, but what do you think?

"Just, ah, put your arms around me, Highness."

I tried to avoid her eyes, figuring she'd be having a hissy fit. Uh-uh; she got on the seat, encircled my waist, and laced her fingers.

The drop-dead-gorgeous-times-ten queen of Amazina was touching me!

Wish I could swap my tight spandex for a pair of baggy Dockers or something.

Since I was feeling like week-old Jell-O now, what would I be like at her place?

"What are you waiting for, Jack?" Sharra asked.

Well, rubber legs and all I managed to get us in one piece to the royal palace, another large adobe structure. Digging inside my seat bag, I withdrew a small foil square that had a circular bulge in the middle.

Hey, you didn't think I was running around leaving my seed all over the universe or whatever, did you?

Sharra studied the packaged condom. "What is this?"

"Uh, I'll tell you . . . later."

"Fine. Then show me another way of introducing the womanmaker fluid."

Introducing the . . . "Can we go to your room?"

"You mean my bedchamber?" She was getting testy. "This way, then. But no more after that. You will show me!"

The hallways and other rooms of the palace were nice; Sharra's bedchamber was opulent. It was absolutely *lined* with the thickest furs. No way could you tell where she slept; everywhere was comfortable.

She faced me in the middle of the room. "Well?"

"You just don't *do it*," I explained. "There's stuff that comes before."

"Show me."

"Uh, it requires touching."

"We have already touched. Show me."

All right, the way had been cleared. I took her face in my hands, and with my heart pumping in overdrive I kissed those incredible lips.

"What is that supposed to do?" she asked when we had separated.

Great, old Casanova Miller bombs out again.

"It's supposed to turn us on; you know, get us excited."

"I still don't understand, but let me try it."

She took my face in her hands and did the same thing. *Wow!* But it still had no effect on Sharra.

We persisted. Five kisses later I was starting to get through to her.

Ten kisses later we were horizontal, and I found out where the queen of Amazina slept.

Fifteen kisses later . . .

Okay, wait a minute. You know me well enough by now to figure you weren't going to get a play-by-play. There's another kind of bookstore you can patronize for that kind of stuff.

Sufficed to say . . . *it was faaabulous!*

For having no prior knowledge or experience, Sharra caught on with astonishing speed. And oh, did she love it!

Less than an hour later she asked me to show her again.

She was impressed by the condom. To have such pleasure and not have to bear a wee woman or a wee nobody! I was down to the last one, but Sharra sent it out to her imitative people.

That afternoon the first Amazin brand condoms rolled off the assembly line.

Sharra summoned Ruta and Beulah and others of her entourage and had me show them, too.

By nightfall ole Jack . . .

Let me capsulize the rest of this.

I spent five days in the Great City.

It didn't take long to prove to Sharra and the rest that *all* men—that's *men,* not nobodies—were capable of the same thing.

Sharra, once I'd convinced her that soon I'd have to move on, took an interest in Dirk, who bore a passing resemblance to Tom Cruise.

(Before that I'd given some *serious* thought to whether I'd really wanted to move on or not.)

By the fourth day men and women were walking hand in hand through the streets of the Great City, talking and laughing on the way to the bedchamber of one or another.

Sharra was given the first bicycle. It wasn't a bad imitation, actually. Before I left people were riding them everywhere, sometimes falling over or crashing, but all in all having a good time.

The *main function* clinics were turned into parking structures for bikes.

All *changing* was discontinued. Men of various Orders showed up to be *un-changed.* Sharra promised to get word to the monks of the Order of Demakk, and beyond.

By the queen's decree all Bimbos, Harlots, Trollops, and the like were dropped from their names. (There wasn't anyone who could explain the origins of *that* to me.)

The vast but mostly empty Great City would be repopulated by wee ones, old ones, and all ones in-between. (Oh, yes, you should've *seen* some of the thirty-somethings!

Future explorations were planned beyond the mountains that surrounded Amazina.

Let me tell you, this had become one happy and productive place!

In her farewell to me, Sharra proclaimed Jack Miller a national hero.

I shook the hand of every former nobody; I was kissed by every female. The whole thing took a while.

Scores of wobbly, bumping, laughing bike riders followed me to the edge of the Great City, then fell behind when I barreled down the orange brick road.

CHAPTER 21

Of Sore Necks and Other Things

Scenario: Study Group Old Guys wondering about Jack Miller's interference in the cultural development of the people of Amazina.

Study Group Old Guy #3: "I was wondering about Jack Miller's interference in the cultural development of the people of Amazina."

Study Group Old Guy #1: "I think you're wrong to categorize Jack's involvement as *interference.*"

My Old Guy: "Oh, indeed. Jack has interfered with nothing."

Study Group Old Guy #4: "I agree with that assessment."

Study Group Old Guy #2: "I, too, was wondering about Jack Miller's interference in the cultural development of the people of Amazina."

Study Group Old Guy #3: "You see, we had a look into the future of that place. Amazina and its people—male and female, young and old—sit at the hub of a thriving world, encompassing many civilizations from beyond the Mountains of the East, the Mountains of the North, the—"

My Old Guy: "Yes, we know that. It becomes a fine place. So what is the problem?"

Study Group Old Guy #2: "But the Universal Laws—!"

Study Group Old Guy #4 (pissed): "Always the Universal Laws! If you had absorbed them properly you'd know that Jack did not screw up."

Study Group Old Guy #1 (puzzled about *screwed up,* but agreeing anyway): "That's right. Had he knowingly interfered with some event upon his own world, *then* Universal Law would have been breached. The two key elements there are that the interference must be done *knowingly,* and only upon his *own world.* So you see, there was no need for you to be wondering about Jack Miller's interference in the cultural development of the people of Amazina."

Study Group Old Guy #4: "His entry into that world, and

his subsequent involvement, were random. Therefore, he became *part* of its development. The future history books of Amazina speak highly—with embellishments, of course—of a stranger named Jack who helped bring order out of chaos. He is referred to as the Sore-Necked Prophet. And see here, he also appears in the history and literature of civilization that he has not yet even visited!''

My Old Guy (huffily): ''Enough of this wondering about Jack Miller's interference in the cultural development of the people of Amazina. He is about to encounter other problems and will need our help.''

Thoughts about this and that while riding along the Ultimate Bike Path:

I've been to some strange and interesting places before, but that last one had to rank way up there.

Things were shaping up pretty nice when I left, but I was wondering about the future effect of my interference in the cultural development of the people of Amazina. Maybe after a while things would change back to the way they were. Naaah, those were cool people, and they sure liked to party.

Does anyone know when the Cleveland Indians last won the World Series? Does anyone care?

Do you have any idea how much my neck is hurting? Toward the end, every third or fourth word that anybody said was putting me through the ceiling. The UT6 had to be replaced, *fast.*

Did you know that when you stacked a year's worth of *National Geographics* they measured approximately three and three-quarter inches? Did *you* care?

I must've still been in the left fork of the *mhuva lun gallee,* because I kept glancing over to the right for a possible merge, which hadn't yet happened. Not that it would've mattered, had I found the blue door back to Pendleton. But there were no blue doors *whatsoever,* and after what seemed a substantial amount of time I started growing concerned. I could keep up this easy cadence for a long time, but not forever.

Hey, guess what, I *know* what Billy Joe McAllister and the girl were throwing off the Tallahatchie Bridge that day. (Write me, care of the publisher, if you want to know too.)

People who gripe and complain a lot are known, among other things, as *kvetches.* Did I *kvetch* to you about my neck already? Wanna hear me *kvetch* some more? Even without anyone saying *harlot* or *forbidden* or *trollop* or *womanmaker*, the damn thing hurt like crazy!

The Old Guy had once said something about being governed by Universal Laws. I mean, there was no way I could have strangled the shit out of little Hitler with it holding up (not to mention my buns being ground into burger). But let's say I'm tooling down the road, not sure where I am or anything, and little Hitler runs in front of me. I send him flying, he hits his head against a tree and dies. Then what? Do the Old Guys resurrect him? Am I still turned into patties for Burger King? Uh-uh; that couldn't happen, because it *didn't* happen . . .

Definitely, I was making myself nuts again. Okay, forget Hitler. What if I *unknowningly* did something in our world's past? Maybe I'm walking along and see this little girl drowning in a lake. Now I just can't stand there and watch, can I? Could you? After I save her, she grows up to be Mother Teresa or Joan Rivers or whoever. On the other hand, what if that kid had been meant to drown by some power greater than ourselves? Do I still lose my riding privileges, and/or my ass? I don't know; it'll have to go on my *List of Things to Ask the Old Guy.*

I'm pretty sure I never told you about Barney.

My parents, Henry and Rose Miller (yeah, you know them), were *not* very fond of animals. Actually, I'm not sure what my father thought about them, but his opinion never counted. At least he took me to the Bronx Zoo once in a while, which I mentioned before. But the closest my mother ever willingly came to an animal was watching Mutual of Omaha's *Wild Kingdom.* ("Observe closely as the rhinoceros in pursuit of Marlin inserts his horn where the sun don't shine.")

In all my years as a fair-haired youth I owned a grand total of one pet, a parakeet which I imaginatively named Tweety. (*Like a hole in the head you need a bird, Jackie! All those feathers and bird doody and other* schmootz? *Such a dirty thing.* Feh! *You can get diseases from it!*) He hung in there for six years, even though I swear my mother tried a few times to give him a one-way ticket out the kitchen window. Tweety's funeral pyre was our apartment building's incinerator in a Quaker Oats box. He was not the most stimulating pet, but he did have an eighteen-word vocabulary (including "fuck you," which a neighbor kid named Davey Feldman taught him).

Didn't *every* kid have a dog at one time or another?

I found Barney in a pet shop two years before Carol and I got married. He was a runty German shepherd, not as impressive as a couple of others they had for sale at the same time. I even had to nurse him through a cold right off the bat. But that didn't matter, because it was love at first sight—on both our parts.

Barney was around during the whole six years I was married to Carol. They were fond of each other, and Barney would've chewed up anyone he thought was threatening her. But he was always *my* dog, and toward the end of the marriage, when I often felt so incredibly alone, he was my only friend. We would walk on the beach or wherever for miles and miles; he loved that.

I had Barney around for more than two years after the marriage ended. He seemed to enjoy things the old way. Then, he got real sick. It was something-or-other; I can't even remember what the vet called it. He said it could go either way in a short time.

It went the wrong way.

Barney was lying in his favorite corner, by the front door. I was watching a movie on television, some priest-cop thing with the Roberts DeNiro and Duvall, when he staggered over. At that point he could hardly walk. He put one paw up on my leg; I rubbed him behind the ears, one of his most-loved things.

He fell over in my arms and died.

My journey toward an understanding and belief of the metaphysical nature of the universe has been a long, slow one. But let me tell you something that happened a year ago.

First off, you should know that I thought a hell of a lot about Barney in the years after he died. I even dreamed about him, usually the two of us sharing the good times, but often *that night.*

Okay, here's what happened a year ago. It was a Friday night, and I was home alone (not a big surprise, huh?). I was reading this creepy horror novel called *Demon Shadows* or something, and I had some David Benoit spinning on the CD player. At one point I leaned my head back and closed my eyes to give them a rest.

When I opened them, Barney was there.

I mean, he was *sort of* there in a hazy broken-image-on-the-television way. He was sitting in front of me, looking up at my face. Okay, I was dreaming, you say; that's what I figured. But first of all, I could hear Benoit's "Some Other Sunset" clearly; no mistake about that.

And second, I could *smell* Barney.

Yeah, his distinct doggy smell, touching my senses.

Barney was there, in my condo, that night.

Shortly after, he was gone. I don't recall snapping awake, as I usually did after nodding off, or feeling particularly tired. On the contrary, I was alert, invigorated, like my body had experienced a sort of warm, fluid *rush.* "Some Other Sunset" was just finishing up.

Barney had come back to tell me he was all right, that I needn't worry about him anymore. And you know what? I haven't dreamed about him since, and the memories have been of the fun times.

The left branch of the Ultimate Bike Path was starting to worry me.

Not only hadn't I seen a blue door yet, I'd also come across a *new* gate, which hadn't happened for a long time. This one was weird: a tall, upside-down profile of a toothbrush with a heart halfway up the handle. I don't mean a Valentine's Day heart, but a *real* one, with auricles, ventricles, arteries, veins, the whole nine yards. Quite a run of them, too, before they disappeared. Something to put down for future considerations. But not now.

Yeah, I really was starting to run out of gas. Even without any way to tell time I was sure I'd been doing this for hours. All the while I hadn't passed a single other rider along the *mhuva lun gallee.* Maybe everyone else knew better.

Since there was no way I could stop and rest along the tunnel, I had no choice but to get off. You know the risk there. Find some place that's flat in all directions and I had a long trek ahead of me. Engage in communication with any of the natives and this blasted thing in my neck could explode.

Still, I was beat.

I angled into the fireworks of the next isosceles triangle and . . .

. . . shifted out of the Vurdabrok Gear as I braked to a stop.

My front tire was a yard away from the edge of a sheer drop off the summit of a craggy mountain.

Well, that was good. I could be back on the Ultimate Bike Path instantly. My only concern was this fog below, which might have been concealing the tops of other peaks. I was reasonably sure I could shift up before plummeting that far, but it still made me nervous.

First things first, though. Another good thing about this place was that there didn't appear to be anyone around for a zillion miles. A brief rest, a snack, and I was outta here with no risk to my neck, or any other part of my anatomy.

There was food in my bag and water in the bottle. Sharra had seen to that. Actually, if she'd gotten her way she would've filled the latter with some of the fantastic wine from the vineyards just outside the Great City. But I had to be more practical. The people of Amazina, on the other hand, were all riding around with wine in their bike bottles. Can you imagine the spills that was going to cause? Can you imagine how little any of them would care?

I had just finished eating and was stretched out supine on the hard ground, looking up at lots of wispy dark clouds, when this guy came flying toward me.

He looked like the creepy Max Schreck in the silent film *Nosferatu,* or Barlow the vampire in *'Salem's Lot* (who also looked like the creepy Max Schreck in the silent film *Nosferatu).* His wings were these big, membranous things that grew out of his shoulders. I stood up quickly, and I suppose I should've been scared shitless, except for two things. First, the guy was wearing baggy polka-dot pants and a T-shirt with a picture of a female winged creature. Second, he was waving at me.

"Howdy do," he said (honest!), alighting softly. "We who soar across rivers of discarded tampons and flushable diapers welcome you with open hair nets and uninhibited tree branches to . . . excuse me, why are you thrashing around like that?"

I made a sign of the cross with my arms to ward him off, but it did no good. My teeth grinding, I put a finger to my lips.

"I'm not trying to be unsociable, but don't say a word!" I gasped. "It's not you, it's me. Good-bye, I must be going. Have a nice life; love your wings. Hope we can chat some other time."

Give him credit, he tried to keep his leathery lips shut. I got on the bike, backtracked far enough to gain momentum, and pedaled like a madman off the edge.

"Did you mean to do that?" he asked, following me down.

Boy, it must've blown his mind when I disappeared.

CHAPTER 22

Banging on the Pipes

I started passing other riders in both directions along the Ultimate Bike Path. Okay, so I wasn't lost, just a bit out of the way.

There were Vulvans, and things that looked like sheet-metal screws with Australian bush hats, and small amoeboid creatures on go-things resembling wheeled electric chairs. For obvious reasons I didn't strike up a conversation with any of them.

You know what I started thinking? How ironical it would be if, with the UT6 making it impossible for me to listen to anyone, I came across the gate that led to the glassy mountain-top of Ralph Ralph. I don't think the universe could be *that* unfair, could it?

So what do you think appeared after about two dozen assorted Elmer Fudds, iridescent snowmen, and Gorbys? Yep, the very same white, diamond-shaped portal I'd been hoping to find for so long.

The one I dared not go near, lest the first nonterrestrial quote from the sage himself send my head a-rollin' down the slope.

To coin a well-worn, colorful phrase: *SHIT!*

What was the diamond-shaped portal doing along this branch of the *mhuva lun gallee,* anyway? I don't think that's where I found it before. And if it was, then *my* gate shouldn't be too far off, which I'm not sure I believed.

Anyway, mulling over this stuff at least helped me keep my brain matter packed together as I rode past it. Another time, I told myself. One thing for sure, it hadn't been beckoning me, like the first time . . . or even the second, when I passed it by just because I wanted to get home so badly.

Okay, it was far behind, and I was fine now. Really. The problem remained finding *my* gate; you know, *the one that would appear often because it was the doorway to* my *place and time in the universe?*

Hey, Old Guy, you wouldn't want me to be thinking of your revered self as a liar now, would you?

Oh, no, a bunch of Bart Simpson heads. Even knowing what lay beyond, they were still unsettling. Well, I wasn't about to pedal at blur-speed, or anything approximating it, since I couldn't risk missing my gate. They would eventually run their course.

Then, one of them reached out and grabbed me.

I don't just mean in a subtle way. The sucker practically *yanked* the Nishiki toward it. I tried to resist, but it defiantly wanted me. Oh, great; this wasn't in my plans. Mouthing a bunch of words that would have done a goon hockey player proud, I popped through the portal . . .

. . . into a gray, hazy emptiness. Yep, same as the first time.

When the haze parted slightly a few moments later, I saw the Old Guy.

Now it could have been *an* Old Guy, but I'm pretty sure it was *my* Old Guy, since this whole study was his baby. No bike clothes this time, but those same big-sleeved pajamas he had been wearing in the white room that very first day in downtown San Diego. He was smiling as he waved me over.

Two things I noticed as I approached: First, the Old Guy was standing in a waiting area, like where I'd had my brief visit with Harry Chapin. Second, there were noises coming from the black cave mouth behind him. They were sounds of flowing water, and metal tapping against metal. Weird.

"Halloo, Jack," he called, then made a *whoops* gesture and pretended to zip his lip (He-Who-Sends-Me-On-These-Crazy-Adventures?). I hope so; if he'd been watching at all since Amazina he knew what I was going through.

Yeah, he had that damn cattle prod-thing again. This time I was glad to see it. He zapped the offending chip of metal out of my neck (*whew!*) and inserted what I assumed was the UT7.

"Thank you," I told him with a deep sigh.

"No need to thank me, Jack," he said. "It is I who must apologize. The UT6 has proven to be one of the most unreliable in the entire series. It's chief designer has been relieved of the project and has been assigned the study of maggot interaction in Namaban dung. I have it on the best authority that the UT7 is infallible."

"I hope you're right. Anyway, I'm puzzled about something."

"What?"

"How . . . can you be here? I mean, I thought you could only meet me somewhere on my world."

He smiled. "This most assuredly falls into the category of the half you could not understand, Jack. I knew you needed help, so here I am. Besides, my choice of this place allows us to resolve something else that has been on your mind."

"What's that?"

"You want to learn how to travel in the Afterwards, do you not? So; now is the time!"

He was right about that, even though I'm not sure *how* he knew. In any case I was over the sore neck business, so nothing was stopping me.

"Which Afterward is this?" I asked.

"It is Plumbers' Afterward," he replied.

Say what, *Plumbers'* Afterward? At least that accounted for the noises from the blackness.

"But I don't know *anyone* who is—or was—a plumber."

"That's the idea, Jack. Not having close ties to those within will make it easier for you to learn how one who is not yet dead gets around in an Afterward."

Okay, the Old Guy knew best. He motioned for me to leave the bike where it was and led me to the opening, where he stopped.

"You *are* coming in with me, right?" I asked.

"Gracious, no," he said, surprised that anyone could be such a doofus. "There are some places that my people would find uncomfortable. Ah, here is your guide."

Another one of those Romero zombies suddenly sprang up. I thought he was the same Doorkeeper from Rock-and-Roll Afterward.

"Have we met before?" I asked.

The smiling fellow said, "No, sir, I'm certain we have not. You wish to have a look around, I understand."

"Uh, right."

"It's important you truly want this, sir, otherwise you will find it most uncomfortable in there."

Did I want this, did I want this? I looked at the Old Guy, then the Doorkeeper, and made up my mind.

"I would *really* like to experience an Afterward," I said firmly.

"Very good, sir. You need but touch my robe and come in."

Who was this, the Ghost of Christmas Past? An arm came out of the blackness. There was some flesh on the hand, but all in all it reminded me of that weird ferryman.

What the hell, I held his sleeve and stepped into Plumbers' Afterward.

Oh, myyy, was this weeeeird!

First thing, I was upside-down. Now I didn't *feel* upside-down; it's just that, glancing out into the waiting area, the Old Guy *looked* upside-down, and I couldn't imagine why he would be, so I figured it was me.

The Doorkeeper, who was also upside-down, said, "Sir, you can let go of my sleeve now. It was only necessary to touch it while you were passing through."

I had a grip on it that would have squeezed blood out of a turnip. Okay, I let go of the security blanket, which immediately sent my *angst* into overdrive. I stared at the Doorkeeper, wide-eyed; he smiled.

"Try breathing, sir," he said.

Oh, yeah, that's what I had forgotten! I took a few short breaths; my body tilted. I took a deep breath; my body went horizontal, and my *angst* fell slightly.

"Now breathe normally," the Doorkeeper suggested.

I did, and he was right. My body kept on turning, and soon I could feel something solid under my feet, which were engulfed by a black mist. The overwhelming anxiety lessened even more, but it was still there.

"How am . . . I doing?" I asked the Doorkeeper, trying to be cool.

"Oh, outstanding. I know of others who, unable to remain in an Afterward for even a few moments, ran shrieking back into the waiting area, their brains fried, and likely to be so for a long time."

Hey, thanks for letting me know that up front! Oh, jeez! I wanted to get really pissed off, but already I could feel my *angst* resuming its climb, so I checked it.

"Okay, now what?"

"Follow me, sir."

"Why don't you call me Jack?"

''Certainly, sir.''

We started *walking,* and I resisted the urge to grab hold of his sleeve again. With each step I was afraid I'd flip over, but I breathed normally, and it didn't happen.

Okay, the Plumbers' Afterward. It was really black in here, but somehow you could see all around. What I saw were sinks, tubs, toilets, and a vast network of pipes, like the web of a giant, metallic spider. Figures darted busily amid these pipes, the hum of their voices added to the tapping, the flowing water, and the seemingly endless flushing of the toilets.

A figure suddenly popped up in front of us; now *that* was unnerving. He was a short, happy-looking guy, thirtyish, with wavy black hair. *Eddie* was what it said on the oval patch of his blue work shirt. He was carrying a huge crescent wrench in his left hand.

''Hiya, Jack,'' Eddie said, holding out his other hand.

Okay, I'd shaken hands with Harry Chapin, but that was on the *other* side. Whatever; I couldn't be unsociable, and besides, I was here to learn the ropes, right?

''Nice to see you, Eddie,'' I told him, nearly wincing from his firm grip.

''Well, gotta go,'' he said, waving the wrench. ''Work to do.''

Eddie left but was replaced by Al, who looked even younger. We also shook hands. After that we seemed to be surrounded by happy plumbers. My hand was pumped by Lou, Mike, Vito, John, Josephine, and so on.

Had this been Chimney Sweeps' Afterward, one whole lot of good luck would have rubbed off on me.

One thing kept puzzling me as we negotiated the maze of pipes. I said to the Doorkeeper, ''None of these . . . people look to be any older than forty. Did they all die so young?''

''On the contrary, most lived to ripe old ages. But in an Afterward you can choose your appearance at the time of your life that most pleased you.''

Oh yeah, huh? That made sense. Why be old and gnarly if you had a choice?

Anyway, we walked past more people in blue and gray work uniforms unclogging drains, changing shower heads, and the like. They kept on shaking my hand, which was fine, until I suddenly felt that old *angst* crawling up again. I told the Doorkeeper.

"Yes, you should leave," he said. "Each time you enter an Afterward from here on, you'll find it easier to remain longer."

Yeah, great, but right now get me out of here! I couldn't shake another hand, and my breathing got so freaky that I was afraid of hyperventilating. It occurred to me that we had walked a long way, and I questioned whether I'd be able to make it back without losing it. Already my body was horizontal.

When we turned around, the cave mouth was right there.

"Touch my robe again, sir," I heard the Doorkeeper say, and I did, all the while focusing on the Old Guy, who again looked upside-down to me.

I stepped out of Plumbers' Afterward . . .

. . . and was face-to-face with the Old Guy.

The Doorkeeper withdrew his hand and sank out of sight.

"Well, Jack, what did you think of that?" the Old Guy asked.

"Unsettling at first, but once you—"

Uh-oh, the Old Guy was fading, like he'd done in the white room. Everything below his waist was gone.

"Hey, wait, I have questions!" I exclaimed.

"Perhaps we'll talk later, by the bridge."

"But that was one of the questions! The *mhuva lun gallee* branched off, and there doesn't seem to be a way back along the tunnel I picked."

The emptiness was up to his chest. "Don't worry, everything's cool. The *mhuva lun gallee* branches often but always comes together again. You only need be persistent, as you've always been."

My brain was swimming with all the stuff I'd thought about asking him. But now the only thing left was his head. "Listen, I—"

"Good-bye, Jack," his hollow voice called, and the rest of him was gone. Well, at least I'd learned that the branching of the Ultimate Bike Path was not an anomaly, that I'd be able to find my way home.

And I'd also learned how to get around—tentatively, to be sure—in an Afterward. What possibilities *that* could open up!

I glanced behind me into the blackness of the cave mouth. Eddie, Al, Josephine, and others were standing there, waving and smiling.

I waved back, then got on the Nishiki and rode off.

CHAPTER 23

Old Friends

More thoughts about this and that while riding along the Ultimate Bike Path.

Did *all* plumbers wind up in Plumbers' Afterward? Did *all* software developers wind up in Software Developers' Afterward? I mean, was it what they wanted to do through eternity? Okay, maybe that was true of software developers. But plumbers, carpenters, dentists, truck drivers, all had lives away from their professions. Wouldn't they want to be in some other Afterward with families and friends? Maybe fishing, bowling, making love, sitting around and sucking on a beer while watching a World Series or Super Bowl that had no end?

Could it be their spirits existed in a number of different Afterwards? For example, Al the Plumber is fixing a toilet here, but over there he's dining at the Sizzler with his wife, and somewhere else he and some high school buddies are cruising the bars . . .

Yep, Jack gets crazy again. Maybe Ralph Ralph can explain the essence of life after death to me. Until then, stop worrying about it.

Great oldies, like the Chi-Lites' "Have You Seen Her?" can almost never be topped, no matter who does what to them.

The next time the *mhuva lun gallee* splits, I'm going to take the *right* branch. Not that I had taken the *wrong* branch, mind you. What I meant was . . .

Forget it.

Remember that toothbrush gate I told you about? There were more of them now, and they were giving off creepy emanations, even worse than the Bart Simpson heads when I didn't know what was behind them. On the one hand I felt they should be avoided completely; on the other hand I thought, Hey, why am I passing these all by? I *am* an explorer . . .

Right?

In his music video, "Me and Julio Down by the Schoolyard," Paul Simon is pitching stickball to Mickey Mantle.

Great fantasy! He slips the first pitch past. Then, the Mick connects with the ball and sends it halfway to Neptune. Wow!

Aha, a blue door! Not mine, but it was the first in a long while. Didn't matter, anyway, because with the thing in my neck replaced I was still on the road. Reality time had no hold on me at the moment.

Now, I was assuming that the UT7 was state-of-the-art, as advertised. It hadn't given me any problems in the Plumbers' Afterward, but then, Eddie and Josephine weren't exactly alien life-forms. A shadow of a doubt would be cast over me until I could test it.

There was a rider up ahead, something that looked like a six-foot pea pod with fuzzy orange bunny slippers on its *feet* or whatever. Its go-thing was a large-wheeled unicycle. I paralleled it, but at a comfortable distance of two yards. You just never know.

"Hey, nice wheel," I called out, which sounded dumb.

The pea pod turned its *head,* which resembled two raisins and a stick of Big Red on a silver chafing dish. Something that looked like a knitting needle emerged from the Big Red mouth.

"After I insert this inside you and suck out the marrow of your bones," it said, "I intend to decorate my go-thing with your toes and the lobes of your ears."

Hey, no problem, the UT7 worked fine. No sore neck or . . .

What did it say? *Oh, shit!* The pea pod started angling over. I flipped it the finger (yeah, tacky, but think about what it planned on doing to *me*), put my head down . . .

. . . and got outta there at something more blurry than blur-speed.

It was just after I slowed down—about twenty zillion miles later—that the two branches of the *mhuva lun gallee* came together. Yeah, finally. To tell the truth, nothing seemed all that different, except for the increasing number of blue doors. There were still plenty of those toothbrush gates, some even more creepy than before. Or was it me? Maybe I needed a dose of reality time more than I'd thought.

But when my gate appeared, I passed it. In fact, within a short period of time I rode by it again. Okay, I was committed to going on. The question was, where? No particular portal seemed too interested in Jack Miller's presence, while the toothbrushes with hearts seemed to be throbbing out the message *just try it asshole*.

So what do you think I did? Give me either kudos for having courage or brickbats for being the aforementioned posterior orifice . . . but I angled toward the most ominous toothbrush gate I could find.

Think of all the ones that said *come on in jack and enjoy yourself* and wound up getting me into deep kaka. How bad could this be? It was assuredly a Class M world, so I wasn't going to explode or melt. And it could be one of the nicest excursions yet.

Then how come, for the first time in a while, I was cutting loose a good old scream as I penetrated the pulsating portal . . . ?

. . . and how come I was still screaming on the other side?

That's easy, you should've seen what was in my face.

It had emerged from a bubbling, smoking pit of what was either molten lava or spaghetti sauce, about a yard in front of me. There were dozens of these pits all around, any of which I could've tumbled into. I should say *half*-emerged, only its head, arms, and upper torso being visible. The thing, drenched in this self-same orange/red goo, looked like a cyclopean refugee from a movie in which Ray Harryhausen had done the special effects. Above its one eye was a horn; not the kind Marlin Perkins runs away from, but one from which Satchmo blew his sweet jazz. It had a gaping mouth with rows of sharp teeth, and long, birdlike claws at the end of an abnormally large number of fingers. The bloodshot eye was staring at me; all in all the thing looked really pissed.

I expected a nasty bellow to pour out of that ugly mouth.

Instead, it blew an E flat from the horn on its forehead.

The first muted toot sent a stream of that spaghetti sauce or whatever-it-was past my head.

The second, louder toot roused similar creatures up from about half the pits.

Talk about doing the slalom on a mountain bike! I dodged raking claws, ducked deadly spaghetti sauce, and wished I could cover my ears against the growing cacophony of their blasted horns.

We told you not to come schmucko but you came anyway so it's your ass in your hand.

There actually was an end to the pits, and once twenty yards past I dared a glance behind. None of the red-hot cyclops-things had climbed out, which I interpreted as meaning they couldn't. They were still blowing those awful horns and waving their *fists* in a gesture that said *next time jack.*

Tough luck, fellas.

But a quick look around advised me that I'd hardly had the last laugh, because this was one *awful place!* Over by those fire pits it must've been one hundred fifty degrees, and even away from them it wasn't that much cooler. Okay, this might not've been Hell itself, but it sure looked a lot like people's perceptions of the Devil's playground.

For example, the sky was the color of the horizon off the southern California coast at sunset on the worst smoggy day. And the mountains all around were black and steamy, like they'd been ravaged by fire. There were broad cracks in the earth, the closest only a few yards away. It revealed a white-hot, bubbling caldron of whatever below; not all that far down, either. Undoubtedly hotter than your average pizza oven.

Yeah, this was for sure a quick stop. Head to the nearest mountain slope and . . .

Something came down out of the sky.

It looked like a giant, mutated sparrow with fangs and a wing span that would enable it to fly over Dallas and Fort Worth at the same time. The sound it made would have had a familiar ring to those in the dungeons of the Spanish Inquisition.

Screw this, I leaped into the crack . . .

. . . and nearly crashed into a wall along the *mhuva lun gallee,* being half-blinded by the perspiration running off my forehead, not to mention the rest of my nearly parboiled body.

Rule-To-Live-By #789 when riding along the Ultimate Bike Path: Never go through a toothbrush gate.

Back in control now I rode along steadily, and pretty soon the last of the toothbrush portals was behind. Good riddance! There was a long run of lemon-yellow Gorbachev birthmarks, none of which interested me. I could've gone faster, but I let them pass at the same speed. No way was I in a hurry to make another entry.

Hey, Old Guys, do I have *testiculos,* or what! Leaping into that molten crack instead of taking the easy way out and rubbing the Bukko. Must've impressed the hell out of you.

Of course, if you could read my mind you'd know that, in my panic, I'd forgotten about the blasted coin.

Ah well, sometimes folks need only run in reverse to become heroes.

I wonder what Holly was doing right now.

Let's see, I'd left Camp Pendleton late Sunday morning, and although long ago it was *still* late Sunday morning there, which meant it was early afternoon in Iowa. At this very moment (a *long* moment) she could be having lunch with Mr. Cedar Rapids.

Who cares?

The Gorbys changed into a random pattern. I mean, *really* random, no two in a row alike for some time. A few Bart Simpson heads were mixed in here, which was odd, since they usually appeared in long runs.

It was one of these that beckoned me in.

Not *yanked,* like the one where the Old Guy had been waiting. This was more gently insistent, and therefore irresistible.

I angled toward it, burst through . . .

. . . and continued pedaling slowly as I shifted down from the Vurdabrok Gear.

No waiting area was visible yet through the engulfing gray haze, but that didn't bother me, because I was going in the right direction. I tried not to speculate about what Afterward this was, figuring it could only make me nuts. That would be revealed soon enough.

I felt excitement churning, not to mention trepidation.

A minute later the silence was broken by something I could not at first identify, even though I concentrated hard on the sound. Then, as the haze gave way and I saw the now-familiar cave mouth across the waiting area, I knew what it was.

The barking of a whole lot of dogs.

Oh, no; no no no. Was it really . . . ?

Henceforth, consider carefully the *thoughts about this and that* you have while riding along the Ultimate Bike Path, for someone is almost surely tuned in.

I barely remember getting off the Nishiki and leaving it on the *floor* of the waiting area, or even walking to the cave mouth. But there I was, staring into the blackness, when the

Doorkeeper popped up. Even knowing that would happen, it still scared the crap out of me.

The zombie (I *swear* it was the same one) smiled and said, "Welcome to Doggy Afterward, sir."

"Yeah; nice to see you again."

He scratched his head. "I don't think we've ever met, sir."

I should've expected that. "Oh, sorry."

"No problem. Do you wish to come in?"

I listened to the barking for a moment. "Yes."

That made him happy. "Very good, sir. You need only touch my robe . . ."

I was face-to-face with him in the blackness, and already I'd let go of his sleeve. My breathing was steady; I felt pretty good. The barking was louder, as you can imagine, but it had a calming effect.

A bull mastiff approached. This was the kind of beast that when jogging, you prayed never came running out of someone's yard after your rear end or ankle. But this fellow sat down, looking up at me, and held out a paw. I shook it, and he ambled off.

The Doorkeeper's smile grew. "Shall we go on, sir?"

"Sure."

"You don't need me, but I'll be happy to accompany you."

"No, I'm fine."

"Very good, sir."

He backed away; floated, I would say. A black miniature poodle was suddenly there, practically on top of my feet. Now, in the past I'd been yapped at, nipped, even peed on by dogs like this. But guess what, it held up a paw, just like the mastiff. I shook the tiny thing and ruffled its curly head. It licked my hand and scurried off.

I walked through the Afterward and was greeted, in turn, by an Alsatian, a cocker spaniel, two basset hounds, a Doberman pinscher, two chihuahuas, a Pomeranian, and an unbelievable assortment of lovable mutts. Even with all the barking in the background, not one of them flapped its gums at me.

Then, I saw Barney.

Okay, I was breathing too fast, and my *angst* was doing cartwheels. I slowed down, and it was better.

Even years after his death, even with a hundred—or a thousand—other German shepherds around him, I would have known Barney in an instant. There wasn't a single feature of his black-white-gray body that I hadn't memorized. The crooked, happy grin on his muzzle was what it had been nearly all his life, not the pain of that last horrible week. His eyes were bright with a mischievous glint.

I knelt down and waited as he trotted toward me.

He sat down on the run, a habit of his that had once proven funny on a freshly polished kitchen floor.

"How're you doing, furball?" I said, and rubbed him behind the ears.

He put a paw up on my chest and licked my chin, which used to gross some people out, especially Mrs. Rose Miller Leventhal. Didn't bother me.

Barney rolled over on his back. My fingers immediately found the infamous *tickle zone* on his belly. One leg thumped like a piston engine.

"Rooo rooo roooo," he said.

He scrambled up suddenly and started off, glancing behind to make sure I followed. I did.

There were no other dogs around, and even the barking was distant. Barney led me through the blackness to a field; *our* field, a patch of scrub, sage, and brittle earth near some hills, a private place where we used to go.

Our old rubber softball with the thousand teeth marks in it lay on the ground; so did the Louisville Slugger I'd had since I was a kid. A year after Barney died I'd splintered it in a game and consigned it to the fireplace.

He sat down next to the bat and ball; hands trembling, I picked them up. He rose and stood poised, like a sprinter.

Our favorite game began.

I popped the ball into the air about fifty feet across the field. Barney raced out, his eyes following its arc, and caught it in his jaws over his shoulder. He brought it back but playfully made me work at pulling it free. I hit it again.

And again.

There were days we played it endlessly; he seldom tired.

After the sixth time he dropped the ball on the ground and sat down in front of me. He knew how much I was being overwhelmed by all that was happening.

Barely in control, I knelt down and rubbed behind his ears one last time. He licked my chin, took the softball in his mouth, and trotted off. Blackness enveloped our field.

I turned, and the Doorkeeper was waiting at the cave mouth.

CHAPTER 24

Great Big Woman Valley

It was rush hour on the Ultimate Bike Path.

I'm not kidding, I never saw so many whoevers and whatevers at one time. Plenty of individual riders, some pairs, but also larger groups whizzing by, one in particular with so many *cyclists* that I couldn't keep count. I saw Vulvans, oh, yes; even passed one in the throes of invigoration, but I kept on going. At least I didn't run into any elephant-flies, pea pods, or the like.

Blue doors went by without me even looking at them, because no way was I ready to go back. I had *lots* of energy to expend, so at least one more excursion was in order. Riding at blur-speed on the *mhuva lun gallee* was okay, but I needed to open up. Some pleasant, nonchallenging world, where I wasn't at risk of being fried, eaten, or otherwise mutilated; yeah, that would be nice.

Along the way I fell in with this one group of about a dozen riders. They looked like marble busts of Aristotle on top of spider legs. At first they'd passed me by on their tricycle go-things, then slowed down for me to catch up. One thing weird about them was their ears, hardly more than tiny pinpricks. I suppose that's why they talked in voices loud enough to drown out a waterfall. Even when I shouted, they strained to listen. But all in all they were an okay bunch of guys, even inviting me to go riding with them in their world, on the other side of an Elmer Fudd gate (I figured that out from their description). At first I accepted.

Then, I heard one *whisper* to another (in a voice that would have shattered glass), "I can't wait to get him back to Jendrigon so that his brain *and* his go-thing can be dissected."

I slowed down to *nearly falling over,* and the Aristotles were far ahead before they realized what had happened.

Okay, the path was too crowded for its own good. I had to get off. The random pattern of gates currently dominated. I felt a tug from one of those black circles with the laser bread slicers, so I angled toward it. Not comfortable with that special effect, I shut my eyes as I burst through . . .

. . . and opened them immediately on the other side.

Hey, now this was *perfect*. Everything in wherever-I-was looked to be the proper color: sky, mountains, earth, trees, all the other foliage. There was one sun bathing the land, the temperature just right. I had broken through—can you believe this?—on a *road,* one which paralleled a clear river that wound amid some grassy hills. I was already way up in the mountains, so I believed, but there were quite a few pretty tall peaks all around.

The gritty but hard road was a piece of cake for the mountain bike's tires. It was about ten feet wide, and as best I could tell, wheel ruts and animal tracks indicated that it was routinely traveled in both directions. At the moment there was no one in sight, which didn't matter. I chose the direction that would take me upriver.

Wow, what a great ride! The air up here was clear and sweet, and would have fulfilled anyone's dream of a pollution-free environment. Birds of all colors sang happily as they flitted in and out of the junipers, stunted elms, and other foliage that occasionally lined both the river and the road. A few times I saw a big fish leap above the rippling surface.

I came across the first inhabitants of this place within a few miles. There were three of them, a man, woman, and little girl, the adults walking in front of a buggy that looked like the kind you see in Pennsylvania Dutch country. They appeared to be human, perhaps a bit on the short side, but that was all. My appearance startled neither them nor the horse-thing that pulled the buggy (a Mr. Ed look-alike, I swear, other than having six legs). On the contrary, they waved nonchalantly, then went on with a conversation they'd been having.

Well, fine, I wasn't much in a chatty mood. I kept on pedaling, and pretty soon there were a lot more people, some fishing or picnicking along the river, others on the road. All were small of stature, though nothing like the adults of Warithess. Nearly everyone greeted me politely, but that was about it.

Smaller paths had been intersecting the main road for a while, and despite its width I was unable to ride as hard and fast as before. Something told me a town would be coming up before long. Great; I could grab a bite and maybe head *down* the road, away from civilization.

Then, the road branched. The left fork curved with the river; *all* the people went this way. The deserted right fork crossed a rickety-looking bridge, then twisted around a hill and disappeared.

There was a sign at the split. The *letters* looked like what you would have after you dipped a writhing mass of earthworms in blue ink and threw them down on paper. I touched the sign. Under an arrow to the right fork it said THE WAY TO GREAT BIG WOMAN VALLEY. The left fork was THE WAY TO EVERYWHERE ELSE.

Great Big Woman Valley? Yep, that sounded intriguing. So when did old Jack-o ever go with the crowd?

I took the right fork.

The bridge over the river, as advertised, was a piece of crap. I crossed on foot, treading gingerly. A foot-long piece of two-by-four broke loose and plummeted into the water, but otherwise I made it without mishap.

Now the road, although just as wide, was not in the best of shape. Lots of holes, deep ruts, stuff like that. It was still ridable, but I had to be careful.

After twisting around the hill the road inclined slightly for a few miles, then leveled as it passed between a couple of peaks. Not tall, but of considerable length, and it took some time— half an hour or more—before they were behind me.

Okay, the road wasn't great, and the only tributary was a narrow stream with sandy, sloping banks. But this valley I'd just ridden into was as idyllic as the place I started from, the same foliage, chirping birds, clean air, everything. And to tell the truth, with each yard the road was in better repair. I sped up slightly but resisted the urge to drop a couple of more gears and let fly.

It was a few minutes later when I ran into my first great big woman.

There were bushes along the stream, and she was kneeling by them, picking what looked to be blueberries and putting them in a basket. Seeing me she rose to her full height, which was about seven feet one.

Yeah, I could be pretty accurate about that. As a kid I went to lots of New York Knicks games, and I knew how tall all of *them* were. I used to stand by the passageway as they went in and out of the locker room. This lady was definitely a few inches taller than Willis Reed.

And no, she wasn't drop-dead-gorgeous, or anything close to it. She was just okay, unless you happened to be a leg man, in which case you would've thought she was *wonderful.* Her clothing consisted of a bulky top and something that looked like culottes, both of the same drab material. She was barefoot.

Now, not having a clue about her attitude, I was poised to pedal off like a bat out of hell. But I didn't, because a nice smile lit up her angular face, and she waved to me.

"Hi, sailor," she called. (I swear, that's what she said!)

"Hello," I said. "Beautiful day."

She looked around. "I didn't notice; they're all like this. You're far from the sea, aren't you?"

"Excuse me?"

"Your clothes; I heard only sailors wear such as this."

That explained it. "Right; yes, I *am* far from the sea. Thought I'd take a tour of the countryside." No sense trying to spell it out any other way, huh?

I had gotten off the bike and was standing alongside it when she neared to within a yard. She looked me down and up, then sighed in a sort of wistful way.

"A bit taller than most," she said, "but . . . No matter. Pardon my lack of manners. My name is Hesper. Welcome to Great Big Woman Valley."

"Thank you. I'm Jack."

"Well, Jack, would you care to have some of these berries, or would you rather follow me to Great Big Woman Village for more substantial refreshment?"

"Is it far?"

She shook her head. "Only a mile."

"Then lead on."

Basket in hand, Hesper set off running. Despite the ease of her strides, you would not *believe* how fast she went. Had the road still been bad, I would have been sorely pressed to keep up.

In any case we reached Great Big Woman Village quickly. It consisted of about two dozen Great Big Cottages . . . wait a minute, that's great big cottages, and some abundant growing fields, on both sides of the stream. Lots of other great big women watched me ride in, and I became an instant curiosity piece. Seeing them, I realized that Hesper could have been the runt of the litter. Most were even taller. Their clothing was the same as Hesper's, almost like a uniform.

Pardon this brief regression to chauvinism, but you leg men out there would have truly thought you'd found Paradise.

There, that's all. Anyway, even though there were many women around it was not difficult to recognize their honcho. She was neither the tallest nor the oldest, but she had this Glenn Close air of authority about her. Others parted quickly to let her through.

"This is Ivana," Hesper said by way of introduction. "She is our Chief Executive Officer. I would like to present Jack, a sailor who is traveling through Great Big Woman Valley."

Ivana tilted her head in a formal way. "May we offer you food and drink, Jack?"

"Yes, thank you."

Hesper and a couple of others hurried off. Ivana led me to what looked like a picnic table, near the stream. By the time I'd washed my face and taken a leak behind a tree, food was on the table. All great stuff, which I washed down with something that tasted like spearmint-flavored beer.

While I ate, the CEO and others asked me lots of questions. Some were about the bike, but most were regarding my experiences as a sailor. Now, I know as much about plying the waves as Golda Meir knew about hog-raising. But in the manner of Indiana Jones I made it up as I went along, and once I figured out these great big women knew as little as I did, it was easy.

You of course realize that I hadn't seen any men here. After what happened with the women of Amazina I should've been wary. But they were treating me nicely, so I decided to pose the question. What it caused was a bunch of anguished looks.

"The people of our region are not partial to tall females," Ivana explained. "By law they cannot banish us from the villages, but our lives are made so miserable that we *want* to leave. So we come here, to Great Big Woman Valley, where we are not bothered."

"What a crock," I said sourly. "But that still doesn't answer my question about men."

"As far as we know," Hesper said, "only females grow like this."

"Too bad you're not a foot taller," Ivana said thoughtfully.

You know, I really *did* like tall women, and none of them

here were *that* bad, especially this one redhead who had been giving me the eye . . . uh-uh, that's not what I was here for.

So I said my good-byes all around and rode out of Great Big Woman Village. A couple of them jogged next to the bike for a while, then pulled back.

"Too bad he wasn't a foot taller," I heard one reiterate.

Great Big Woman Valley was not a great big valley, and I got across it quickly. The road now snaked downward in the shadow of some rugged-looking slopes. I had already decided that as soon as I came across the first long straightaway, I was outta here. Sure, this place was nice, but I was okay now and ready for some reality time.

That straightaway wasn't long in coming. I'd just rounded a curve when there it was, running on for some distance before disappearing between two tightly pinched slopes. Let me tell you, the sucker was *STEEP*. Slick it down with ice and snow and you'd have the perfect venue for an Olympic ski jump. This might not've been like leaping off a cliff, but it was close to it.

Well, it had to be done. The road would take some watching, because in the last couple of miles it had begun to deteriorate again. But I could handle it, since I would be hitting my desired speed in a matter of seconds.

Resisting the urge to yell *banzai!* or *geronimo!* or something just as idiotic, I started down the hill.

In a matter of seconds I *had* reached my desired speed. I pushed up on the thumb lever.

Nothing happened.

Shortly after that I was *beyond* the desired speed; *nothing* continued to happen.

Thirty-seven point five mph; thirty-eight. I couldn't shift into the Vurdabrok Gear.

Forty mph; *oh, shit.* Forty point five, and this was with squeezing the brakes!

Okay, Miller, don't look at the speedometer anymore.

Actually I couldn't, being too busy negotiating the road, which had grown nastier. So far so good, but at this speed all I needed was for the road to curve.

I reached the part where the slopes pinched together, and guess what, *the road curved.*

Not too severely, but still, even riding the brakes it was going to be chancy. One good thing was that after it curved, the road leveled as it crossed a mountain meadow that was covered with amber waves of grain or some such thing. Even veering off the road I might be able to utilize this stuff for slowing down.

Forty-two mph; *damn, why did I have to look!*

I didn't see the rise in the road until it was too late. Skiers, snowmobilers, skateboarders, and the like would have loved this natural ramp.

Not bike riders going forty-two mph.

Somehow, while flying through the air, I got separated from the Nishiki. The last thing I remember was . . .

I don't remember.

CHAPTER 25

Jack and the Bean . . . ? *Naaah*

The first thing I do remember upon coming to was being up close and personal with a horse's rear end.

I was lying on the back of a cart with a cold wet cloth on my throbbing head and an outstanding view of the aforementioned posterior under the driver's bench. The tail was swishing flies away as the six-legged creature plodded along. I also noticed a pair of booted feet hanging down.

"Hey, what's happening?" I called out groggily. "Someone talk to me."

The driver called "whoa!" and made a sputtering sound. I tilted my head with considerable effort, glancing up at the same moment he turned and glanced down.

I swear, he looked like a short, blue-collar version of Sir Winston Churchill.

Jowly, serious, a lot younger-looking than all those pictures you've seen of Winnie in history books. He eyed me with about as much interest as a New York cabbie would give to a mugging in progress on the street, then spoke in a voice that generated equal enthusiasm.

"You're all right, I suppose."

"Yes. Do I have you to thank for that?"

"Of course. I saw you and your whichawho flying through the air. Then you landed in a field of wild wheat near where I was working, four miles back. You were knocked out, but the wild wheat cushioned your fall, so I don't think anything was broken."

"Nothing was, or you would've heard me screaming by now," I said jokingly.

He scratched his head. "What is *screaming*?"

"Never mind."

"I don't think there was any damage to your whichawho either."

My *whichawho*. Now I got it: the Nishiki. It was there, atop mounds of wild wheat, and it looked to be in good shape. That was a relief . . .

On the other hand . . . *the Vurdabrok Gear didn't work!*

Well, that wasn't this guy's fault. "Listen, pal, I owe you one," I said.

He shrugged and yawned; *sor-ree* if I was boring him. "I must take this load back to town. You may ride along, or get off here. In either case, make up your mind quickly. And my name is Latimer, not *pal.*"

Now mind you, he wasn't saying any of this in a nasty tone of voice. He sounded so deathly, nasally bored that I thought he might fall asleep sitting there.

"If it's all the same," I said, "I'll go with you. I still have chimes ringing up in the clock tower."

I don't know if that puzzled Latimer, because he didn't show it. He turned and called "Gee!" to the horse, and the cart took off with a jolt, which really rattled my cage.

Lately I'd been coming better and better prepared for these excursions. Before leaving the last time I'd slipped one of those little tins of Tylenol into my seat bag. Shortly after downing a couple the bells stopped ringing, and I dragged myself up. Yep, the Nishiki was fine outwardly, except for some wild wheat clinging to it in places. Deciding to clean it later—wasn't *that* the least of my problems?—I sat down on the bench next to Latimer, who didn't utter a sound but whose expression held the enthusiasm of a bunch of bar patrons watching C-Span.

Remember me saying that Great Big Woman Valley was even more idyllic than my first stop on this world? Well, the place where I was now had both beat. I'm not kidding; the blue of the sky and streams, the yellow of the wheat, the green of the grass and trees, and the multihues of flowers were the bright colors that a preschooler would make with a box of crayons. Even the grazing herds of six-legged cow-things had a sort of unreal look, though not so the men and women who either tended them or worked in the wheat fields. They were, like Latimer, the most bored-looking folks I'd ever seen. You'd have thought a stranger would generate some interest, but they hardly looked up as we passed. Same for their dogs, wanna-be collies with (what else?) six legs. Not even a yip or a yap from them.

Let me amend one thing: Not all around here was Crayola bright. A couple of miles ahead the fields and such ended at the base of a rather ominous mountain. Clinging to the side of this mountain, half a mile or so up, was a dense gray cloud. At one point I noticed Latimer glancing at it, kind of scowling. Nope, he didn't appear too thrilled. When he saw me looking at him the humdrum expression returned.

Anyway, considering my circumstances I really didn't care about much else. I mean, *what was I going to do about getting out of here?* Forty-something mph and I couldn't use the Vurdabrok Gear; I'd say there was a definite problem with the Nishiki.

So what happens? Does an Old Guy show up here in wherever-the-hell-I-was and fix it? If so, why hadn't it been done already? Maybe they weren't watching just now. Great; that would mean I'd have to rub the Bukko. Hey, no fair! I was only supposed to use it to save my ass. They couldn't charge that against my account.

Maybe there was some big Universal Complaints Department I could appeal to in the event that happened.

"I suppose you're hungry," Latimer whined, and it had been so long since he'd last spoken that I nearly flew off the bench.

"Actually, I ate not too long ago," I told him, "but I could use a drink."

He reached into a pocket and handed me a pint-sized bottle three-quarters full with a green liquid that looked like Scope mouthwash but fortunately wasn't. It tasted like watered-down cremè de menthe laced with cloves. I downed about half the contents, not quite sure if I'd just gotten drunk or what.

Shortly after, we came to the edge of the town. It really was weird seeing that gloomy cloud hanging straight above it, while all around were blue skies and such. Plenty of people were afoot, but as before I was virtually ignored.

Before entering town Latimer reined Mr. Ed to a stop. Telling me to wait, he climbed down and went over to talk to another guy. I got off the cart too, because there was a sign nearby, and I was curious to know what it said.

The "words" were really weird. It looked like someone had taken Hebrew letters, tried to mix them with Chinese characters, gotten pissed off, and made diagonal slash marks through the whole thing. When I touched the sign the mess changed to this: YOU ARE IN LETHARGIA.

Well, that made sense, huh? A town called Marina Del Rey

or Daytona Beach or something might have caused me to raise an eyebrow, but Lethargia fit this place just fine.

I rejoined Latimer, and we rode into town. It was a surprisingly big place, if not the most inspired from the standpoint of architecture. The buildings were all of the same design and material, but at least they varied in size.

One of the largest was our next stop. A mill, I figured, since we unloaded the wild wheat, while others were doing the same. At this point I took the Nishiki off the cart.

"Where are you going?" Latimer whined.

"To find an inn, or someplace to crash. Thanks again for all your help."

This was true. I still hadn't recovered from the fall, and the stuff he'd given me to drink was getting to my head. Besides, it was late. With a decent night's sleep I might better be able to decide where to go from here . . . assuming I *could* go anywhere without a twenty-second gear.

"Why don't you stay at my house?" Latimer offered with minimal enthusiasm. "Lucinda won't care; I won't care either."

"Are you sure?"

"Yes, I'm sure we won't care."

"Then I accept."

I mean, how could you turn down a nice invitation like that? He got back on his cart; I cleaned the wild wheat off, climbed on the seat, and followed.

Even this passing oddity did not awaken the good folk of Lethargia from their lethargy.

I didn't mention this, but nearly everyone I'd seen in and around the town, man, woman, and child, resembled either Winston Churchill or Danny DeVito. Latimer's wife, Lucinda, was in the latter category. She was working in an anemic-looking garden when we approached their house, which stood isolated past the far edge of town, toward the base of the mountain. When Latimer pulled up in front of what I suppose was the barn, Lucinda walked over slowly.

"This is somebody-or-other and his whichawho," Latimer told his wife. "He's going to spend the night."

"I don't care," Lucinda whined.

Yeah, a pleasure to meet you too, ma'am.

"How was your day?" Latimer asked.

"I picked a tomato," Lucinda said. "No, wait, it was two tomatoes."

"And?"

"I pulled up a couple of weeds and swept the porch steps. Oh, and I sewed your overalls."

Life in the fast lane; isn't it a bitch sometimes?

"Nothing else happened?" Latimer asked.

"No, I . . . yes, wait a minute. Our daughter was stolen by the giant."

Say what! Their daughter was stolen by the *giant*? Definitely the fifth item of importance, behind weeds and tomatoes and such. *What was with these people?*

Latimer and Lucinda, standing shoulder to shoulder, turned to face me. "Woe is us, woe is us," they whined lifelessly. "Our daughter was stolen by the giant. Woe is us."

"Uh, right," I said, wondering why they were telling this to me. "Where did the giant take your daughter?"

They aimed a finger up the face of the mountain. "He took Eloise to his castle," Lucinda said, "which is in the clouds."

Well naturally, where else would you expect a giant's castle to be? Reluctantly I asked, "What will he do with her?"

"No one is really sure what he does with the sons and daughters of Lethargia that he has stolen," Latimer said.

"Then he's taken others?"

"Yes. Eloise is the sixth since the giant appeared."

Lucinda shrugged and yawned. "Perhaps it is best we don't know what he does with them."

"But she's your *daughter,* for crying out loud!" I exclaimed.

Latimer, who had unhitched Mr. Ed and sent him off to graze, said, "Let's continue this over dinner. I'm hungry."

Jeez, I couldn't believe these two! They walked side by side to the house, again whining "Woe is us," although I didn't have a clue why. I followed, pushing the Nishiki, and when they went inside I spent a few seconds chaining it to a heavy rail along the front steps. Sure, Lethargia this might be, but I wasn't taking any chances, especially with a *giant* running around.

They were already stuffing their faces when I entered the cottage. The first thing I noticed was this family portrait hanging on one wall. Lucinda and Latimer, looking totally bored, were flanking a girl of fifteen or so, who did *not* look like either Winston Churchill or Danny DeVito. Cute kid, actually, sort or resembling Patty Duke when she did that old television show. And unlike her parents she wore a smile, which brought life to her face.

I'm sorry, but this kid didn't deserve to be written off!

"How do I get up to the giant's castle?" I asked them insistently.

They both stopped chewing mouthfuls of cheese and stared at me. "Why would you want to go there?" Lucinda whined.

"To see if I can bring Eloise back . . . not that you seem to want her."

Latimer's expression changed to something verging on indignancy. "Of course we would like our daughter returned. But there is no way to defeat the giant. He is a terrible—"

"Has anyone ever tried?"

He scratched his head. "I don't think so."

"Fine. Then I ask again, how do I get up there?"

Latimer's new expression read *hey fella butt out of our lives will you,* but on Lucinda's face there was something akin to hope. "We know one way, but it must first be approved by the Chief Executive Officer of Lethargia."

What was with this *chief executive officer* business! "Bring the dude here and I'll talk to him," I said.

"I'll go and fetch Oscar," Latimer whined.

"We'll *both* go and fetch Oscar," Lucinda added. "Uh, somebody-or-other . . ."

"Jack; my name's Jack."

"Yes. Have some food, Jack. We won't be long."

They left, and I decided that I *was* hungry. I passed on the cheese, which smelled awful, but tore off a hunk of bread and smeared it with something that looked like gray, lumpy cream cheese but tasted (fortunately) like Peter Pan peanut butter with the chunks in it. I took it outside, where I contemplated the Nishiki while eating.

"Okay, Old Guys, listen up," I finally said. (This time I didn't gaze skyward, but looked toward the base of the mountain.) "Through no fault of my own the Vurdabrok Gear appears to be kaput. That's *out of order,* so don't bother sticking fingers in your ears. If you're tuned in, here's the scoop: I'm headed off to do something. No big deal, rescue a bunch of kids from an evil giant, maybe slay him in the process; usual thing. Could you *please* take care of the bike while I'm gone? I don't want to stay in Lethargia one minute longer than I have to. Yes, you'll do it? Good. And please leave me some sign that the job was done. A repair order, along with the parts replaced, would be fine. Okay? Thank you. Over and out.''

If you don't think I felt stupid doing that . . .

Anyway, Lucinda and Latimer were back quickly, as promised. The guy with them, about sixtyish, looked like a *cross* between Winston Churchill and Danny DeVito. His expression far out-bored the other two.

"This is Oscar, our Chief Executive Officer," Latimer said. "The somebody-or-other is . . ."

"Jack," Lucinda finished.

Oscar made a grunting noise but neither met my eyes nor offered a hand. Looking at the Nishiki he said, "And this is the whichawho? I'll learn more about it later; maybe . . ."

"Listen, Oscar," I said, "did they tell you what I wanted?"

The CEO faced me. "You wish to go to the giant's castle?" he whined.

"Yes."

"It is highly irregular."

"Nonetheless, that's the plan. What do I need? Your blessing? A map? The code to detonate a nuclear device under the big guy's ass? Tell me."

"My grandson was stolen by the giant," Oscar said.

"Then you have something at stake. Come on, what's the deal?"

I was staring him down; so was Lucinda, for that matter. Oscar thought about it for a few seconds more, then shrugged and reached in his pocket. The box he withdrew was the size of my Tylenol tin. He opened it and shook the contents out on his palm.

There were three jelly beans.

A pink one, a green one, and a black one. They were small, the kind you had to shove into your mouth by the handful in order to really get your teeth into them.

"What are these for?" I asked, afraid to hear the answer.

"You plant them in the ground," the CEO said. "Latimer knows the spot, as do most Lethargians."

"Then what?"

Oscar's expression was one of those *boy are you a dumb*

asshole things. "A beanstalk will grow overnight and reach up into the clouds. You then climb it."

Oh, yeah, bullshit and a half! A jelly beanstalk! Was I buying this? Uh-uh. These dorky people had more of a sense of humor than I gave them credit for. They'd been pulling my leg the whole time, I bet.

But Lucinda, who could read my doubt, said, "He's telling the truth."

I had trouble disbelieving her, but I still thought Oscar the CEO was doing a great deadpan.

"Yes, I am," he whined, "and I suggest that before it's too late, you get your ass moving." (I swear that's what he said!)

Now truthfully, I had to bite my lip to keep from cracking up. "Too late for what?" I inquired.

"Let me explain," Latimer said. "It is getting on toward dark. The beans must be planted at dusk, before the rising of the moon, otherwise we must wait until the *next* night."

It *was* getting late, and I was too tired to deal with this nonsense. One thing for certain, nothing was going to happen tonight. I yawned, which all of them related well to.

"Okay, look," I said, "go ahead and plant the beans, and we'll check it out in the morning. Till then—"

"No," Oscar said.

"Excuse me?"

"He means that none can put the beans in the ground save the one who will first be climbing the stalk," Latimer whined.

I grabbed the jelly beans out of Oscar's hand. "Fine. Lead on, Macduff."

"My name is Latimer, not—"

"Never mind!"

I followed Latimer; Lucinda followed me. Oscar went home. I figured he would have to come along to do a benediction or whatever. Bad call.

Fifty yards from the base of the cliff, Latimer stopped. "Here, right here," he said, that nasal sound making me want to gnash my teeth.

"How far down?" I asked.

"It doesn't matter."

"How much space between them?"

"It doesn't matter."

Okay, I didn't care either. The ground being moist, I poked three holes with my index finger, dropped a bean in each, and covered them up. Great timing, because the sun had just called it a day.

"Lead me to a bed," I said.

They gave me poor Eloise's room. I only had a minute to think about her, and this weird place, before I bombed out.

Lucinda was standing in the doorway when I woke up at dawn. She didn't say anything, but walked over to the window and drew back the curtain.

Over toward the mountain a beanstalk of huge proportions had grown overnight, its top reaching into the clouds.

No shit!

CHAPTER 26

The Giant's Castle

Yeah, well, go figure. I keep telling myself to stop questioning whatever happens in these weird worlds along the Ultimate Bike Path, but I go right on doing it. If *this* didn't make a believer out of me . . .

Lucinda had collected my clothes to clean the night before. I was dressed in a tunic and shorts that belonged to Latimer; bulky things to begin with, so they fit me okay, despite my having six inches on the guy. I'd retained my bike shoes, otherwise I would've had a total peasant look.

The woman with the Danny DeVito countenance left the room as I was urging myself up. I had another peek out the window to make sure what I'd seen was not the product of the blow to my head, or the green stuff I'd guzzled. Nope, none of the above, because the jelly beanstalk was still there.

I walked into the front room, where Latimer and Lucinda were having breakfast. Again with that smelly cheese! Yuck. Well, what the hey, I wasn't going off giant-killing on an empty stomach. I had some more bread, liberally smeared with the stuff that looked like rancid cream cheese, for which I was developing quite a taste. Both of them were swigging that mouthwash, but I chose to wash down my breakfast with this naturally brown milk, which tasted nothing like Nestlé Quik, but was tolerable.

After breakfast we walked outside into a chilly dawn, where I told my hosts, "I'd like to take along some weapons."

"Weapons?" Lucinda whined. "What kind of weapons?"

"Sixty-millimeter mortar would be nice. Maybe an M203 grenade launcher. Tell you what, I'll settle for a thirty-thirty."

They looked at each other and shrugged. Latimer went into the barn. He returned with a dull hand ax and a skinny club that looked like a sawed-off baseball bat.

"Weapons," he said.

Wow, I felt so safe.

We walked to the beanstalk. Now here was a surprise: about

two dozen of Lethargia's stimulating citizens were already there, or on their way. They had formed a circle around the base, no one closer than five yards. Oscar was among them.

"There is still time to change your mind," the CEO whined. "If you do not set foot upon the beanstalk within an hour, it well merely go away."

Now *that* might've been something to see, but no way. For an answer I walked over to the stalk and climbed up about eight feet. The requisite gasps of astonishment were unsurprisingly absent.

"Anyone care to join me?" I called to the throng.

They met that challenge with a collective yawn. Many walked away. Figures.

Forget them. Think about the poor kids up there. Try *not* to think about the fact that most of them might have been the giant's lunch a long time ago.

I continued up the beanstalk.

In my lifetime I'd read about namesake doing this very thing. I'd seen Abbott and Costello climb it; I'd seen Mickey, Donald, and Goofy ascend—in their sleep, no less. I'd even seen a Japanese version of the story (Yukio *and the Beanstalk*?). But now, it was *me*.

I stopped for a moment and touched the Bukko.

The vines that had grown out of the three jelly beans (??) were as thick as the legs of an elephant. Not only had they intertwined, but they were covered with both knobby protuberances and indentations that were up to six inches deep. The bottom line: climbing the thing did not prove to be a death-defying challenge.

My only problem was forcing myself not to look down.

Yeah, I know; I'd gone off cliffs, plunged into the flaming bowels of the earth, all that stuff. But to tell the truth, I still had a problem looking out the second-floor window of my condo.

Fortunately the first cloud had descended during the night, and within a short period of time I was ready to penetrate it. This time I looked down on purpose, observing that nearly all the people of Lethargia had gone back to their homes. Only Lucinda, Latimer, and Oscar remained at the base.

I climbed into the cloud.

Man, it was cold and clammy! Should've taken some more clothing; too late to worry about it. I had a water pouch that Latimer had given to me. It had started out as a Scope mouthwash pouch, but I'd made him empty the stuff out and refill it. Didn't bring any food, because they'd assured me it wouldn't be necessary.

It wasn't, assuming you liked jelly beans, which I did.

Yeah, the fruit of the vine was thick clusters of jelly beans, their colors covering the full spectrum. Some were odd; like, an *olive* jelly bean? Those I left alone. But the reds tasted like cherry, the yellows like lemon, and so on. I munched them all the way up; who knows, maybe I'd have a better chance at whipping the giant while in a hyperactive state.

Eventually I popped out of the first cloud, where a sliver of sun warmed my bones. The next one wasn't too far overhead. I slowed down to take advantage of the exposure.

Birds were flitting all around, though at the moment none were close to the beanstalk. Like I'd noticed yesterday, these birds were more like bright caricatures drawn by kids.

This one in particular interested me. As it started winging its way closer I had a good look at its disproportionately large yellow head and skinny little claws. He looked like Tweety Pie, real calm at the moment without Sylvester trying to bite off his ass. Alighting on a jelly bean cluster, he looked me over.

Here is what I expected him to say in his cutesy Tweety Pie voice: "I tawt I taw a puddy tat."

Here is what he actually said in a deep, stentorian voice: "You gotta be one motherhumping asshole to be headed up that way."

I tell you, Sylvester would've heard that voice and had a massive coronary.

Did you ever notice how nice Sylvester was in the cartoons *without* Tweety Pie?

Next time, I hope the cat wins.

Anyway, the little yellow smart-assed commentator flew off, and none of the other birds approached. Good, who needed them? I continued up, and the second cloud took me.

I didn't mention this, but after yesterday's swan dive into the wild wheat my body was sore. An hour in the Jacuzzi sounded like a wonderful plan, certainly better than busting my buns climbing a beanstalk through cold, damp clouds. At least the head wasn't pounding anymore.

It took a lot longer to get through the second cloud. On the way I got to thinking, just how *giant* was this giant? The one Abbott and Costello met was Buddy Baer, a big guy to be sure, but not abnormal. Willy the Giant in *Mickey and the Beanstalk* was quite a bit larger than Mickey, Donald, and Goofy, but then, wouldn't *we* as normal humans seem like giants to a mouse, a duck, and a dog? (*Is* Goofy a dog? A-hyuck, I don't know.) But then, are we to assume that Mickey, Donald, and Goofy are human-sized to begin with? If not, how can a mouse, a duck, and a dog be the same size, unless Mickey was really a large rat and Goofy a chihuahua . . .

Maybe the thin air up here was making me crazy. Whatever. I finally emerged from the cloud, right where the beanstalk snaked within inches of the edge of a broad, colorful plateau. Was the giant's castle here? I couldn't tell, because the beanstalk kept going up, disappearing in another cloud fifty yards overhead. Looks like I had a choice to make.

Then, on the side of a cliff across the plateau, I noticed a big letter *G*, with an arrow pointing down. Okay, that made life easy. I got off the beanstalk.

Even after the first quarter mile or so across the plateau's Crayola green-yellow grass and Crayola red-orange shrubs, I still hadn't spotted the giant's castle. But I *had* made up my mind about one thing: his size. Twenty-three feet, give or take a foot. Don't ask me how; I just *knew*. Yeah, pretty big, but not exactly King Kong or the Sta-Puft Marshmallow Man. Probably not too bright, either. I'd find a way to do him in, save Eloise and whoever else.

Then, emerging from a grove of Crayola fluorescent green trees, I saw the castle and immediately changed my estimate.

The sucker was fifty feet tall if he was an inch.

I mean, this was one humongous castle! Even from a mile away I couldn't *believe* the size of the doors and the numerous barred windows. Did I say a *mile* away? As big as it was, I might've still had *five* miles to go.

No, I think my initial guess was right, because I reached the first of three dozen or so steps in about twenty minutes. But what steps! Seeing them up close I again changed my estimate of the giant's size.

Seventy-five feet, at least.

Each stone step was eight feet tall, and you had to cross twice that distance to get to the next one. Some *big* feet must have trod these babies. Getting up all of them would have been a bitch, but fortunately I didn't have to. Paralleling the stairs was a wide ramp with one of those universal signs denoting

WHEELCHAIR ACCESS. Quite steep, but I managed, and soon I was standing at the front door.

There was a knocker on the door; not a padoodle or Jacob Marley, just a knocker. But it was *way the hell* above my head. And even if it were in reach, do you think I was going to announce my coming? *Hello, Mr. Giant, I'm here to take away your prized possessions and hack you into bite-sized nuggets.* Uh-uh.

So I crawled through the space under the door, which was tiny in proportion, but plenty wide enough for me to fit.

Guess what, I was inside the giant's castle!

The stone-walled corridor averaged five yards in width, and I don't even want to *guess* how high the ceiling was. A *hundred*-footer could've gotten around in here. There were plenty of nooks and crannies along the base of the wall, as well as the legs of tables, sideboards, and such, where I could hide. *The size of this furniture!*

Anyway, with ax and club poised (now wasn't *that* stupid?), I set off to explore the castle. The giant was probably not afoot, otherwise this place would've felt like San Francisco *circa* 1906 or 1989. I moved along in silence for about half a mile, passing a few doors and looking under them into dark chambers.

Finally the silence was broken by what I swear was . . . music. Strings and a flute, I think, but pretty far away at the moment. Still, each step was bringing me closer to it.

Then, up the corridor in the direction I'd just come from, I saw someone. It was a man, and he was close. He waved at me and put a finger to his lips as he continued on. My first thought was that a Lethargian had followed me up. Or maybe it was one of the kids who had been stolen. If so, there was hope they might all be alive. I waited, hands nervously squeezing my weapons.

Actually, the fellow hadn't been as close as I'd thought. The illusion was because he was *tall.* I'm talking *way* beyond anything they had in the NBA. He was about seven feet six, whipcord-thin, with a shock of blond hair and an endearing Ed Begley, Jr. personality. Even so, I was wary.

He stopped a yard away, smiled broadly, and asked, "Have you come after the giant?"

"Uh, right," I said.

"Well, me too! Why don't we hunt him down together?" He held out a hand. "My name is Sigmund."

I hesitated a moment, then switched the ax to my other hand and shook his. Nope, he didn't try anything funny.

"I'm Jack."

"Nice to meet you, Jack." He indicated my weapons and grinned again. "Trust me, *those* won't do you a bit of good."

"Then you've faced the giant before?"

He shook his head. "But I know all about him. If I'm right, he can be outwitted."

"Fine, but I'm still taking these along."

"As you wish. Come on."

I followed Sigmund along the base of the wall, under more pieces of furniture that dwarfed even *him.* The music was getting louder. Great beat; sounded like something by Carlos Santana.

"Where is it—?" I began.

"Shhh!" he admonished. "Over there."

The massive door he pointed to across the corridor had another smaller door built into it, this one only ten feet high and four feet across. Sigmund looked furtively in both directions, then hurried to the other side. I followed.

Yeah, this was definitely the source of the music. I wanted to peer through the keyhole; there wasn't any. I thought about bending down and looking under the larger door.

Before I could do that Sigmund threw open the smaller door, ran in, and shouted at the top of his lungs, "Hey, giant, come on out and fight!"

Do you *believe* what this guy just did? I heard screams from inside as I followed him blindly, again making like a warrior with the ax and stick.

Then, the screams turned to laughter.

There were six teenaged kids in the chamber, all of whom Sigmund had momentarily scared the crap out of. One pair had been playing the instruments I'd heard; another had been sitting and reading books. Eloise and a third boy stood breathless in the middle of the nicely decorated room. They had been dancing.

"Sigmund, why'd you do that?" one of the grinning boys asked.

Right, that's what *I* wanted to know. "Sorry, I couldn't resist," he said. "Look, I brought a visitor . . . uh, Jack, you can put down your weapons. This is what you came for, isn't it?''

I nodded absently. ''But . . . what about the giant?''

This really broke them up. ''*I'm* the giant, Jack,'' Sigmund said. ''There is no other.''

''*You?* But *look* at this place!''

''Oh, there were giants here once, in ancient times,'' a girl said. ''We've been reading about them. This castle had been abandoned for centuries until Sigmund moved in.''

''Then . . . it was Sigmund who stole all of you?''

''We weren't stolen,'' Eloise said. ''We're here because we want to be.''

I scratched my head. ''This is making me crazy.''

Sigmund grinned. ''We'll explain everything. But first, refreshments and entertainment! You came the hard way, Jack, so you must be tired.''

The pair that had been reading left, but were back quickly with all kinds of goodies. Sigmund joined the orchestra, which consisted of a pan flute and something that looked like Mr. Spock's Vulcan harp, with a set of conical, hand-played drums. They jammed happily; the other two couples danced exuberantly. I stuffed my face.

Eventually they wore themselves out, then joined me for food and drink. ''Now, will someone tell me what's going on?'' I asked.

''I was the first of our town to find my way up here,'' a boy named Ichabod said. ''A couple of nights later I went down and told Velda, and she came shortly after.''

''The rest followed at regular intervals,'' Velda said, ''and there are many more our age and younger who want to come. We made up the giant story because it seemed like the easiest way to explain our disappearances.''

''But why did you want to leave Lethargia?''

Eloise looked at me with her head cocked. ''Do you really need to ask that, Jack?''

I shrugged. ''No, guess not. It's pretty boring down there, huh?''

They all nodded, and Ichabod said, ''Much worse than boring. None of us want to become like our parents.''

''Up here there are things to do,'' Velda said. ''We have lots of fun.''

''But we also learn a great deal,'' a girl named Rima added.

"There are many books from ancient times, and newer ones brought here by Sigmund."

"Your motivations are understandable," I said. "But have you ever stopped to think how your leaving under such allegedly sinister circumstances has affected your parents?"

"Do you really believe they care?" a boy named Lamar asked challengingly.

"On the surface it hardly shows at all. But inside I know it's eating them up. I especially felt that from your mother, Eloise."

They looked at one another, and it was clear they were chastened. Before any of them could respond a voice at the door said, "Jack speaks the truth."

Lucinda came walking in, followed by Latimer, Oscar, and about a dozen other Lethargians. All of us stood. The Lethargians cast a dubious eye at Sigmund, then faced the kids. Both groups shuffled their feet nervously.

Latimer finally said, "After you left, Jack, we had a hard look at ourselves and were not proud of what we saw. Here you go after our children, and we do nothing! So we followed you up the beanstalk."

"We were outside this door and heard everything our young people said," Oscar added. "Now we are doubly ashamed of the dull lives we have lived, and of the example we have set."

"This is going to change," Lucinda said. She looked at the kids. "Maybe you can guide us."

"Of course," Eloise told her. "We . . . also want to apologize for leaving you the way we did."

Okay, the two groups ran together, and it was a wonderful scene as they got to know one another again. While all this was going on, I took Sigmund aside.

"I still don't understand what part you play here," I said.

He smiled wistfully. "I came here to explore the castle, and to be alone with my thoughts for a while. When the young people began appearing, it was a revelation. They enjoyed having me teach them things, reading my books. And they liked having fun. So I wound up staying, too. You see, the place I come from, while not as bad as Lethargia, is boring enough."

"Where is that?"

"A place in the mountains far to the west that you have probably never heard of. It is called Great Big Man Valley."

Say what! Great Big *Man* Valley? ''Don't tell me; the people of your region don't like tall men, so they make your lives miserable, and you all migrate there.''

''Yes, that's right.''

''But it's only *men* there who grow tall, so there are no great big women for you, which is why you're not exactly despondent in Great Big Man Valley, but not particularly overjoyed with life.''

His eyes were wide. ''Jack, you have astounding insight.''

I clapped him on the shoulder and grinned. ''Sigmund, have I got some girls for you and your buddies!''

The guy went absolutely ape-shit when I clued him in about Hesper, Ivana, and the other lonely ladies of Great Big Woman Valley. I swear, he just about danced on the walls of the giant chamber!

Needless to say, I was surrounded by a *lot* of happy people. The kids introduced their parents to Sigmund, who then bade all of us farewell. He was eager to get back to Great Big Man Valley and spread the word. They all agreed to get together again.

The kids knew something their parents didn't. They had not gotten up here the archaic way, via the beanstalk. Inside the mountain, not far from the rear of the castle, was a winding stairwell, which ended in a rift not far from the spot where the jelly beans were planted. Now, you could also utilize this to get down, but the kids had an even better way.

A slide! A *killer* slide, larger and steeper and more fun than any slide you'd ever hurtled down in any theme park in the world. I rode atop a blanket for ten minutes before reaching the bottom, where I flew headlong into a thick layer of mattresses and other soft stuff. (Fortunately the kids had told me about it, or I would have been screaming all the way.) The adults enjoyed it too, and everyone was laughing their heads off. It took a while before we composed ourselves and paraded from the rift.

Guess what, the jelly beanstalk was gone.

Now naturally, not all the citizens of Lethargia had as yet caught the *Get A Life* fever. They looked upon their peers with something of a jaundiced eye. But I believe change was going to come quickly.

Uh-oh, what the hell was going on? Even my hosts were surprised at what awaited us as we approached their house.

Some guy was sitting on the ground with my Nishiki, which was in about a hundred pieces!

From behind his clothing identified him as a Lethargian. Oh, great, what did they know?

"Hey, what are you doing?" I shouted, now running. "Take your hands off—!"

He turned around. It was the Old Guy.

No, it was *an* Old Guy. Sure, they looked identical, but I could tell.

"Hello, Jack," he said, his smile as bad as my Old Guy's when he first started trying. "It's a pleasure to see you face-to-face for the first time."

Okay, it was Study Group Old Guy #3 or #4. "What happened to the Vurdabrok Gear?" I asked.

He shrugged. "A rare anomaly. We've never seen its like. Anyway, I'll have it repaired soon, and it will never happen again." He scratched his head. "I think. In the meantime, go about your business with these people. It will be done before long."

To tell the truth, he really didn't look like he knew what was going on, but I tried not to notice, figuring it would make me crazy. Somehow the whole day had nearly passed, and I was beat. Once again I was the guest of Lucinda and Latimer, although there were many others who would have been happy to share their homes. With Eloise back, I slept in the living room.

Before turning in I went outside. My Nishiki, glistening in the moonlight, was back in one piece. Now if it only worked . . .

Most of Lethargia saw me off the next morning. My destination was the same hill where I'd first learned the Vurdabrok Gear was gone. Why not?

At the edge of town Oscar the CEO pointed at the sign. He and the others were looking at me, smiling and clapping their hands. I tried to act gracious, even though I didn't know what in hell was going on. When I inched my way over and touched the sign, I saw that it had been changed. It now read YOU ARE IN JACKTOWN, A HAPPY PLACE.

Hey, was that cool, or what!

Anyway, I rode to the hill, trudged about halfway up, and stopped. Taking a deep breath, I started down.

At thirty-one mph I knew that I was headed home . . .

CHAPTER 27

This Thing Called Love

The Ultimate Bike Path had served me well for now.

I had denied reality time for too long. Despite the distasteful doses it sometimes meted out, it had to be met head-on.

Still, the *mhuva lun gallee* held on a little while longer before thrusting the blue door in my way and saying *see ya jack . . .*

. . . and I braked to a stop on the Santa Margarita River bridge, where the Old Guy—*my* Old Guy—was waiting for me.

"I was certain you would return this time, Jack," he said. "Sorry about the little foul-up."

"*Little* foul-up? Do you know what would've happened if I'd gone off a mountain or something?"

"We would have made certain you came to no harm."

"Assuming you were watching!"

"And if we weren't, you could have rubbed the Bukko."

"*Assuming* I had more than one point four seconds and wasn't frozen with fear!"

He nodded. "Having made a study of your race, I can understand why you're so . . . *bummed out.* I promise you, Jack, the Vurdabrok Gear is now in fine working order. That will not happen again."

"Yeah, well, I hope you're right."

"You . . . still intend to travel the *mhuva lun gallee,* do you not?" He was really concerned.

"Of course."

"Oh, I'm glad! You did so well on that last world, as you've done on many others. Our study group may grow significantly in the future."

"Glad to hear it, but . . ."

"But now you need some more of your reality time, right?"

"Yes."

He looked rather sheepish as he asked, "Must you go home this minute, or do you have a little time?"

"What did you have in mind?"

"If the subject doesn't disturb you, I thought maybe you could try and explain to me about this thing called *love*."

Well, what the heck. We sat under the Santa Margarita River bridge, and for the next forty-five minutes (I know, because my watch was moving) I thoroughly confused the poor fellow by trying to talk sensibly about the world's greatest and most confusing preoccupation. To tell the truth, the more I heard myself prattle on about love, relationships, bells and whistles, commitment, broken hearts and such, the less I came to realize that *I* understood.

When I said good-bye to the Old Guy, I think both our brains were fried.

Anyway, no reason for you to ride along any farther right now. I have a hot date with a Jacuzzi, after which I'm going to let reality time run its course for a while. Maybe next week I'll know more about those book projects of mine that are hanging in midair.

Maybe next week I'll hear from Holly Dragonette . . .

In any case, you'll be among the first to know.

I promise.

◆ ◆ ◆

Coming Soon!

The Twenty-second Gear

The further utterly impossible
but totally feasible adventures
of Jack Miller